PREMONITION

The Ability to See the Future

CASSIE GREUTMAN

PREVIOUSLY:

Previously in the world of Penchant for Trouble:

To sum things up, I, Trish Penchant, am fae. I live with human foster parents because, to put it nicely, my bio parents are crazy. They've proved it over and over, though not as strongly as when my dad forced my fosters, Dan and Nina, to eat food in Faerie, thereby making them lose all memory of me. Which had to be rough since I'm their favorite thing.

Seriously. I'm just as surprised by it as you are.

My sister Starren traveled with me to Faerie, and we were able to get help from someone who owed me a favor. After a whole lot of trouble that included my foster mom dying and me somehow taking her wound and saving her, we got Dan and Nina's memory back. But that put me in the precarious situation of having foiled one of my father's master plans.

He doesn't take that well.

So now all of my people are watching out for me, waiting to see what happens next. I have people. Again, as surprised as you are. On the human team, Dan and Nina are hovering a bit. Rebecca, my friend/maybe more's mom, is handling things better than I would have expected, and my poor friend Rosie still doesn't even know I'm not human.

Yeah, I feel really bad about that, but it's safer for everyone.

As for the fae, Jaden is being his usual adorable/just the right amount of protective self and still thinks he owes me for saving his family, Cray is jumping at every shadow, and Starren...

Who knows. It's Starren.

Now that you're all caught up, let's see what happens next...

CHAPTER ONE

A look over my shoulder didn't reveal anything the last three hadn't. But I couldn't shake the feeling that someone was watching me. Not a big surprise. I hadn't had a moment of peace since my parents had threatened me in an alley a month ago.

The creepy feeling didn't go away. I'd learned to trust my gut after the last year of dealing with the fae and all of their crazy, so I shuffled along a little faster. Not fast enough that whoever, or whatever, following me would notice, but fast enough to get me a little farther away.

Hopefully.

Why had I walked down a dark alley alone? Pretty stupid. But, I was used to taking care of myself. And looking for Storm.

My dog/dragon had disappeared while I was in Faerie trying to get Dan and Nina's memories back. The thought that someone may have figured out what he was had crossed my mind far too many times. But there hadn't been any news stories or a panicked exodus from Fort Wayne, so I assumed that hadn't happened.

Maybe he'd just moved on to someone else who needed him. Or more likely, someone else who fed him. He was probably sitting under some kid's table right now, cleaning up the scraps from lunch. Starren had never let me keep him in the house. But Nina... she gave in to almost anything. If I could find the sorry looking creature, she'd let him live in the house for sure.

As long as she didn't find out what he actually was.

Another glance showed a man had come out of hiding. He shuffled along at the same speed I was moving, never looking up from behind his brimmed hat. Couldn't assume anything about that though, it was still chilly out here.

There weren't a lot of homeless in Fort Wayne, but it also wasn't unheard of. I just needed to make sure that I didn't jump to conclusions because of the things I'd been through recently.

"Storm?" I whispered. "Storm? This would be a great time for you to come out of hiding."

If I was outside of Sanctuary right now, I wouldn't have anything to worry about. Whatever happened to me, I'd heal. Okay, the pain wasn't great, so I still preferred not getting hurt in the first place. But still. While Sanctuary was the safest place for me in the entire world, or two worlds for that matter, it still wasn't very safe.

The man didn't seem too worried about me noticing him at this point. His head went up, eyes following me as I walked. The next question was if he was just some run-of-the-mill creeper, or if one of my parents had sent him.

My money was on the second option.

I spun around to face him. "Hey. Looking for someone?"

He didn't seem worried at all that I'd called him out. He smiled, a weird, somewhat predatory smile. "Not anymore."

I widened my stance, going into fight mode. "Well then, bring it on."

"Oh no, not here. Not like this. I'm not allowed to hurt you. But if you don't come with me now, you'll regret it later." Something about the way he said it made me shiver a bit. Good thing there was a chill in the air, or I might have been embarrassed.

"And how are you going to make me regret it? Which parent sent you?" It could be either one. My evil dad or my somewhat crazy mom.

"You'll know when the time comes. But I wanted to give you a chance to cooperate before going to more... drastic measures."

He waited there like I was just going to say okay, let's go. I crossed my arms and gave him the look Nina always called the stone face.

He didn't seem to care.

Giving me a lazy wave, he put his hands in his pockets and turned around, going back down the alley in the direction we'd both come from.

What a weirdo. And good luck making me regret not going with him. Even without my healing and nature abilities here in Sanctuary, I would make a formidable opponent. Mr. Nelson and Starren had seen to that.

And speaking of Mr. Nelson, I was going to be late for martial arts class. Being late meant staying after class and cleaning up, along with whatever other punishment he came up with that day, so I upped my shuffle to a half jog. The gym was just around the corner. Rosie should be waiting for me.

Giving that guy any more head space would be stupid. I struggled to shove him out of my mind, but it wasn't working very well. I'd seen a lot of fae goons following me around lately, but hadn't been too concerned. Until things escalated today, and one of them actually talked with me.

It would be fine. Sanctuary. He couldn't hurt me.

How in the world they were all getting here now, I didn't know. Someone was letting them through one of the tunnels, or a portal. But why? Fae presence on Earth was highly regulated. I had never bothered with a newspaper before, but now I was glued to them every day. As soon as Dan threw it in the recycling, so he didn't notice me doing something so out of character. An article stood out this morning, about another strange sighting of some weird creature just outside the city limits.

Yeah, not bigfoot, this was Indiana. Something fae.

Who was letting them through? Anyone's guess. Though there was always a chance it was someone else, my parents were at the top of the suspect list. They'd both threatened to come after me here.

And I wouldn't put it past either of them to do just that.

The question was, how much was I responsible for this? And a follow up, what I was obligated to do about it?

No one in this city even knew that they were here. They didn't know why all these strange things were happening, but I could tell people were starting to know something was wrong.

I darted into the dojo, looking over my shoulder. The guy hadn't followed me, which was almost weird also.

Now I was just being paranoid.

I spent the class just going through the motions. If I wasn't already much better at this than average, I'd have been in trouble. As it was, Mr. Nelson waved me over at the end of class.

Moving toward him slowly, I worked on an excuse. Nothing helpful came to mind.

"You seem distracted today," Mr. Nelson said. "Everything okay?"

"Right as rain." I added a big, cheesy grin to make sure my fae blood took it as sarcasm and not a lie.

"If you say so. But I'm available if you need to talk."

"Hunky dory, but thanks. Can I go now?"

He waited a second, studying me, but then nodded. I took off before he could change his mind, and headed in to get out of my workout clothes.

I finished changing and went out to the lockers.

"Hey, Trish," Rosie said from the other side of the room. She waved and headed my way. I hadn't even seen her there.

These classes were the only time I had to get away from everything, away from Dan and Nina, who, even though I loved very much sometimes got a little overwhelming, away from Starren who expected the world from me, and away from Jaden, whose expectations I still didn't understand, period.

I kept stuffing my sweaty clothes into my bag as Rosie walked over. I liked Rosie. A lot. She would probably be the only person I would call a friend in the city, other than the obvious ones. I could be me around her, without having to be a foster daughter, or potential girl-friend, or that girl who broke Faerie.

But right now, I couldn't put her in danger by being around me. None of the crazies I'd seen around town had made any overtures toward me until today. In Sanctuary. Where only the desperate came to hide, and where the fae didn't have any powers.

"Wanna get pizza?" Rosie asked.

I paused. Shoot. I did love pizza. So much. Enough that if I said no, she'd know something was up. "I... ah... I have a ton of homework."

"So much homework you're worried about it even with Easter break?" She bumped me with her shoulder. "What's going on? You avoiding me?"

Well, yes, I was. And awkwardly, I couldn't lie about it. Being fae meant I couldn't lie about anything.

"I'm just going through a bit of a rough patch." Oh great, now I sounded like Dan, my foster dad. He always had odd sayings like that, and I couldn't help but pick some up.

"Okay. But you do know that's when you need friends the most, right?" Her blue eyes bored into me, but not in some demanding kind of way. Like a trying-to-be-there for me kind of way. And then guilt ate at me. She had been there for me, even letting me stay with her a few days when Dan and Nina had forgotten who I was and I'd had to find a place to crash until Starren and I got an apartment.

But how could I tell her? I'd have to take her outside of Sanctuary if I wanted to show her my powers, which I would probably have to do to make her believe me instead of thinking I was crazy. And stepping one foot out of Sanctuary could mean disaster.

So far my parents had followed the old laws and not had me dragged kicking and screaming out of the city and taken to wherever their respective strongholds were at the moment. I'd like to keep it that way.

But if there was a chance of that, did I really want to spend what time I had avoiding the people I cared about?

"Pizza sounds good. Thank you. Just let me text Nina." I popped out my phone and shot off a quick text. Nina would be giddy about me going out to pizza with Rosie. She wanted me to have normal friends.

I just wanted some peace. And security. A certainty that I wouldn't lose everything at any moment, whenever the other shoe dropped and I got swept up in whatever mess the fae race was in at the moment.

And I knew they were in a mess. They always were.

Throwing my bag over my shoulder, I looked her in the eyes. She smiled back at me, and for the first time in a while, a sense of peace washed over me. "Where are we going?"

"Anywhere. You pick. I'm just glad we're getting the chance to do something. We haven't hung out since you disappeared that last time. That isn't going to become normal, is it?"

"Nope. Not normal at all. It won't happen again." I said it. Relief went through me. If I said it, then I truly believed it. No more disappearing.

We walked out of the gym together, headed for Rosie's beloved car. I checked my phone for a text from Nina. "Go," with a bunch of exclamation marks. No matter how many times I tried to convince her that I wasn't normal and therefore would never have a normal life, she tried her best to make it happen for me.

I loved her for it. And for so many other things. I was fully convinced there were no better people on Earth or in all of Faerie than the two who had taken me in. And I still didn't know how I'd gotten so lucky to get them.

I could admit that now. The defensive anger of believing that at some point they would see who I truly was, not the fae part, the me part, and want nothing to do with me was gone. If they still loved me after everything they'd seen, there wasn't anything I could come up with that would make them stop loving me.

I didn't understand it. But oh, did I need it. People always think foster kids are going to be grateful to their foster parents just for taking them in. That's not how it works. Not with all the baggage most of us have. It takes time to prove that some random strangers who took us in are going to be better to us than our own flesh and blood, who were supposed to put us above themselves.

Ugh. Too deep for right now. I was supposed to be relaxing with Rosie. But I just couldn't seem to stay in a good mindset. Not with all of the things lurking just outside the city limits.

The last time I'd crossed the city line, Vilan and his death hounds had almost killed my sister Starren and my aunt Wren. I wasn't taking that chance again, unless I had no other choice.

Such as the city getting dangerous enough that I had to leave it to keep everyone safe.

My phone buzzed and I pulled it out. A text from Jaden, asking if I would please meet some people tonight. I flicked the notification away. I don't know why he wouldn't stop with that. I'd told him twenty times that I wanted nothing to do with his fae rescue system. That I wanted nothing to do with the fae at all.

Rosie nudged me and my attention snapped back to her. Shoot. She'd probably been talking, and I hadn't been listening. "What?" I asked.

"I said some weird stuff has been going on around here. But now I'm just more worried about you. Where's your head always going lately?" She paused for an answer, but I adjusted my backpack and marched toward her car. "You wanna drive?" Rosie asked.

I paused, checking to make sure I'd heard her right. This car meant the world to her. She never let anyone drive it, especially someone who'd only had their license a month. "What?" I asked, sounding dumb.

"Do you want to drive?" she asked again, slowly. "Whenever I'm struggling with something, driving clears my head." She patted the hood of her bug. "Especially this baby."

No way I was going to chance damaging her car. "I'm good, but thanks."

"Okay then. It wouldn't get you out of talking anyway." She smiled.

I waited until she hit the unlock button before putting myself back into interrogation by jumping in beside her, throwing my bag in the back seat.

The pizza had better be extra good today.

We drove in silence, which was unusual for Rosie, but not unheard of. I didn't want to re-bring up the subject of all the weird going on, because every time the weird got brought up was one more chance for her to find out how much weird actually was going on.

And how much I was involved.

Strangely enough, I'd mostly gotten over the fear of people's reactions when they found out what I was. Everyone in my life had taken it pretty well.

Of course, they'd found out under less than ideal circumstances that made them more likely to believe me. If I just blurted everything out to Rosie in Sanctuary where I didn't have any powers, she'd probably think I was nuts.

Or not. She did seem to like conspiracy stuff.

"How are things going with Mason?" I asked.

She eyed me for a second, then went back to watching the road. "Mason and I broke up two weeks ago."

Shoot. Screwed up again. To be fair, I was rather caught up in everything my biological parents had brought to the fae. They hadn't gone through a very cordial separation, and they'd turned that into all-out war between their followers.

I'd managed to keep myself out of that whole mess by staying with a human foster care family on Earth for years.

It had caught up to me.

But there I was again, drifting off.

"I'm sorry, Rosie. You two seemed like you'd make a good match."

She shrugged, pulling into an empty spot near the pizza place we always ate at. "Wasn't meant to be. I can deal with someone not believing the same things I do, but not when they ridicule me."

"Then you're better off without him. You can tell me anything, you know that? Whatever it is that made him think you're crazy, it isn't going to bother me at all. I guarantee it."

That earned me a smile. Smaller than normal, but it was there.

"Thanks, Trish. Seriously. I know I'm not crazy, but I can't get anyone to listen."

Aliens. She was probably about to tell me about aliens. But who was I to say they weren't a thing? I mean, really, if she counted anyone with origins on a different planet, I was an alien.

Wow. That was confusing.

She turned the car off, but didn't make a move for the door handle. My stomach growled, and internally I threatened it to stay quiet. I didn't have enough friends that I could afford to lose any. Especially not this one, the normal one.

"I saw..." she closed her eyes and dropped her head back against the rest. "See, I think I'm crazy too, when I say it out loud."

"It's okay. Seriously." I wasn't good at the encouragement stuff, but I had to give it a go. "You can tell me." At least it wouldn't be about me. Or any fae. Powers didn't work here, so she couldn't have seen any of us doing anything weird.

"Okay. Here it is then. Mason was on duty for his first night ever, just as a trainee, you know?"

Okay, night. Aliens. This was good.

"So I went to the edge of town to his parent's farm, to wait on him. Surprise him, you know?"

Edge of town. Now things were getting a little sketchy. No way she'd seen what had happened with me, Starren, Wren and Vilan. No way.

"And while I was waiting in my car with pizza, I saw a man walk over the city line, and vanish." She held up two balled fists, then flipped her hands open in a show of magic. "Seriously. I know that sounds crazy, but he did!"

Whew. I collapsed against the door of the car, stomach nearly forgotten. It wasn't me she'd seen, getting attacked by death hounds and a gorgeous mercenary.

Rosie dropped her forehead in her hand. "You don't believe me either, do you."

Weighing everything carefully, I decided to just go for it. I couldn't lie to her anyway. "I believe you. One hundred percent."

She grinned and leaned over the center console to give me a one-armed hug. "Yes! Somehow I knew you would."

Ouch. That meant she thought I was weird. I deserved it. I was pretty weird. Didn't quite fit with the humans, and one hundred percent didn't fit with the fae. Any fae.

Scratch that. I had to take it back. Jaden was... amazing. We'd just go with that. He was the only fae I would consistently claim though. My sister Starren could be a bit much.

But to get back on track, this was disturbing. Really disturbing, actually. Some fae out there really wasn't being careful about entering and exiting Sanctuary. Really wasn't being careful, or really didn't care. "Was he going into town, or coming out?"

Rosie beamed at me. She really had thought I would dismiss her story. "Going in! Which made it even more scary. He could be anywhere in the city, doing whatever he wants."

I'd thought I'd known the answer to that question. Thought I'd just been keeping the conversation going. But this was actually a scary development. A fae could use his abilities in Sanctuary? That wasn't supposed to happen. Now I was going to have to talk to someone about this. Probably Jaden. It was a good reason to go and talk to him.

I didn't actually need a good reason, I just liked to look like I had one. Just so he didn't get any ideas. The thought of us being anything more than we were scared me to death, and that was difficult considering I healed from almost anything.

So far the only people who had stuck by me in my entire life were Dan and Nina. I still hadn't figured out why they did, but I was eternally grateful. Taking a risk on another person seemed pretty dangerous. So I just kept things where they were.

Awkward, that's where.

"And since then, I've been trying to find other people who have seen strange things. We're starting a group. There aren't that many in Fort Wayne, but I've found a lot online."

Okay, that gave me pause.

Rosie rolled her eyes. "Yes, I know, lots of crazies online. But some of them have very genuine stories. Like this girl in Florida. She went through a portal to some other world. At least I think she did. She doesn't seem crazy."

I couldn't help myself. I bolted upright, gripping the door handle. "A portal?"

"Yeah. It took her to some medieval world. She has so many details I can hardly believe she's making it all up. And pictures. I know pictures can be faked, but these didn't look like it. At all."

A deep breath escaped out my nose. Okay. A medieval world. Obviously not Faerie, so the girl was crazy. Crazy as far as I knew.

Wait, were there other worlds than Faerie and Earth?

Who would I even ask about that? Maybe Starren. Yeah, she knew every possible threat to Faerie, so if there were other worlds, she was probably monitoring them. Or had been, back when protecting Faerie had been her main concern. Funny how much things change.

Okay, Rosie was starting to look concerned. Maybe she thought this last bit of info was just too much for me. "Wow, that sounds amazing." Lame. But what else could I say?

"I know, right? Wouldn't it be so amazing? I told her about how the man disappeared, and she said maybe he went into a portal. That's exactly how it happened to her."

Oh crap, what if he had gone into a portal? Now I needed to know. But portals weren't visible. I'd have been crashing into walls the first time I'd used a portal if I hadn't had Starren to follow through.

"So where exactly did this happen?" I wasn't an actress. I'd been able to hide the fact that I was fae from the world, but that was it. This time, I couldn't let Rosie get involved, but I had to know what was going on, so I did my best to act somewhat interested, without looking too interested.

Tried.

"Mason's parents farm." She said it slowly, like I hadn't heard her the first time.

"Uh, yeah, got that, but where exactly? Did you see any kind of landmark or anything?"

Yeah, now she looked suspicious. Shoot. Maybe I needed to learn to hide things better. Oh ick, no, then I'd be more fae. I did not want to be more fae.

"Uh..." Rosie scrunched her nose up as she thought. "Close to one of the road signs. Want to go take a look now?" She reached toward her keys to start her car back up.

"NO!"

Her hand twitched and she stopped moving, blinking at me like I was crazy.

"Sorry, that came out much more forcefully than I meant. I'd really like to get pizza." And would really, really, really, not like to leave the city limits with a human friend. Not leave the city limits at all, of course, but especially not with her along. I would be considered free game, and she would be considered a casualty of war.

"Okayyyy." Rosie dropped her hand but didn't reach for the door handle. "I know you like food Trish, but this is pretty important to me."

She'd been a solid friend. And had never asked anything of me until now.

And of course, it was something I couldn't deliver on. Because of a reason I couldn't explain.

I tried to say 'maybe later,' but it was too much of a lie and I couldn't get it out.

"How about we eat and then figure out what to do? It's going to be dark soon." Stringing unrelated sentences together in ways that implied something without making me a liar had become second nature. I hated it. There was nothing more fae than telling a lie using the truth.

"Okay." Disappointment, in one word form. Rosie rarely used one word. She didn't run her mouth for no reason, but she always said what she was thinking. I loved that about her. She did reach for the door handle then, body language all sad.

Ugh. Somehow I was always hurting feelings. I never meant to, and it was always for a good reason. But that didn't help much.

The door slamming said maybe not all sad. Great. I'd made my one friend mad. Starren was my sister, Jaden was... whatever, and Cray was like a brother. So that left Nina, who was my literal best friend, but also my foster mom, so I wasn't really sure that counted.

Oh wait. I'd forgotten Wraith. Sure, two friends. One human, and the other a mythical monster who fed from human fear and terrified even the scariest of fae.

My life was weird.

I jumped out of the car, slamming the door behind me. "Rosie, come on, wait up." I jogged to catch up with her, but she just kept marching, body stiff.

Time for some uncomfortable truth. "I believe you, seriously."

Progress. She'd slowed, just a little.

"I believe you, but I'm... scared." She didn't have to know of what. I basically lived scared, so that would always be a true statement.

She stopped and whirled around, pulling me into a hug. "I'm so sorry I made you tell me that, of course! I was so freaked out too, seriously! We should wait until it's early daylight to go out there, just in case there's something weird going on." She rolled her eyes. "We already know something weird is going on. But we're going to find out what."

I gave her a smile that even felt sickly. How in the world was I going to get myself out of this one? Crossing the town line had not gone well for me in the past. Or the human who was with me at the time. Even though my Aunt Wren was some epic soldier, she'd still gotten hurt that day. It wasn't really fair to take humans to a fae fight.

I'd lost Nina once because I'd taken her into danger. Not that it had been my choice. I'd tried pretty hard to leave her behind, but it didn't matter. I never wanted to feel that terror and agonizing pain and guilt again. Ever.

Even without my powers, I was better equipped to deal with all the crap the fae threw at us. So protecting my human family was my only priority.

And getting my bio parents to leave me alone. But I still didn't know how to do that.

Rosie tugged me toward our favorite pizza place and I followed along. There wasn't a wait, which was unusual, but something I could get behind. We were sliding into a booth before I even really had a chance to come up with a reason I couldn't go out and look around with her.

At least a reason that didn't involve me telling her I wasn't human.

"I'll check with Nina about heading out there with you tomorrow." Using my foster mom? A stroke of genius. I could tell Nina what was up, she'd freak out and tell me no way I could cross the border, and we'd be all good.

Not that I really liked when she told me what to do, but in this case it would totally work.

I fiddled with the menu, waiting to place my order for what I already knew I was going to get, when someone caught my eye on the other side of the room.

Non-descript really. Nothing that should be catching my attention so strongly. But he was. He glanced up at me and I just kept looking at him. His eyes darted away instantly.

Okay, yeah, he was watching me. The guy from the alley. How had he known I would come here? He was already here when we'd walked in. Why was he here? Why didn't he just say or do whatever he needed to back in that alley?

I couldn't stop staring for a moment. But then a look around the room nearly sent me hyperventilating.

The one weirdo wasn't just one. I took stock. At least six of the people in the room sat alone, strange for this place, and seemed off. They were here for me. And not horribly worried about me noticing, either. Stupid, coming to a place I always did. Too obvious.

Were they all fae? Nothing screamed fae to me, but many fae looked perfectly human.

They just weren't great at acting human.

Maybe I was being paranoid about it being the whole room. After the things I'd been through in the last year, that was to be expected. At least that's what Wren had said last time I'd told Nina about something weird I'd noticed and she went straight to call her Special Forces sister.

"Rosie, how set are you on pizza?" I asked. A blessing in disguise that the waiter was taking so long to get out here.

"We're already here, Trish. They have a bunch of other stuff to choose from, you don't have to get pizza." She didn't even look up from the menu.

And then the guy from the alley made sure to catch my gaze, and gave me a toothy grin.

"You know, I'm really not feeling too good right now." The fact that it came out made it not a lie. My stomach clenched on cue.

This time Rosie looked up instantly. "What's wrong? Your stomach? The flu has been going around really bad at my school. I hope I didn't give you something."

"It hit me suddenly." Which was true. But I couldn't get the other part, where I said I had no idea why, out. Sometimes I forgot I was fae and not human. Nothing wrong with that, in my opinion. "Can we just go?"

"Of course." Rosie stood, hovering over me as we made our way back to her car. I watched over my shoulder and what seemed like half of the rest of the room took turns standing and moving to follow.

Crap. Crap. Now Rosie was associated with me. I'd known this was a bad idea, and went along with it anyway so I didn't lose a friend. How selfish.

Two men behind us bumped into each other, and then got into a heated discussion under their breaths. People were starting to notice.

I flung the door to the restaurant open and practically flew out. Rosie followed closely behind.

"Seriously, Trish, are you okay?"

"I just need to get home. Thanks."

"Okay. If you say so." She hit the unlock button and her car beeped at us, the lights on her bug blinking. I ran and jumped into the passenger side, not even caring at this point if she thought I was crazy. She'd put up with plenty of crazy from me in the short time we'd known each other, hopefully this wouldn't be the breaking point.

But if it was, she'd be safer anyway.

Fidgeting while Rosie took her time with her seatbelt, I kept my eye on the restaurant. Sure enough, the argument must have gotten resolved, because four fae muscled through the door in formation.

What had happened to the other two I'd pegged, I didn't know.

"Would you mind dropping me off at home?" I asked Rosie.

"I was planning on it." She looked in her rear-view mirror and started to carefully back out. I bit the inside of my mouth in an attempt to not yell at her to hurry. She wouldn't know why.

Really, I didn't know why. What were these fae going to do to me, right in the open, right in Sanctuary? In fact, that thought almost made me jump out of the car and confront them. But then I came to my senses. Rosie didn't need to see me out there screaming at a bunch of adults.

That would be hard to explain without lying, or telling the truth. And I definitely wasn't telling the truth. 'Hey there, friend, I'm not actually human, I'm part of an evil race of ne'er do wells who love to cause trouble.'

Yeah. Avoid that.

Rosie finally pulled away from the parking space. I watched over my shoulder to see the four people who had followed us out of the restaurant watch for a moment and then disappear. Not literally. That didn't happen in Sanctuary.

I caught my fists clenching and unclenching and forced them to stop. I had to learn not to show any signs of weakness. My enemies would pick up on every little thing.

My enemies. My parents. Same thing, and that just felt so wrong.

"Turn left here," I told Rosie.

She looked at me oddly, but obeyed. She'd driven me home a hundred times and knew the best route by memory. But today, I didn't want to take the best route.

As sneakily as I could, I looked in the mirror, tabbing every car behind us. "Okay. Turn right."

Rosie looked in her mirror as well as she did as I'd asked. She didn't ask any questions, but her hands whitened on the steering wheel.

After another check behind us, I relaxed. A little. No one seemed to be tailing us. I'd learned all about that not too long ago when my Aunt Wren's friends had tailed Starren, Wren, and me on the way to D.C.

"Ah, okay. This was a nice route, huh?"

Rosie stared me down. She wasn't calling me out, but she definitely wanted me to know she didn't believe anything I'd just thrown at her.

Oops.

She already knew weird things were going on. I didn't need to add anything to that. As much as I hated it, I was going to have to keep my distance for a while.

We pulled up in front of my apartment building and idled for a second. I twisted around and grabbed my bag out of the back seat. "Well. Thanks. See ya." I reached for the door handle, but Rosie grabbed my arm.

"Something is going on, Trish. That's obvious. I wish you trusted me enough to tell me what."

Her eyes bored into me and I had to blink several times to snap out of the panic that put me in.

"Is it your foster parents? Are they treating you okay?"

That threw me for a loop. "Of course! Seriously, you never have to worry about that."

Rosie blew out a big breath. "Okay, good. I so didn't want it to be that. I love Nina. But I don't know Dan, so..." She paused and stared out the window for a second. "I didn't know for sure what your home life was like. Especially since you stayed with me for that bit. And then stayed with that... weird girl."

I almost snickered at her description of Starren. Weird didn't begin to cover it, and Rosie didn't even know.

"All's good on the home front. They're the best foster parents I've ever had. The best anyone could ask for." Wow, that was opening up far more than I was usually comfortable with. But I couldn't have her thinking something was going on with Dan and Nina. If she reported us for something, they could get in real trouble. They were still on somewhat shaky ground after my disappearances back when we lived in D.C.

I didn't want to shut Rosie out. At all. But my base nature was secrecy. Partly because I was fae? Probably. But a whole lot because of being a foster kid. You just didn't let people know how you felt about things. If they knew you cared about something, they had power over you.

Scary. And I didn't like it.

I was trying to change that about myself, but it was a long, slow road. And so far, Dan and Nina were the only two people in this world, or the other, that I truly trusted with anything.

Jaden was close. But there were still things about myself I didn't want him to know. He liked me for some reason, and I didn't want to mess that up, even if I didn't know what to do with it.

"Okay, now where did your head go?" Rosie asked, pulling me out of my thoughts.

Shoot. I did it again. I did it all the time, and just couldn't seem to get past that. Spacing out could be very dangerous when you had enemies. Or parents who wanted to use you for their own gain.

I turned to face Rosie, looking her in the eye. "There's some stuff I just can't talk about. I'm sorry if that hurts our friendship. But I'm just not ready." This could be it. I could have just blown the only regular friendship I had. The only one without strange things tying me and the other person together.

But no. Rosie smiled, reached forward and took both of my hands. "That's okay, Trish. As long as you're honest about it."

Honest. I hadn't been truly honest with her from the beginning. Being fae sucked. Why couldn't I just be human. Why couldn't Dan and Nina be my biological parents. Life didn't make sense.

"Rosie, you know me better than any human my age." Hopefully throwing 'human' in there didn't tip her off. But I had to add it or I couldn't say it. And I had to say it. I didn't want to burn any bridges that I didn't have to.

Ugh, I was all over the place on this one. Burning bridges would be better for Rosie. Would keep her safe. But I just couldn't do it all the way. Maybe blocking bridges would work. Yeah, that sounded much better.

Rosie snorted. "Better than anyone your age? That's kind of sad, Trish. I don't know anything about you."

Uh oh, dangerous territory here.

"How old you are, I've met your foster parents, I know you moved here recently, but that's it." She grinned. "Oh, and the fact that you love pizza. Can't leave that out." Her face went thoughtful. "And that you can kick some serious butt at the gym. So I know some facts. But you don't ever let anyone see the real you."

I got out of her car, leaning in the window. Another car idled over at the intersection. I was too exposed out here, I needed to get inside. "You know a lot more about me than most. I appreciate your friendship." And then I turned and ran before things got mushy. I could blame this on Nina. I would never admitted out loud how much someone meant to me a year ago.

"I appreciate yours too!" Rosie yelled after me out of the window.

I didn't turn back, but I may have let a grin out a bit more than I'd have liked.

"Oh wait! You forgot your backpack." Rosie jumped out of her car and headed to meet me, backpack in hand.

The car at the far intersection rolled forward as Rosie headed my way. Instead of slowing down as he got close to the T in the road, the driver accelerated, getting the large vehicle going far faster on the city street than it should. Toward Rosie's back.

"Rosie!" I screamed.

She turned in time to see the car and tried to jump to get out of the way, but it was too late.

The sickening crunch of impact filled the air. Her body tumbled across the sidewalk and into a small patch of grass outside my apartment building before coming to a stop. And not moving.

CHAPTER TWO

I bolted for Rosie, tears flowing as I skidded to a stop beside her, leaning over her but not touching so I didn't make anything worse. "Rosie, can you hear me?"

A groan answered. She was still alive. How alive, I still couldn't tell. I took her hand, squeezing it. "I'm here."

The driver revved its engine, slowly pulling up beside me.

"Call 911!" I screamed, not even looking up from Rosie's still face.

The engine revved again, and I took just a second to see if the idiot inside was on the phone. He wasn't. It was the guy from the alley. He smiled at me.

"I got permission. Your father says hello." And then he peeled out, leaving rubber on the road.

Other people were beginning to arrive. Several had cell-phones out, but I couldn't tell if they were just taking videos or actually trying to get help. There. One of the women was talking to someone.

I turned back to Rosie, shoving everything else out of my head for the moment.

Rosie groaned and I nearly sobbed in relief.

"Trish?" Jaden's voice, from somewhere behind me, sent my heart pounding. Someone was here to help.

"Jaden! Help!"

I'd never been so glad to hear his voice, and that was saying a lot.

He shoved past a few gawkers, muscling his way in close. I clutched her hand tighter, not knowing what to do. No open wounds. Whatever was wrong was on the inside.

"Help her!"

He didn't answer, just dropped down to the ground beside us and put his hands on both sides of her neck.

"What are you doing?"

"We can't let her neck move." His breaths were short and fast, betraying the fact that he was probably as freaked out as I was, but was handling it much better.

"He just hit her!" The words spilled out of my mouth, without my consent.

He didn't try to tell me it would be okay. He didn't ever even try to lie to me. And he couldn't give me his usual hug with his hands full, but he stared me down, dark brown eyes boring into me.

"It's my fault." The broken words just kept coming. By now people surrounded us, but I didn't care. Rosie was just trying to be a good friend. And that guy had tried to kill her. I couldn't even say fae or human for a hundred percent sure. But he worked for my father.

Thinking about the man was bad enough. But he'd just done as he was told. Thinking about my father...

"Don't go there, Trish," Jaden said. His words broke me from my thoughts. I was useless in this situation.

"Help is coming, just hold on," a woman's voice came from behind me, as she squeezed my shoulder. Sure enough, a few seconds later the sound of distant sirens caught my attention.

I willed them forward as my grip on Rosie's limp hand tightened even more. It would probably be painful, if she was awake. If I could heal her right now, I would. Even with all these people watching. But even outside of Sanctuary, I hadn't figured out how I'd somehow taken Nina's wound on myself when Wade had shot her.

"Who would do something like this?" someone in the crowd asked.

"Did you get a good look? A license plate number?" another asked.

I didn't answer. Couldn't. Could only concentrate on the sound of sirens, getting louder and louder. Under normal circumstances, I avoided the cops at all costs. For some reason I always got the feeling that they were going to find out about me somehow. Like their profession made them sensitive to secrets, and one would sniff out mine. But now, I urged them on, internally begging them to get here faster.

"Trish," Jaden broke me from my thoughts.

I tore my gaze away from Rosie's still form, but didn't say anything.

Tears filled his eyes. "I don't know if that's the police or an ambulance."

His words didn't get through the cloud in my head.

"Trish. I'll stay if you want me to, but I shouldn't be here if the cops are." One of the tears in his eyes spilled down his cheek.

Of course. Of course he couldn't be here. On Earth, Jaden Martan was dead. If the police wanted a witness statement, and asked him for his name, he'd have to give it. He couldn't lie. And if for some reason they ran his name, it would come up as deceased.

"Go. You have to go."

He looked nearly panicked for a moment, but let me take over holding Rosie's neck. He stood. "I'll get Nina." And then he took off, leaving me behind.

Anger was my default mode. My defense mechanism, as I'd been told more than once. It fought for control at the moment. Anger at whoever had done this. Anger at my father. Anger at Jaden for leaving me, even though I knew he had no choice. It was leave me now, or leave me later when he was carted away for lots of questions.

And if they took him over the city border...

He'd be a ghost again. A ghost that everyone saw disappear. From a normal teenage guy, to poof.

A new man shoved through the crowd of onlookers. He saw what I was doing right away. "Are you trained to hold c-spine?"

"Ah, no?"

"Let me take over." He dropped to his knees beside Rosie and gently took her head from me. "I'm Rob. I'm an EMT, just happened to see the crowd."

"Why isn't the ambulance here yet?" someone asked.

"The station is nine minutes from here. And that's if traffic cooperates."

I watched him check for breathing and slide a finger down to feel for a pulse without being able to hear anything going on around me, numb. I backed up a little, hating myself. But there was nothing I could do to help now. Nothing.

The crowd pressed around me, squeezing me out a bit.

I let them.

"Trish!" The one voice that could get through to me right now. I turned and was enveloped in a bone-crushing hug, my face pressed into a soft shoulder. Nina. I burst into tears, not able to do a thing to stop it.

We followed the ambulance to the hospital in tense silence. It went lights and sirens, which could have meant anything from she was doing better and they were just worried about internal injuries, to she had died and they were doing CPR.

Nina was kind enough to not ask any questions. I couldn't have answered at the moment anyway, with the sight of Rosie going down replaying over and over in my head. Nina just kept staring at me with her sad, horrified eyes, and reaching over to squeeze my hand.

It would be my luck if we got into an accident on the way to the hospital. That was just the way things went for me.

I didn't even have either of Rosie's parent's phone numbers. I knew her mom and step-dad fairly well after staying with them for a bit, but I didn't know her dad at all.

Nina let go of my hand to make the final turn into the hospital parking lot. My seatbelt was off and the car door open before she even had the key all of the way into the off position.

"Come on," I said, impatiently.

Nina gave me a look, but complied. We rushed inside together.

Reaching the front desk, I leaned in close, giving the receptionist less than ten seconds to look at me before I started to bounce on my heels.

The receptionist held up a finger, stuck in some conversation on the phone.

When she finally hung up, I blurted out a string of words that hardly made sense. "Rosie. Rosie Hurkley. Is she okay?"

Scooting in beside me, Nina gently pushed me out of the way. "She just came in by ambulance. Eighteen year old, hit and run. We haven't heard anything yet, and really need to."

Nina knew Rosie from the gym. Not well, but Nina treated everyone like family. And there was also the fact that she felt like she owed Rosie for taking care of me when she couldn't. Not that it was their fault or anything, but Nina was like that.

"One second," the receptionist said, picking up her phone. "I'll find out for you. Mother and sister?"

I couldn't lie. Nina could, but wouldn't. I'd never seen her lie. I looked at her, pleading, but she kept her mouth shut.

The receptionist noticed our lack of answering and moved the phone to her shoulder. "Are you related to the patient?"

"No. Just friends. My daughter here was with her when she was struck by a car." Nina pulled me in close.

The receptionist hung her phone up, face full of sympathy. "Then I'm so sorry. But because of HIPPA, we aren't allowed to give you any information. You'll have to wait until an authorized family member arrives."

I gripped the desk in front of me until my fingers ached. "You can't even tell us if she's still alive?"

Face sad, the receptionist shook her head no. "I'm sorry. There's nothing I can do. If you want, you can take a seat and wait. Surely someone from her family will be here soon."

I opened my mouth to chew her out, but Nina tugged on my arm. I snapped my mouth closed and followed her toward the waiting room, not looking her in the face. If I had to look at her sad, sad eyes one more time, I was going to lose it. I'd turn into a mess of snot and tears, right here in the middle of the hospital.

Nina tugged me over to a small alcove, and pushed me into a seat made for two. She sat next to me and put her arm around my shoulders. I tried to shrug it off, because it made me want to cry, but she kept it there until I collapsed into her side.

Keeping the tears at sniffle level, I snuggled into her warmth. She gave me a minute to calm down before going into the questions I knew were only a matter of time before they came.

"What happened?"

"It was a message."

Nina leaned away from me to get a look at my face. "What?"

"From my father. The guy that hit her stopped and said my father says hi before he took off."

"What!" Her voice echoed around the fairly quiet waiting room, making the receptionist and two other people look our way. Her yell turned into a whisper. "What are we doing here? You could be in danger! We need to get you somewhere safe."

I shouldn't have told her. But I was over keeping secrets. I hadn't kept any secrets from her since my big one had come out. Some stuff hadn't come up, but I hadn't been intentionally keeping anything from her. I mean, sure, I had taken off and told her afterward, but I hadn't tried to hide it.

"He won't do anything to me. He needs me. He's trying to scare me into coming back." I stood up and started to pace in front of Nina. "I just need to know Rosie isn't dead because of me. I should have cut our friendship off weeks ago. I shouldn't have been friends with her in the first place. This is my fault."

"Don't say that." Nina stood and stopped my pacing. "Don't let other people's choices change who you are."

Over her shoulder I saw a cop come through the ER door. He walked up to the receptionist and said something to her. She pointed my way and he nodded his thanks before heading toward us.

"Uh, Nina."

She paused and turned to see what I was looking at. She sucked a deep breath in through her nose and closed her eyes for a second. "We should have expected that. Just stay calm and tell him what happened. You don't have to tell him that the guy spoke to you."

The officer marched over toward us, nodding at Nina, and then at me. He was really tall, like I'd expect someone in law to be. But maybe that came from too much TV. "Hello. I'm Officer Reynolds. I'm here about the hit and run."

Immediately I got defensive. I'd never had much trouble with cops, but anyone looking at me too closely might notice I wasn't normal.

Stupid paranoia. I'd lived with Dan and Nina for a year before Nina found out, and that was only because I'd gotten shot with an arrow. But telling myself repeatedly that I had nothing to worry about didn't seem to help.

Nina must have felt my anxiety, because she reached over and squeezed my arm. I instantly felt just a bit better. Not a lot, but a noticeable amount.

"You were the only witness?" Officer Reynolds asked.

"Oh, yeah, sorry," I answered.

"It was a shock," Nina answered.

"Of course. No need to apologize. I'm sorry to make you think through this again." He pulled out a notebook and flipped open the cover. "But it's very important that we get on the search as soon as possible. Did you notice the make or model of the car?"

Could I trust him? I didn't know. He could be working for either of my parents. He could even be fae. He looked like he was about thirty years old, dark eyes, dark hair.

But looks didn't mean much.

"I don't know cars well. It was small. And blue." Stupid. I should have done better about looking at the car. I'd seen enough movies to know that. But all I could see at the time was Rosie, crumpled on the ground.

"Nothing else at all?" The officer's eyes were kind when he asked, but that just made me grumpy. I didn't like pity. At all. I could give him a description of the driver really easily after our interactions. But that seemed like a good way to get humans into trouble that they weren't prepared to deal with.

"It was a man. Driving. But that's about it."

The officer raised an eyebrow. "About it?" Shoot. He'd caught me in my evasion. "We aren't going on much here. There's a good chance that whoever did this is going to get away with it." He softened just a little. "Did the... accident... seem intentional?"

He had me there. I looked at Nina, basically begging for her to step in. How could I get out of this one? I couldn't even say I didn't know. The driver had been very specific that the whole thing had been to get at me.

"You really think it could have been intentional?" Nina asked. "Why would anyone do that to Rosie?"

"That's what I'm trying to find out. And the only one who can answer that for me at the moment is your daughter."

So much for Nina getting me out of this. "Rosie gets along with anyone. I can't think of anyone who would be upset at her." No lies. Rosie only had friends. She'd gotten hurt because of me, not because of her.

He wasn't buying it. He stared me down for what felt like forever, but then stepped back. Pulling a card from his pocket, he handed it to Nina. "If anything comes up, call me right away." Then he looked back at me. "If you don't think that this was an accident, then it was one of two things. The person who did it was after Ms. Hurkley, and if so may try again. Or the second option." He leaned down close so we were at eye level. "It was intentional, without a specific target. Which means whoever did it may do it again. Either way doesn't look very good."

I blinked several times, trying not to give in and just blurt out what I knew about the guy who'd hit Rosie. But if I did that, then this officer might get into bigger trouble than he was prepared to deal with. Like, my dad.

No human was equipped for that.

Heck, I wasn't equipped for that, and I was impossible to kill. Maybe. I hadn't lost my head yet to see if that would do the trick.

I wanted to tell him I hoped he found the guy, but it wouldn't come out of my mouth. Apparently I didn't actually want him to find the guy. Probably so he didn't die. "Good luck." Ah. That came out fine. Super vague. I could be hoping he won the lottery.

The look he gave us totally said he didn't think I was telling the whole truth. Valid, since I totally wasn't. But he nodded politely to me and then to Nina. "Thank you for your time. We'll be looking into this very seriously."

And then he left. I heaved a sigh of relief.

"Are you sure that was the best plan? Keeping the cops out of this?"

Nina's question hit a soft spot, because of course I wasn't sure. But I didn't know what else to do. The guy that had hit her had probably been fae, and therefore probably had some fae ability. A nasty one, if he worked for my father. Basically everything about my father was nasty.

"It's the best I can come up with for now. I don't know what else to do." I would be checking into this myself. As soon as possible. And if I found out that my dad had truly sent someone to hurt someone I cared about... It wasn't going to turn out well for him.

The sliding door the cop had just left through opened again. I tensed, waiting for trouble. But it was a different kind of trouble. Mrs. Hurkley, Rosie's mom. Crying.

Shoot. I didn't do emotions. Especially not painful ones. They brought up too much from the past, blending all the pain into a rock around my neck, weighing me down.

"Trish!" Mrs. Hurkley rushed over. "What happened? How is she?"

I couldn't even answer. She's been so kind to me when I'd stayed at her house. Had tried to be a mother figure, even though I hadn't wanted one. I turned away, staring at the floor.

Nina swooped in, grabbing her into a tight hug. "Violet. We don't know. The nurse isn't allowed to tell us a thing because we aren't family."

"Aren't family? Of course you are." Violet stormed off toward the counter, with Nina following her. When had she and Nina become such good friends? I shouldn't be surprised. Everyone felt that way about Nina.

I trailed behind, close enough that I could overhear, but far enough away that hopefully no one asked me anymore questions. I just needed to know that Rosie was still alive, and then I was out of here. She was safer if I wasn't around.

And I still had a man to find. One who would be taking a message back to my father, whether he wanted to or not. A message that I would come up with, as soon as I could think straight.

"Maybe we should wait until you can talk with the doctor," the nurse said.

"All I need is to see my daughter. Now. And I'd appreciate knowing exactly how worried I should be. Because at the moment, I'm past worried. I'm close to flipping out. And trust me, you don't want to see that."

Very true. I'd seen her flip out once while staying with them, and it hadn't been pretty.

A woman in scrubs walked out of the ER door. She headed right for the desk, looking us all over but going for Mrs. Hurkley. "Violet Hurkley?"

Mrs. Hurkley flung away from the nurse. "Yes? Yes, that's me, do you have news about Rosie?"

"I'm Rosie's physician. She's doing okay. Far better than we were afraid she would be doing, when we heard what the squad was bringing in."

Everything she said after that faded into the background. Rosie was alive. Rosie was going to be fine. I ran out of the hospital, flinging the door open when the automatic setting was too slow.

A couple people sitting on a bench outside eating gave me odd looks, so I moved around the corner into an alcove. Rosie had almost died because of me not handling my problems. Because of me ignoring things, trying to live a normal life.

My breaths started coming faster, and my heart roared in my ears.

A normal life wasn't for me. I should know that by now. But somehow I always started to think it was a possibility. I straightened, pushing off the wall.

Time for me to face my demons. Or in this case, my parents.

CHAPTER THREE

After all the stink they made about the fact that eventually I would join one or the other, my parents were making it hard to find them.

Sure, they both had people watching me. I knew they did. But I couldn't exactly walk up to everyone I saw and ask if they were fae and if they would tell my evil father something for me.

No, setting up a meeting without anyone in my family knowing would take a bit of thinking.

I wasn't good at thinking.

No way I was bringing Starren in on this. She would have the best insight into how to find Mother or Father, probably would even know which person to grab off the street who was actually fae. But I couldn't burden her. Not after everything Father had put her through, and after all the neglect from Mother.

Dan and Nina were obviously off the table. If they knew I was trying to contact Quintin, my father, they'd freak out. Rightfully so. But I didn't have a choice. He'd forced my hand.

Jaden would do anything I asked of him. I didn't have to think twice about that. But he didn't have any more fae knowledge than I did, and had family of his own to worry about.

I'd just drop a note if I knew the right people would find it, but it could be my mom's people instead of Quintin's. Stepping over the border would just be lunacy.

Which left Cray. Who wasn't going to want to help me, but wasn't going to have a choice. It had been a long wait for Dan and Nina to go to bed. Thankfully it had already been late when we had gotten home, and I'd been able to convince them I was going to get some sleep. It had taken another hour of them out whispering to each other in the kitchen, but finally things had quieted down enough that I could go and talk to Cray alone.

I snuck down the hall between our rooms, careful not to make a sound. Nina had been watching me like a hawk since we got home from the hospital. No doubt she was worried about my emotional state and all that.

Valid. But I wasn't. In fact, I was shutting all that down for now. I'd deal with it later. After I had the whole king and queen of the fae fighting over me thing figured out.

Ha. What chance did I really have against those two? Not much, but I was going to try anyway. If I didn't, who knew what message he would send next, or who else would get hurt.

I still hadn't figured out what I was actually going to say to Quintin when I saw him, but I wasn't much of a planner. Even if I did have a speech ready, whatever I was feeling would spill out of my mouth instead anyway.

Good thing Starren wasn't home tonight. She'd gone to check on Cumat, who'd she'd helped rehome when we'd gotten back from Faerie, but wouldn't tell anyone where.

Closing my eyes, I opened Cray's door and slipped in blind, not wanting the knock to wake up Dan, who was a really light sleeper, but also not wanting to see anything I shouldn't.

"Cray?" I whispered loudly.

"Huh?" a mumble came from the direction his bed should be in.

I stumbled that way. "Hey, Cray, wake up!"

"Huh? Somethin wrong?" his words were slurred, but at least he was speaking.

"Are you dressed?"

"Yes?"

"That sounded like a question."

"I'm dressed."

I opened my eyes to find him blinking at me, glasses missing at the moment.

He reached over and patted his desk for a second before finding them and mashing them on his face. "What are you doing in here? What time is it?"

"I need your help." That woke him up. I wasn't good about asking for help, even when I really needed it. "I need to speak to Quintin."

His eyes widened. "Quintin?" Okay, now his voice was really high. "Why in the world would you want to talk with Quintin?"

"Shh, keep your voice down. You know Dan's sleeping habits."

His voice still came out in a squeak, but at least it's at a much lower wave length. "What could you possibly want with Quintin?"

"Rosie today. It wasn't random." This was the first time I'd admitted that out loud to anyone other than Nina. Not even Jaden, who'd stopped by earlier to see how I was doing. No, I especially couldn't tell Jaden, because he'd want to help, and I couldn't just keep throwing him into danger all of the time. He'd be upset if he knew, but he didn't need to know.

Cray's eyes widened and he looked away. "I was afraid of that."

"You were afraid of that?" Now it was my voice going too high. "Afraid of what, specifically?"

"That things would escalate. Your parents aren't exactly reasonable people."

True. Without even a pause, I one hundred percent agreed with that. "You should have warned me."

"And made you paranoid for no reason? Plus, would you even have listened to me? I don't think so."

That was a good point too. Cray always had some paranoid theory about what could happen. I probably would have just brushed it off if he'd said anything. "So what do I do?"

"Why in any world are you asking me? I don't know what to do. I can't even decide what sandwich to get at the cafeteria most days."

"I'm asking you because you're my friend, Cray, practically my brother, and you know the fae far better than I do. I'm terrible at being fae."

"Yeah, that's why we're friends. I don't like the fae very much."

"What do you think they'll do next? Either one of them. I can't handle it if something else happens to someone because of me." Shoot, that last part just slipped out. Once this opening up stuff got started, apparently it didn't get shut down. I'd have never let Cray have even a small glimpse into my feelings a year ago. But it was too late now.

"I don't know specifically. But you know it won't stop. Fae are big into all that prophecy stuff, if they both think you're the path to the crown, you aren't getting away from them. Ever."

Ever. Such a strong word.

"Sorry I don't have any better advice. I'll think about it, but I'm afraid you're going to have to do something drastic."

"Drastic? How drastic?"

"Choose a side. Or..." he paused, looking squeamish. "Never mind. That wouldn't work. But don't do anything stupid until we have a plan. There will be plenty of time for stupid after, when you run off and ignore our plan anyway."

I snorted. "Then what's the point of making one?"

"The point is that you have people who care about you and who want to be involved. I'll text Jaden and Starren, we can all meet and figure this out." He grabbed his phone off his end table and started typing. "With all the different perspectives, we have to be able to come up with something."

"Sure, sure."

Cray squinted at me, not satisfied with my non-committal answer. "I'm serious, Trish, if you pull any of that dumb stuff you pulled when you ran off with Starren..." Apparently he couldn't come up with something terrible enough, because he just ended his sentence with a glare. It was a Cray glare, so not very intimidating, but it was one of the best I'd seen from him.

"You're not my actual brother, Cray. You don't get to tell me what to do." It came out much harsher than I meant it to, pent up feelings from the day flowing out of me. Cray looked like I'd just knifed him in the back, but he kept it together.

"The family you choose is stronger than the family you're born with. You don't have to listen to me, of course. But I hope you'll at least consider what I've said."

I grunted, but didn't give him a real answer. If I said I would, that meant I had to, and I really didn't want to.

"Thanks, Cray. I'm sorry. You are my brother." It was the first time that had come out of my mouth. He started to beam, which left me scrambling for the door. Truth bomb and then exit, so I didn't have to deal with the aftermath.

Shutting the door to my room behind me, I grabbed a set of clothes I'd left out earlier.

Fort Wayne was a pretty safe city. But a teenage girl skulking around in the middle of the night even in a safe city wasn't a great idea. Not great ideas were my best kind. I changed quickly and slipped out of the apartment, hardly breathing as I closed the door behind me.

Oh for the D.C. days when I had a convenient window I could throw myself out of, wait a second to heal whatever I'd messed up, and then go about my business.

This time I'd made it away without anyone noticing. Hopefully. But maybe not next time. We really needed to get moved out of the apartment and into the new house. Ground level floor, baby, and a beautiful sliding window.

The trip downstairs didn't take long. I flew out the apartment building door, and right into someone. "I'm so sorry!" I said, stepping back.

Then I saw who it was. Jaden straightened up in front of me, looking down.

"What are you doing here?" I asked.

"Want to ask in a different voice?" Jaden answered. "That's no way to talk to a friend. Especially one that's been sitting out here all night waiting for you to sneak away and do something stupid."

Ouch. Not the something stupid part, everyone knew that was true, but the other part. The part where I'd gotten so predictable. "Maybe I just needed to clear my head. Get some space. Look for Storm."

"Yeah. Sure. Then you won't mind if I hang around."

I glared up at him but it didn't seem to have any effect.

"Go on. Go about whatever you were doing. I'll just be here, waiting to call 911."

Stomping off, I pretended he wasn't following me. This presented a problem. A serious problem. I was about to do something stupid. Of course I was. But I really didn't want Jaden involved. If he came along, he might find out about something else stupid that I'd done, not that long ago.

Recent enough that I still didn't know if it was going to come back and bite me in the rear or not.

Jaden wouldn't be able to hear me talking with Nara in my head. I hadn't heard from her in a while, and I'd taken that as a good thing since she worked so closely with my mom, but at this point I was getting desperate. Maybe my mother would be willing to help me with my father.

No violence or anything, I didn't need that happening, just advice. She's known him... Actually I didn't know how long. I didn't know anything about their relationship. Kind of sad, but not my fault.

Nara's power must not work like a normal power, because it had worked fine in Sanctuary before. But that was when she wanted to talk to me. I didn't really know how to get ahold of her.

Maybe I should just try talking. "Nara?" I said in my head. No need to let Jaden know what was up.

No answer.

"Nara?" I tried again.

Still no answer.

Was she sleeping? Intentionally not answering? Or could she not hear me? And the worst question of all, did I have to cross the city line to get communication started?

Ugh. Crossing the line had always been bad news so far. I'd almost lost Nina and Dan with one trip, nearly gotten my Aunt Wren killed trying to heal a gunshot wound on another, and then there was the last time, which had led to another trip to Faerie.

Gross.

I started walking toward the closet spot in the boundary. Knowing exactly where the line was before had always been to make sure I didn't cross it. And now it would be to cross it intentionally.

Things tended to get complicated around here.

Jaden trailed behind me, hands in his pockets, not saying a thing. He didn't need to. I knew how dumb this was, I just didn't feel like I had any good options.

It took much longer than it should have to reach the boundary. Even with the fact that I was ticked off that someone I cared about had been hurt, I still had to force each foot to move, to control each step.

I stopped at the line to take a deep breath. This section of the boundary was wooded, with very little traffic, which was great, just in case something happened. But not great, because something was much less likely to happen if there were humans around.

"You sure about this?" Jaden asked.

I straightened my shoulders. "As sure as it gets."

"Are you going to tell me what you're doing?"

"Not unless it works."

Jaden sighed, but stepped over the line in front of me, looking both directions. I stepped out behind him and we both waited a second in silence, breaths held.

Nothing happened.

"Nara?" I said internally. I waited for a full minute, but there wasn't a response. "Seriously, Nara, come on. Answer me." How could there still be nothing? Maybe she was back in the prison that blocked powers. Or maybe she was... Nope. Not going there.

An eerie howl sounded off to our left. I froze, but Jaden somehow kept his head about him. He grabbed my arm and jerked me back across the line just as a death hound bounded out from the trees.

"How did it know we were here?" I asked Jaden.

He loosened his grip on my arm, but kept his hand there like he was afraid I'd go running back into danger. I couldn't really take offense at that. Putting myself in danger seemed to be a normal occurrence.

The death hound bounded up to the line, and even though I knew he couldn't cross it, I cringed a bit. Somewhere out there, Vilan must be waiting for me to slip up.

"Did you get any pizza?" Jaden's question was so out of the blue that I just turned and blinked at him.

"Huh?"

"You tried to get pizza with Rosie, but then the pizza place was full of fae and you had to leave. Did you get any pizza first?"

"Ah, no."

Outside, the death hound called a mournful call, its white eyes closing for just a second. Its call was answered by another hound's voice, off in the distance.

"What? Where'd he get another one?"

"He's always had two," Jaden said.

"Yeah, but one got killed in Faerie on my last trip. It was really sad."

Jaden looked at me like I was crazy.

"What? I can be sad when an animal dies. I can't help that its master is evil."

"I don't think you told me about that part of your trip. But anyway. Pizza?"

My stomach growled in answer. I hadn't eaten anything all night, hadn't even thought about it. Which for me was saying something. "We can't go back to Dot's."

"And why is that?" He turned and walked away. I followed.

"The guy that hit Rosie followed us from there. They know it's one of my places to go, apparently."

Jaden stuck an elbow out. I hesitantly took it. Because my hands were cold, of course. No other reason.

He smiled and tugged me forward. "I know just the place."

'Just the place' was a dive bar only a few blocks away from the apartment building. The sign blinked *J nny's*, and it was dark enough that I couldn't tell what the missing letter was supposed to be. We got odd looks when we walked in, until the smoke cleared enough for them to see it was Jaden.

"Hey! Back already?" a waitress asked as she bustled by, her voice raspy from years of smoke inhalation.

"Yeah, needed some food and everywhere else is closed."

She nodded toward a back table, far away from the actual bar. "Keep your friend over there. You might be able to pass for an adult, but she sure don't look old enough to be in the bar side."

"You got it, Martha."

The waitress threw one menu on the table and walked away.

Apparently he was here often. How had we never talked about this? But then, really, how much had we talked lately? And we always seemed to talk about my stuff, not his. Did he have a life outside of what I knew about him?

I didn't know if I should be insulted or happy, so I defaulted to happy. He was building himself a real life here. A life that included human friends, regular people.

So he was doing better than I was, and he was a ghost.

"How long have you been coming here?"

"Do you remember when I was working all those odd hours after we first got here?"

I nodded.

"This was the only place open when I got off work. And they let me pay off my tab by doing odd jobs."

Another look around the room didn't reveal anything out of the ordinary. I should have checked better when we came in, but something about Jaden being around was finally allowing me to drop my guard a bit. This day had been...

No words. And now that I was somewhere that felt fairly safe with one of the people I felt the most safe with, my eyelids began to droop.

The waitress walked over. "You want your usual appetizer, Jaden?"

"She hasn't looked over the menu yet," he answered.

"Just get what you always get, with a second helping," Martha suggested.

The side of his mouth quirked up, and he looked at me. "Mac and cheese bites?"

"Eww, no."

"That's what I thought." He looked back up at the waitress. "We'll just take a large chicken club pizza. Thanks."

Martha nodded and swiped the one menu off the table.

We waited in silence as she buzzed away. Then Jaden leaned over the table catching my eye even though I tried to avoid it. "How was the dojo today?"

"I... what?" His question threw me off. No how is Rosie? Now how am I? What about what next?

"Did you have a good session at the dojo today? Weapons on Fridays, right?"

"It went great?" My answer came out as a question. The side of Jaden's mouth quirked up. "Why? That's a weird question right now."

"I just thought you might like to talk about something else for a bit. Something other than the crazy."

I almost smiled back, but then I remembered what happened after the great session at the dojo. "That's really sweet, but right now, I need a plan of attack. Someone hurt Rosie. Someone sent by my father. I can't just sit here and eat pizza and chat about my day."

Jaden rubbed the back of his neck. "I get that. I was just hoping to give you a couple minutes of normal before moving on."

"Moving on?"

He looked over his shoulder and waved a man toward us. The guy had been leaning against the bar since we walked in, flannel jacket, worn and torn jeans, the exact type I'd expect to see in a bar.

The man ambled over and flipped a chair around, straddling it as he nodded to me.

"Trish," Jaden said. "This is Phillip."

I nodded back, not sure where Jaden was going with this.

"He's fae. As is-" he took another look around the room. "Everyone in the bar at the moment."

I jerked around, taking another look at everyone I'd dismissed when I'd walked through the door. Eight other fae? In one place? I had to catch myself before I started to hyperventilate and let this Phillip know how much that freaked me out. I bit my lip to keep from chewing Jaden out. Had he set me up? Brought me here to his little fae rescue operation when he knew I wanted nothing to do with it?

"Hey now, Jaden. You're not supposed to be spreading that around." Phillip didn't sound happy. And anyone that big was intimidating when they weren't happy.

"You know I wouldn't tell anyone unless it was completely necessary."

Phillip leaned back in his chair, studying me for a second. "Then she's the one."

"She's the one."

After that he studied me some more. To the point that my uncomfortableness turned to being weirded out. "Okay, I'm the one, no idea what that means. Who are you?" I twisted to look at Jaden. "Is this the real reason you brought me here?"

Jaden rubbed his neck. "That, and you really did seem hungry."

"You're the one that has Sanctuary no longer feeling like a Sanctuary," Phillip grumbled.

Rude. It wasn't my fault my parents were crazy.

"How long have you been here?" See, I could control my mouth. Sometimes. Jaden and I'd had this conversation enough times that I wasn't going to get into it with him right now.

"Two weeks."

"Two weeks? It's changed that much in two weeks?"

"Okay, I haven't seen the changes, but I've heard about them. That this used to be a nice, calm place to live. And now the fae to human ratio is really getting mixed up."

"He's a refugee," Jaden clarified. "Left Faerie because of everything going on there."

"Everything going on?" I asked. Normally I avoided talk of Faerie, which Jaden knew. And so if he was the one bringing it up...

"All-out war between..." his rude expression went a little squeamish. "All-out war."

"You don't need to hold anything back with her," Jaden said. "She knows what her parents are."

"Monsters!" the man half-yelled.

The sad thing was I didn't know if to disagree or not. I knew how I felt about them, and while it should hurt to hear others felt that way too, it didn't, because it was exactly what I expected.

At least the guy had the decency to look slightly ashamed. Slightly.

"The fae have always been... let's say they don't play well with others. But for the last thousand years, that means that they scheme behind each other's backs, occasionally have a rival assassinated, you know, all the back alley fae stuff. But now, everyone is choosing sides. And if you don't, you're taken out by one side or the other."

This wasn't my responsibility. It wasn't my fault. They were my parents for Pete's sake, not the other way around. But that didn't stop the guilt that went through me.

"Everyone else is being forced to pick a side," Phillip said. "It's time you do too. If you choose one, the other will have to back down. Whoever has the girl has the throne."

"That prophecy is a load of crap," I said. "I don't have any power here."

"Whether it's actually true or not doesn't matter. People believe it's true, and therefore it has power. Why do you get to stay here in peace while everyone else suffers? Whole sections of both armies are trying to defect. Do you know what happens to the ones who don't make it here?"

"Okay, that's enough," Jaden interrupted. "This isn't why I set up this meeting. You were just supposed to give her a run-down on how things are, not guilt trip her."

"Sorry. I don't know what else you want me to say."

"It's fine. Go." Jaden watched the man walk away. I fidgeted, never quite able to hold still. Once Phillip was out of hearing range, Jaden leaned in close, face sober. "I have an idea but I'm not sure you're going to like it." His words were not very reassuring. In fact, I was normally the one saying that people aren't going to like what I was going to do next, so they were less than not reassuring.

"I'm not going to like it? Like I don't like the fact that you brought me here, after I've told you about a hundred times that I don't want to get involved? Yeah, I'm probably not going to like anything else you have to say."

"I'm sorry, Trish. It was wrong of me. Seriously."

I studied him for a second, just to make sure he knew that I wasn't just letting him off the hook. "Okay. What's this dumb idea?"

Jaden grinned. Not quite his normal grin, but I'd take it. "Because you like to be the one causing all the trouble." He got serious. "I need to get over the line, Trish. I need to find somewhere safe to sleep for a bit, see if anything comes to me."

"Are you crazy? You'll get killed!"

"It's the best way to know what's going to happen. Living here, I haven't been able to practice with my ability. I have no idea what, if anything, I'll see. But I need to try. If war is coming to Earth, we need to be ready."

War on Earth? Surely the fae weren't crazy enough to...

Who was I kidding. Of course they were.

"I'm sorry to involve you, but I need someone to watch my back while I'm asleep, and I don't have anyone else to ask. At least anyone who would actually be any help."

"Are you really apologizing for asking for help to do something to help me?" I leaned back away from him, stalling a bit. Going across the line was crazy. But some tips about the future could be invaluable. "How long do you need to be asleep?"

He rubbed his neck, looking so tired. "I hate putting you back in harm's way. But I don't know what else to do. Because I don't have control of my ability, I have no idea how long it will take. Or even if I'll have a vision. It's always been completely random. But with something this important, surely I'll see some type of future."

"You putting me in harm's way? Do you remember how many times I've gotten people in trouble?"

"Let's not argue about this, Trish. I owe you far more than you owe me."

I fumed for a second, trying to come up with a response, but he held up a finger.

"No. I'm serious. Let's make a plan and stop wasting time arguing. I can't do it without you, unless you convince Starren to come with me."

"Starren? That would be such a bad idea."

"On so many levels." I got another small smile from him, and my heart warmed. It made me want to think of something clever or funny to say to keep that smile there, but I didn't come up with anything in time.

"Okay then. Over the line it is. When? And where are we going to hide to give you enough time to have a vision?"

"That's a great question. One I wish I had an answer to."

I sat up straight, hit by a thought. "The old farmhouse! The one we got into a fight with Starren and Wade at." That seemed like so long ago. Wow, things had changed since then. For one thing, my sister wasn't trying to kill me anymore, so that was nice.

Jaden considered me for a second. "As good a place as any, I guess. Though a little farther over the line than I'd like."

"Me too. I guess we could pull over the border in your truck."

"I'd never fall asleep. Unless..." He thought about it for a second. "I can throw a mattress in the bed."

I shrugged. "Worth a try. How tired are you right now?"

"You want to do this right now?"

"Why not? It's night. Neither of us are going to be able to sleep at home anyway, thinking about this."

He considered. "Fine. Let's do it." He stood up. "Anyone have a mattress sitting around? It's time for me to get the best sleep of my life." He smiled at me, the real kind, and I almost melted. Okay then. Stupid, here we come.

CHAPTER FOUR

We bumped along in Jaden's old pickup, him with a white-knuckled grip on the steering wheel, me staring out the back window, hoping not to see someone following us, but expecting the worst.

Not a word had been said as we'd thrown an old mattress and some blankets in the bed of the pickup and stopped at my place for just long enough for me to sneak in and grab my sword. I also left Nina a note, just in case. There had been too many close calls lately, and if something happened to me, I wanted her to know that I loved her and Dan, even if I had a hard time saying it.

Jaden turned left a third time in the last five blocks, twisting around toward the city limits. He glanced in his rear-view mirror even though he knew I was keeping an eye out.

I didn't blame him.

"Are you even going to be able to sleep?" I asked to break the silence.

"I hope so. Someone gave me something to help in case I can't fall asleep on my own. That stuff puts me right out, to the point I won't be able to wake up for anything for about an hour."

Wonderful. Not only would I be in charge of keeping him safe while he was asleep, but now I wouldn't be able to get him up if I needed to in a hurry. Hopefully it wouldn't come to that. The help sleeping, or the waking up in a hurry.

I wouldn't hold my breath.

There. The city limits sign. I knew where every single one in the entire place was. Knew where the limit was even on the roads too small to have a sign. I gripped the handhold in the door of the truck so hard that I probably left permanent indentations.

Jaden stopped with the nose of the truck just at the edge of the line. He stared ahead for a moment, lost in thought. "We'd better switch places. Just in case we're seen."

That said something about how tired I was. I hadn't even thought of that. Only fae would be able to see Jaden outside of Sanctuary. To humans, he'd be a ghost. We switched places in near silence, the only sound in the night that of the truck doors slamming closed.

How long had it been since he'd crossed the border? Did he feel different when he wasn't whole? I watched him for a second, but it wasn't the right time to ask. When he met my eyes and nodded, I put the truck in drive and took a deep breath before coasting forward, inch by inch.

Three feet. Four. So far so good.

A horn behind us nearly sent me through the windshield. We'd both been so focused on what might come at us from the front that we'd missed some quiet electric vehicle pull up behind us. The driver waved us angrily on. I ground my teeth, keeping it together for peace-loving Jaden, and pulled off to the side of the road so the car could pass us.

"Is this far enough?" I asked Jaden.

He cocked his head. "How are your aches and pains?"

I evaluated for a second. "Gone."

"It's far enough."

We waited a moment in silence, both tense. I couldn't know for sure what he was thinking, but I was remembering the last time I'd crossed the line on a 'short errand.' That time was just supposed to be long enough for me to heal a gunshot wound.

It hadn't turned out that way.

Even though I strained to hear, the baying of death hounds didn't break the silence. No weird figures in the dark.

"We'd better just go for it." Jaden broke the quiet night sounds. "The longer we're here, the more likely we are to be found."

"Or we could just turn around. Go back, and try something different." I wasn't normally the one advocating for a less risky option, but it was Jaden who would be in the most danger if we took the next step in the plan.

"Give me a better option right now, and I'll take it." He waited a second, but I didn't have one. I could try talking to Nara, but that was a last resort. She was loyal to my mom, and I wasn't sure I could trust her. Jaden got tired of waiting for an answer to his question. "Then I'm doing this." I almost protested, but he must have seen it in my face. "It's not just for you, Trish. It's for everyone in the city. Including my little sisters and my mom."

Here I was, being selfish again. I hadn't even thought about the fact that if someone came after me, his family could be collateral damage, just like Rosie.

"Okay then. Let's get it over with."

He jumped out of the cab and made his way to the bed of the pickup. I followed, not jumping up behind him but leaning on the wheel-well. "I'll stay in the driver's seat. Be ready to go if someone does show up."

"That would probably be best." He eyed me for a second. "Don't take any chances. They're after you, not me. Get out of here if you have to." He laid back and popped some pills in his mouth, swallowing them without water and then giving me a crooked grin. "I already know I'm going to need these. Might as well not waste any time."

It took him a second to get comfortable, shifting around on the mattress until he apparently found exactly the right spot. He stopped moving really quickly, and, contrary to what I'd told him I was going to do, I jumped up in the truck bed and moved over to sit by his head.

He looked completely out already.

"Jaden?" I asked quietly. He didn't answer. I slid my sword out of the sheath hanging on my back and snuggled in closer to him.

Enough awake to notice me sit down, he shoved a corner of the blanket at me. I pulled it over my legs as his breathing evened, and then slowed to the point I couldn't hear it anymore. I leaned down over his face to watch for his breath, the brilliant moonlight helping me make out a whisper going over his lips.

He'd better trust whoever he'd gotten those pills from. The last thing we needed was another enemy. Or to have an enemy we didn't know about try something. We had plenty of people to worry about already.

Amazing how some people looked so serene when they slept. Like they didn't have a care in the world. I probably didn't. Not that I really knew, but I had to be one of those ugly sleepers, for sure.

Settling in against the cab of the truck, I took a deep breath in through my nose, and let it out my mouth. Nothing bad was going to happen. A person only had so much rotten luck in a day, and I'd already seen one of my best friends get hit by a car. Another one wasn't going to get hurt in the next twenty-four hours.

It just couldn't happen.

A few minutes went by. I watched the woods lining the road ahead of us intently for the first bit. As nothing happened, I relaxed, just a little, and stared up at the stars.

Getting me as a babysitter was a bad idea on so many levels. One of which being I got bored way too easily. I flicked the blanket off my lap and shivered at the chill air that replaced the warmth. If I stayed under there much longer, I might fall asleep, even under these circumstances.

The first sign that something might be off came with a jerk. Jaden spasmed, and I dropped back down beside him.

"Jade?" I asked quietly, using his little sister Jaime's nickname for him. No surprise, he didn't answer. But he did calm back down. I sat by him again and pulled his hand out from under the blanket, clasping it between mine. Why I couldn't do this when he was awake was beyond me.

The contact relaxed him, and it was another minute before he called out. I couldn't understand whatever it was he said, but I could feel the emotion behind it. Desperation.

"It's okay, Jaden. I'm here." Again, my voice seemed to calm him a bit. But how long would that last? I took a wary look around the truck.

Something was going to hear him. And with my luck, it would be something I really didn't want to deal with.

Jaden whimpered. Surely he had seen enough by now. Were the pills he'd taken something magical, something that would be stopped by crossing back over the city limits?

Worth a shot, if it came to that. But if I drug him across now, and he missed the end of whatever he was seeing because I had chickened out...

No signs of danger yet. Nothing that should make me jump in the driver's seat and gun the truck backwards across the line. I kept his hand in one of mine and gripped the hilt of my sword in my other.

No one would touch him.

Something rustled in the trees down the road. I slowly tucked Jaden's hand back under the blanket and stood, grip tightening on my sword. This was Indiana. No reason to get nervous about something in the trees. It could be a deer. A stray dog. Maybe even a friendly coon.

The only sound breaking the night at this point was my breathing. Everything was extremely still, extremely quiet.

Like something dangerous was nearby.

A weird fog trickled out of the trees. That grip on my sword began to hurt a bit, the leather biting into my hand. I knew that fog. And hopefully it was a friend. I'd never met anyone like her before, so there was a good chance it was, but what if it wasn't? Even Starren was afraid of hyran, and until the moment I'd found that out, I'd thought Starren incapable of fear.

The scritch of scales across pavement made me bite my lip. The first thing I saw were her eyes. Every time, their white irises nearly hypnotizing.

Shoot. Should I make a break for the cab of the truck? Did I just stay here and wait? How would she feel about Jaden? As far as I knew, they'd never met.

She was close enough now that even if I'd wanted to, I wouldn't be able to get away. I relaxed my painful grip on my sword a little. I wouldn't be able to stop her from doing whatever she felt like doing, I might as well present myself as the friend I hoped I still was to her.

The sound of a car coming up behind us caught my attention.

The fog thickened, and Wraith's watchful gaze disappeared. She knew how to get by in the human world. And fog was common this time of year.

The car inched by and was gone.

I let out a breath. Not that I thought Wraith would trash the vehicle and kill whoever was inside, but I didn't really know what to expect from her.

"Trisha." Her voice hissed through the fog, and suddenly there was her pale face, equal height with mine even though I was standing in the bed of a truck and she stood on the ground.

As far as I knew.

She grinned at me. No use trying to hide my fear, she could taste it. Whether the grin was the enjoyment of that fact or an attempt to put me at ease, I had no idea. "It's been too long."

"It's only been a few weeks," I retorted.

"True. But I haven't had a laugh in all that time. I don't think that's healthy."

"Laughter is good for the soul." I relaxed a bit. So far, so good.

Wraith leaned in over the truck, inspecting Jaden. "Is this the boy you like?"

"Uh uh, we aren't talking about that."

She cocked her head to look at me, it twisted sideways like an owls. "Then what should we talk about, my friend?"

"How about why you're here? In the human world, in the open, ready to be seen at any moment?"

"I'm not worried about being seen." She grinned and her needle teeth reflected the moonlight. "It's almost time for the fae to come forward. If it happens by accident by me being here, so be it."

The fae were starting to think about revealing themselves to the public? That did not sound good.

"Aren't you afraid of what they'll do to you?"

The grin got wider. "What exactly would the humans be able to do to me?"

A great question. One I had no idea what the answer was. Surely a missile would take her out, right? I looked her over.

Maybe not.

"Okay, but what about the first part of my question? Why are you here?"

Her face went serious, which felt really weird. She always acted all jolly around me. I got the impression that wasn't her normal state, but we'd always gotten along really well for some reason.

"I'm worried about you, little fae-who-isn't-fae. You have powerful enemies. It's time to bring in your powerful friends." She looked down at Jaden, still knocked out cold. "What happened to him?"

"He's just sleeping."

The grin came back. "I'd hate to see his dreams right now."

For her to mention dreams... did she know his ability?

"I tend to make dreams take a dark turn." Oh. Her whole feeding on fear thing. That made sense. But hopefully it didn't affect Jaden. Poor guy didn't seem to be having the most pleasant of dreams even before she'd slithered up.

"There are things nearby that even I may not be able to protect you from," Wraith said. "If you are done with your little tryst with lover-boy, perhaps we should cross back into Sanctuary."

Things she couldn't protect us from? That sounded bad. Really bad. "Okay. I'll drive." I looked her up and down again. "I don't think Jaden's truck is going to be able to haul you." It was probably just a crappy little truck even twenty years ago when it had been made. Today I'd be surprised if it hauled a couch well.

"Pick me up once we cross the border." And with that, she disappeared into the fog.

"Wonderful," I muttered under my breath, then clamped a hand over my big mouth. I didn't know how well she could hear, and insulting her would be worse than stupid.

An odd chuckle bounced around the fog, and I got the strong impression she knew exactly what had just happened.

I watched the fog, muttering as I tripped around getting out of the truck bed and into the cab. I shoved my sword into its sheath and tossed it in the passenger seat, where Jaden should be sitting right now.

Putting the truck in drive, I coasted forward and put the windows down, straining to hear a sound from Jaden or any traffic that might be on the road, invisible behind the fog wall.

It took a nine-point turn, but I got the truck pointed in the right direction and cruised across the city line. As soon as the windshield cleared it, the fog was gone. I looked in the rearview mirror. The fog was just as thick behind us.

Okay, so I could just take off and leave Wraith behind. In one way, that seemed like the best option by far. But on the other hand... Ticking off a giant snake-creature who'd told me she was here to help didn't seem like a good idea. I didn't really want to change her mind.

The fog curled around a humanoid shape coming up the road behind us. Who the heck was that?

And then, it all dissolved.

I shivered.

The woman walked toward me, her gait slightly awkward. She pulled open the truck door on the passenger side, giving me my first good look when the dome light blinked on. Short grey hair, a pudgy face, with a mole on her cheek. This woman had to be at least seventy-five. She shoved my sword out of the way, and climbed in. The dome turned off when she slammed the door, plunging us into darkness.

"Well," Wraith's voice came out of the old lady's mouth. "What are we waiting for?"

Waiting for me to snap my jaw closed, that's what. I did, and pulled forward. At this time of night, things were pretty dead. I didn't have to concentrate on the road nearly as hard as I pretended to, but there wasn't anywhere else to look at the moment.

"So?" Wraith asked, gesturing to herself in a way I couldn't imagine any old lady doing. "What do you think?"

"You got the look right. You could be anyone's grandma."

She looked pleased with herself. "Thank you. I've spent a lot of time around humans, you know. I really am an expert." She studied me for a second, not blinking. Okay, that was totally wrong for a human. "Even more of an expert than you, I'd wager."

"Could be," I said, no solid answer in my words. Getting into an argument right now would be disastrous, and I still didn't know her well enough to not accidentally push any buttons. I was, unfortunately, very good at that.

What now? Did I take Jaden home? How could I explain the situation to his mom, Rebecca? Did I take them to my place? Letting Wraith around Dan and Nina just seemed like a really bad idea. Maybe she could stay with Carver? Ouch, another bad idea. Starren wouldn't let anything that could even possibly hurt Carver that close to him. And Wraith and Starren already really, really didn't like each other.

Okay then. The bar it was. Wraith could help me drag Jaden in somewhere warm while he slept off whatever he'd taken, and maybe I could find someone to take Wraith.

I drove well below the speed limit, but not so slow to cause road rage to the few drivers out at five a.m. Every little bump in the road, and there were a lot of them, I looked in the mirror to make sure I hadn't lost Jaden.

We passed a cop and I gave him a little wave. Getting pulled over right now would be a disaster.

"What's wrong?" Wraith asked. "You were nervous, then extremely scared."

"We just passed a cop. If we get pulled over, I'm dead when he calls Dan and Nina."

"Eh, just one human? You don't have to worry about being dead. You could probably handle him on your own. If you couldn't, I'm here. Nothing would happen to you."

Was she trying to be encouraging? It sure sounded like it. "I didn't mean literally dead. Just in a lot of trouble."

"Ahh, I see. But the threat is gone?"

I checked the mirror for the hundredth time. "No flashing lights."

Wraith just blinked at me in a face that looked like it should be wearing glasses. Maybe Cray had an extra set sitting around somewhere.

"And no flashing lights is a good thing?"

Some human expert. Every human above the age of five knew what flashing lights meant.

When I didn't answer she looked back out the window, tapping her nails on the arm rest. The tapping caught my attention and I glanced down. Even in the dark I could see the gleam of two-inch hot pink nails.

Pick a lane, Wraith.

Jaden had taken so many turns on our way to the city limits to make sure we didn't have a tail that I was having a hard time finding the way back. The sunrise began to light up the sky behind us. If I didn't hurry, I'd have Nina all over my case soon.

Did I want to hide this from her? Well, crossing the border, yeah. Having a fear-eating fae monster along for the ride, yeah. That I spent the night out without telling her? Yeah, okay, so I didn't really *want* to tell her any of it. But even if I wasn't fae and could lie, I really didn't know if I could lie to Nina.

"What's got you so quiet?" Wraith asked. "You're usually a talker."

Ouch. But I did tend to ramble around her. She made me nervous. "I'm trying to decide what to do next." I wrestled the truck into a right turn. The power-steering didn't work, which was one of the reasons Jaden had been able to afford it in the first place.

"Ah, yes. What is the plan of attack? I'm not sure which one will be harder to take out, we should probably start with the easier one first, make sure we don't drive them into teaming up.

I turned and blinked at her, mouth hanging open. "What?"

"Your father's military strength is far superior, but I do believe your mother's ability is stronger. So it depends on if we're going to do a full-on assault, or some back-handed sneaky assassination attempt." She grinned. "I think you can guess which I would prefer."

The more destruction, the better to her. I shivered. She was here to help me kill my parents? That was crazy. There was no way I was going to do that. No way I was even going to try, let alone succeed.

"Uh, I'm not ready for murder."

Wraith stared at me, an intense, reptilian stare. "I can see I brought it up too early. Carry on."

Yeah, like some time going by was really going to make me ready to kill anyone, let alone my biological parents. Sure, I'd only known my dad a short time and we weren't on the best of terms, but murder? There had to be a better way to stop them.

"We'll get everyone together and talk about this as soon as we can."

"You mean I'll have to see that sister of yours again?"

Was this hyran a bit crazy? Such mood swings. "She does know the most about the situation."

"She knows your father best. You know your mother best. I know the situation best, I just came from Faerie."

True. I pulled up in front of Jenny's and put the truck in park. The place was closed by now, but there was movement inside still. Someone was cleaning up. I opened the pickup door. Wraith reached for her handle. "No, you just stay here," I said. "I'll be right back."

"What makes you think you can tell me to stay in the truck?"

"You're here to help me, right? That means I make the decisions, and you help make them happen. Stay in the truck. Watch after Jaden."

She gave me a pouty look and crossed her arms in front of her, but didn't move to get out of the truck. I slid out and took off before she could see or feel my relief that she'd obeyed. Most of the fae didn't like hyran, and I couldn't say I blamed them if Wraith's behavior was typical of her kind. She'd taken a liking to me for some reason, but that didn't mean I didn't see how she treated others.

The door into the bar was locked. I knocked on the window, and a man wiping down the tables threw the towel he was using over his shoulder before coming over to open the door. It took him a good thirty seconds to unlock all of the locks. Seemed a bit excessive for an old bar, but considering their clientele, I couldn't blame them.

"Whaddya want?" he asked. He looked tired. Like the permanently tired kind of tired, not just the he was up past bedtime kind. He wore a grease stained t-shirt but didn't seem to notice the cold. His head sported a bit of stubble and a bandana.

"Uh, hi, I need somewhere for my friend to hang out until he wakes up. I don't have anywhere else to go."

He started to swing the door closed. "We're closed."

I stuck my foot in the door. "It's Jaden. One of your regulars. I think. I can't take him home right now, he just needs to sleep a bit longer, and it's too cold to leave him in the truck." I didn't know exactly how long a bit longer was, but hopefully not long.

"Yeah, I know Jaden. But we're closed." He looked pointedly at my foot. When I didn't pull it back, he gave my toe a kick.

There was a small whoosh of air and suddenly there was an old woman next to me, smiling an insane smile. "Dear, I do believe my friend here has asked for help. It wouldn't be polite to tell her no now, would it?" Wraith's wicked smile looked so wrong in the face of an old woman that I almost started hyperventilating.

"Uh, no, not polite at all, come on in." The man scrambled backward out of the doorway, giving me the impression he could see past Wraith's old lady act.

Wraith glided in the door and gave the room a quick glance, wrinkling her nose. Like Alcatraz where we'd first met was so much better. "The young man in question is in the bed of the pickup right outside. Be a dear and bring him in for us?"

If her strength was even a fraction in human form that it was in her regular body, she could have tossed Jaden over her shoulder with no more trouble than someone hefting cotton candy. But that would have looked pretty insane if any humans passed by, so I appreciated her restraint even if it wasn't there for that reason.

The man skirted Wraith as he passed us, slipping through the door and scurrying to the truck. He grunted a little, but didn't seem to have too much trouble hauling Jaden inside. His body flopped around, and I had a flashback to Rosie when the paramedics were rolling her onto a backboard. He looked as dead right now as she had then.

I scooted in close to the guy, straining to see Jaden's chest rise and fall, but couldn't with all the jostling going on.

"There's a cot in the back where we throw people to sleep it off sometimes," the man said. "I can put him there if you'd like."

"As long as he's safe and isn't going to wake up with a backache."

"A backache won't be my fault." The man gave me a longsuffering look. "I think you took care of that part yourself."

Wraith giggled and I sighed. The man hauled Jaden to a small back room. I kept an eye on him until Jaden was lying in a small cot, his legs hanging over the end. Wraith giggled again and I looked at her. "Aren't you supposed to be scary? Maybe you should look like a teenager instead of a grandma."

Her face went serious. "Have you seen how teenagers get treated? Nah, grandmas get to do whatever they want, say whatever they want."

"And if you slip up and mention the fae, I'll just tell people you're senile," I added.

That made her crack up again, and showed me exactly how easy it would be to get people to believe she didn't have everything quite right upstairs.

"Now. What to do with you."

She sobered up again. "I'm here to keep you safe. To do that, I need to be close enough to you to help if you get yourself into danger again." She grinned. "And when aren't you doing that?"

"So that's a no to living with Carver then?"

"Such a nice boy. But no. I will be within ten of your human feet of you at all times."

Ten feet? No way. I would not be able to handle that. Ten feet was ridiculous. I opened my mouth to tell her that, but her eyebrows went up and her lips pursed, and I remembered that I really should be slightly afraid of her, even if she looked like a grandma right now. "Okay."

We stared at each other for a second before I looked down.

"How do you look like that anyway?" I gestured toward her. "Glamor doesn't work in Sanctuary."

"It does for those of us who are older than the Sanctuary spell." She cocked her head. "But enough about me. How long until your sleeping handsome wakes up?" She preened at her little joke, but waited for me to answer.

Older than the spell? Just how old was she? I noticed her watching me and realized I hadn't answered her. "I don't know. He didn't know. He took some sleeping pills someone gave him. It could be a minute, it could be a year." I glanced over to watch his chest rise and fall. "I sure hope it isn't a year."

"Maybe you should just give him a little kiss, see what happens." She herded me toward Jaden, but I slipped around her and crossed my arms.

"Let's decide what we're going to do about you, and by the time we get done with that, he'll probably be awake." My phone dinged and I cringed. That meant it was late, or early, enough that someone was awake. No doubt someone I didn't want to talk with. I pulled my phone out of my pocket. 5:30 a.m. Of course Dan was the type to be up at 5:30. Nina was probably still sleeping, she wasn't a morning person.

Whew. He didn't know I wasn't in my room, he was just letting me know he had to leave for work early today. Okay. This might just work. Let Nina meet Wraith first, and then go on from there. Did I tell them that she was fae? I almost had to. While they were good about helping anyone in need, it would probably stretch even their generosity if I kept bringing random people home and asking for their help housing them.

"I'm Nina's problem, which makes you her problem too. I don't know where else to go but home. As soon as Jaden's awake, we'll head that way."

Wraith smirked. "Good. I'd love to meet the people you call family."

Wasn't that wonderful. I was taking one of Faerie's most deadly creatures home to meet the parents.

It wasn't much longer before Jaden woke up. Unfortunately for the poor guy at the bar who just seemed like he wanted to go home, Wraith ate everything in sight until that happened.

"I thought you fed on human fear," I said, watching her down a fourth helping of onion rings.

"I do, I do. But that doesn't mean I can't taste the deliciousness that human food is."

I shrugged. Who was I to judge? When not in Sanctuary, I could eat as much as the high school football team if I wanted to.

A sound made me glance toward Jaden. He'd shifted on the cot a bit, the first time he'd moved since he'd been tossed there. I rushed over and almost took his hand, catching myself just before our skin touched. "Jade?"

He groaned and his eyelids flickered, but he didn't move.

"He's going to have a nice hangover if he took what I think he took," Wraith announced around a mouthful of mac and cheese bites.

"And if he did take what you think he took, how long until he's ready to go?"

"Once he starts to wake up, he'll wake up fast. Any minute now."

"Okay then. Time to get him out to the truck."

Wraith looked down at her mostly empty plate, disappointed.

"They have to-go boxes, I'm sure."

She cocked her head at the bartender. He nodded, obviously uncomfortable at being the object of her attention, and rushed to grab a container.

"How does he know to be scared of you?" I asked.

"You already know what I am, so you don't feel it. But my kind give off a certain... aura, I think you'd call it in English. An aura that lets others know we aren't to be trifled with."

"Do you think you could tone it down a little? We don't need every fae we run into scrambling to get away."

She considered that for a moment. "I've never wanted to tone it down before. If anything, I've always gone the other way." She smiled a very unpleasant smile. "It's amazing what a little bravado will do for you even when you're outmatched. I'll see what I can do."

Her? Outmatched? She'd said when we were in Faerie that there were things there even she didn't want to tangle with. I really didn't want to know what those were.

"Trish?" Jaden asked, without opening his eyes. His voice was froggy, like he'd been asleep for two days instead of just a few hours.

"Yeah, I'm here." I did take his hand then.

He blinked, and then squinted at me, like the low fluorescent lights in the bar were too much. "Got any ibuprofen?"

"The bartender has to have some here somewhere." I moved to go ask, but he just held my hand tighter. "It can wait."

Wraith glided over and looked down at Jaden. "Such a handsome young man," she said.

Jaden's grip on my hand tightened and he awkwardly tried to pull me to the side of the bed, putting him closer to Wraith. "Uh, who are you?"

"Oh honey, has Trish never mentioned me? I would be so hurt to learn that."

He shot a wild look my way and I nodded. I had told him about her, and he'd thought I was crazy for trusting her. This probably would have gone better if I could have prepared him for the situation when he wasn't waking up from being drugged.

"How are you... Why..." He glanced at him and I could practically hear him think *yeah, here we go again.* "Never mind those questions. Just what are your intentions?"

The look in her eyes got so intense that even I wanted to shrink back from her. Somehow Jaden didn't flinch.

"To protect Trisha. Whatever the cost."

Okay, that was kind of weird. Our little friendship should not extend to 'whatever the cost.' She was fae and couldn't lie, as far as I knew, which meant that what she said was true, but didn't give me any insight into her motivations.

Jaden met her scary eyes and nodded. "Okay then. We need to call a meeting."

"A meeting?" I asked.

His jaw clenched. "This whole thing just got a lot bigger."

CHAPTER FIVE

This was a war council, which made me really uncomfortable. I'd called Nina, Starren, Carver, and Cray, asking them to meet us in the gym at Jaden's apartment building. No one ever used the space. It was a small room, but much bigger than our tiny apartment, and I didn't have to show Wraith exactly where I lived until Nina said it was okay. I hated to include her, but shuddered to think what she'd do to me if she found out I hadn't.

On top of the people I'd called in, there was Jaden, Wraith, and me. Dan was trying to make it, but he didn't know if he could get away from work before lunch.

Nina was waiting when we got there, looking perfect of course, even though I'd woken her up when I'd called and was still in her sweats. Cray had already arrived too. He was a bit disheveled, but very awake. Carver walked in right behind us, doing a double-take at Wraith.

"Honey?" Nina hurried over. "What's going on? Why were you out so early? Is everything okay?" She nodded to Wraith. "Hi, I'm Nina."

Wraith controlled herself surprisingly well and just nodded back. She had to know how much Nina meant to me after helping us get her memory back, which likely explained her behaving herself.

"I'll tell everyone at once," I said. More to give myself a few more minutes to gather my thoughts than because I didn't want to have to tell the story twice. I glanced at Jaden. His body was here, but his mind was far away. What had he seen? He'd refused to speak in the truck on the way here.

"Just Starren, then?" Nina asked.

I nodded. Starren lived with us too, but worked swing shifts at a small gas station down the road. She was their most valued employee, because shoplifting on any shifts she worked was zero. They had her working a lot.

The door opened, and there she was. She stopped dead when she noticed Wraith. "You," she said, her tone not very complimentary.

"And you," Wraith answered with a scary smile.

And here I'd thought they'd started to get along when we'd spent the night in Wraith's cave when we'd been to Faerie last.

"What's she doing here?" Starren's hand sat ready to grab one of the many knives she had hidden on her person.

"I'm here to protect Trisha, just like you are," Wraith answered.

Wait, what? Starren wasn't here to protect me. I'd helped her after she had to run from our father. She only stayed because she didn't have anywhere else to go.

Starren didn't ask Wraith what I needed protection from. We all knew. But she did relax, just a little.

Might as well get things started now that we were all here. "Everyone, meet Wraith. She's going to be staying with us for a while." I looked her over for a second. "We're going to have to think of something else to call you while you're here."

"Hazel!" Wraith butted in. "I always thought my human name would be Hazel."

"Human name?" Nina eyed her, but didn't make a move.

Wraith smiled and her teeth showed far too much. Somehow, right now she was making even a granny face look scary. Now Nina did take a step closer to me.

"Is this the–" Nina whispered to me.

"She can still hear you," I answered in a normal tone.

"Oh," Nina smiled and nodded toward Wraith, who gave her a wicked grin back.

"Okay then," I said loudly, even though I didn't need to be loud at all. The entire room had gone quiet, watching Wraith. "We should get started." I motioned Jaden over. His face was wan, like he'd been in a bunker for a month instead of just having the best sleep of his life.

"We went outside the border tonight." Okay, Jaden wasn't easing people into that, just getting it out there. A storm-cloud basically took over the room. Nina went white and her face tightened, telling me how angry she was. Starren's face got that neutral look that Nina called the stone face. While that meant I couldn't actually tell what she was thinking, I was pretty sure that meant she was mad too.

Cray and Carver didn't say anything at all, but they didn't need to. Both of them were now taking furtive glances around, like the border could have followed us here.

"It was for a good reason," I interjected.

"It always is, Trish. But that doesn't mean you should do it." Nina's voice was the high pitch that meant I was in serious trouble. It was so hard finding the right balance between us as mom and daughter. She wanted to protect me, but I also needed to protect her. And I was better at it. At least physically.

"Jaden had a vision."

The already quiet room went deathly still. Most of the people in the room didn't know what Jaden's ability was. It wasn't a polite question to ask a fae. No one really wanted others to know what they could do. But for this to mean anything, people had to know.

"He sometimes sees the future in his dreams."

"And this time it was like my ability was making up for the months I've been in Sanctuary. I saw..." the room collectively held its breath. "A lot."

I smiled at him, trying to be encouraging. Not one of my strong traits.

"The most relevant to us, someone is going to out the fae."

A chorus of voices went around the room, loud enough I couldn't understand any individual.

"Shut up!" Starren yelled. When the room quieted again, she asked Jaden, "And the result?"

"All-out war between the fae. Once they have no reason to hide, Quintin and Raiena go at each other in earnest. The death count…" he grimaces. "I don't know. Devastating."

"And the humans?" Nina asked. Her voice was quiet, strained.

"They do their best to exterminate the fae."

Starren growled somewhere behind me, and I heard Cray squeak. War between the fae and humans? For some reason in the back of my mind, I'd begun to think that maybe it wouldn't be such a big deal for the humans to know about us. They loved superhero movies and supernatural stories, surely it wouldn't be that big of a leap to accept at least the fae that looked human.

Growing up, being discovered had been my worst fear. Once I'd actually got to know some humans, and they'd found out about me, every single one had been wonderful. Rosie didn't know, but she seemed to think there were aliens, so fae weren't a huge leap.

Really, we were from a different world, didn't that make us aliens?

But apparently it would go the way my mom had always warned me it would go. War and death, for both sides. Because the fae wouldn't go without a fight, even if they didn't stand a chance.

"Humans have tanks and planes, bombs and ships. What are the fae going to do against that?" I asked.

Starren grumbled and Wraith wheezed out a laugh.

"Oh child, still making an old woman cackle," Wraith said.

"You're just showing your ignorance," Starren said. "How many fae do you truly know? Ten? Fifteen? Some of the old ones have wanted Earth for centuries. And you don't want to see what they're capable of."

Nina hugged me close with one arm, her face even more white than before. Poor woman. Until she'd taken me in, she'd had a good life. A stable life. I'd ruined all that. Even if it was by accident, it made me hurt knowing she would have been better off without me.

Even now, Rosie had proven that the people in my life were targets. How could I keep her safe when I didn't even know what the threats were? I looked around the room full of people I cared about. How could I keep any of them safe?

"This isn't a doom and gloom meeting," Carver snapped for the first time. "It's a planning meeting. What leads up to this fight? What assets do we have, and what do they have? Did you see any of us specifically, and what were we doing? Obviously we don't have an army, so precision strikes are our only recourse."

Starren's grin was nasty. "I'm very good with precision strikes."

"Before we talk about going and striking anyone, we need to try to talk to them. And maybe we should warn someone in D.C.," Nina said. "We can't let the world get attacked without warning."

"It's not going to be without warning," Jaden answered. "I don't think."

"You don't think?" Nina asked.

"It's not like my visions are a movie or something. They don't just play in chronological order. These visions could take place years in the future. I see bits and pieces, in whatever order they feel like happening. And not only that, if we change things, that changes the future, which means some of them won't be right anyway."

"If you try and tell any other humans about Faerie, you will die." Starren's voice was monotone, with no inflection. I glared at her. She should know better than to threaten Nina. I was about to follow through on the glare when she kept talking. "The fae have people integrated in all types of human authority. They would know as soon as you tried anything, and Sanctuary doesn't apply to humans."

Okay. She wasn't threatening Nina. I convinced my body to loosen up a little. It had been a long night, and I hadn't slept in... forever. I needed to keep a lid on my temper.

"You would be dead within an hour of trying to out the fae," Cray added from his corner, cementing my change of heart about Starren's comment. She was actually attempting to protect a human. Strange. But no one could resist Nina, not even Starren. Unless she was doing it for me, but we didn't really have that close of a relationship. I'd hoped we would become like real sisters after confronting both of our parents together and nearly dying together multiple times, but nothing had really changed. She still acted like I was an obligation that she didn't really care for.

"So what do we do?" I asked. I was a person of action. Not very good at planning, I jumped in and figured it out on the way, just like that fateful road-trip from Chicago to Fort Wayne, where Nina had found out about my healing ability. This situation called for a lot more finesse. So much more rode on this than just me getting ripped away from Dan and Nina.

I glanced at Nina. Never mind. So many more people depended on this, but for me, the stakes were almost the same. I looked around the room at all the people who cared about me. Okay, not exactly the same. How I'd gathered all these people by accident, I had no idea.

"There is an option we haven't truly discussed," Starren said, with uncharacteristic hesitation in her voice. "A... permanent solution."

"What does that mean?" Carver asked.

"She means she wants to do to them what she did to the Council," Wraith interjected gleefully.

"What?" I asked. "You want to kill them? Kill our own parents?" Was she crazy? They might have their problems, but did that really mean we had to kill them?

"I don't want to, Trish. It's just something we need to consider."

"No. No way. That is one hundred percent off the table."

"Then we're going to have to call a meeting," Starren said grimly.

I gestured around the room. "Isn't that what we're doing?"

She cocked an eyebrow at me. "With Mother and Father."

I wilted. "Oh." One of my worst fears, come to life. This was what I'd been trying to avoid by getting Jaden involved.

Nina put her arm back around my shoulder. "Is that safe? Those crazy people might just snatch Trish and take her to who knows where."

"Not if the meeting is in Sanctuary," Carver said.

"I don't want them here," I interrupted. "It's not safe for anyone." The image of Rosie's unmoving body nearly made me gag. It was worse now, with no sleep. I couldn't force it down, and I could feel my eyes start to tear up.

"They know where we are, Trish." Cray's voice was soft, kind. "Bringing them here to talk isn't going to change anything."

It would for me. Any semblance of normality that I'd built for myself would be gone. "I won't meet them in Sanctuary. Maybe the old farmhouse."

Nina spun me around. "No way. You aren't crossing that border. Not without me, and neither of us wants that."

"She'll be fine," Wraith broke in. "I'll be with her. There are things both Quintin and Raeina could call on that could best me, but not if they don't know I'm here. They won't be expecting it." She straightened to her entire four-foot eleven height. "I guarantee her safety, Nina of the humans."

I had no idea what that meant, but both Carver and Starren looked surprised. It took a lot to make Starren surprised at all, let alone to make her show it.

"And how, exactly, is that supposed to make me feel better?" Nina asked.

"If she's with me, you have no need of worrying about her safety." Wraith's crazy smile made her look more like she belonged in a loony bin than in the apartment building.

"Trisha is the safest she's ever been if Wraith is around," Carver said.

Starren glared at him, but didn't argue.

"Do you think those ogres would have tried to kill us if she was around?" Carver asked, gesturing at Wraith.

"Would someone please explain this to me?" Nina asked loudly.

"Sanctuary makes her look human," I said. I didn't even try to keep my voice down. She could hear anything in the room, there was no point embarrassing myself by pretending she couldn't. "She's actually a very..." how did I put this delicately? "Fierce fae. She can protect me better than anyone." I looked out over everyone. "Now. How exactly do we go about getting a meeting set up?"

No one would meet my eyes until I got to Starren. She stared me down for a moment. "Is this truly what you want?" she asked.

"No. But I don't know what else to do."

"When and where." She said it like an answer, not a question.

"Tomorrow, to give them plenty of time to get here," Jaden said. His face was pale, eyes dark. His ability had given us a lot tonight, but it had also taken a lot from him.

"Tomorrow then. At the farmhouse." Starren eyed Wraith. "We'll take plenty of fire-power. Even Mother and Father wouldn't be so disrespectful that they would break a council."

Wraith cackled. "No, your father needs you to do that for him."

"Not that kind of council," Cray interrupted. "A meeting council."

"You think I don't know that, boy?" Wraith's tone went sharp. "Let an old woman amuse herself."

That was enough of this. Time to break things up. "That's it, meeting adjourned. I need some sleep." I gestured for Jaden, and he half stumbled over. He obviously needed someone to make sure he made it upstairs, or he might fall asleep on the elevator.

"I got it," Starren said. She shoved Cray out of the way to make room for Jaden.

I watched them leave the room, jealous of Starren for a second, but a head full of wispy white hair popped up in my face. "Where are we going now?" Wraith wrung her hands, barely capable of containing her excitement.

"I'm going to my apartment, to sleep."

Wraith cocked her head. "Sleep? How much do you need to sleep?"

"At least four or five hours. I should have slept like nine hours last night and I got exactly zero."

"What am I supposed to do for four hours?" Wraith whined.

Wow. That was actually a great question. Where did one store their reptilian monster protector while they slept? I looked over at Nina, who was holding the door for Jaden and Starren.

Nope. Not leaving my mother with a crazy fear-eating fae, even if we were friends. My mother. I couldn't just think things like that. My biological mother was alive. Wanted me. That had to count for something.

I walked out behind Jaden and Starren. She propped him up against the wall and came over to snag me, pulling me over. Wraith followed right behind me and raised an eyebrow, but I waved her off.

"If you cross the border again," Starren hissed. "You take me. That is not a suggestion."

I made a little wave toward Wraith. "I've got extra back-up now."

"I don't trust her. And you shouldn't either. You shouldn't trust anyone but you, and me." She glanced toward Nina, who was scooting around Wraith to catch up with me. "And that one."

"It wasn't about trust, Starren. Of course I trust you to protect me. What I didn't trust was you staying calm if we ran into Mother or Father."

She relaxed a little. "Still. I'm here to keep you safe. I can't do that if you don't tell me what's going on."

I blinked, trying to control my face. If she'd said it, she had to mean it. This whole time I'd thought she was in Sanctuary because she didn't have anywhere to go after defying Father. But she was here to protect me?

That was news I would have to digest for a bit. I really didn't know what to do with the information other than put it in a box for now. Maybe if we both survived all this, we'd have to have a chat.

Wow, Nina and her talks were really getting to me.

And without a goodbye, Starren walked off, grabbing Jaden and tugging him along.

"Come on, Hazel," I said to Wraith. "It's time for a nap." I stumbled out of the building without checking to see if she followed or not. It wasn't like I could make her do anything, so I couldn't put any of what little energy reserves I had left into keeping an eye on her.

As I made my way toward our apartment, trying to figure out how not to leave Wraith with Nina.

Shoot, Nina, I'd zoned out and left her behind. I glanced over my shoulder. Nina and Wraith were walking together, eyeing each other and then eyeing me.

"Hey, Wraith?" I called back to them.

"Yes?"

"Can you make the same promise for Nina that you did for me?"

Wraith squinted at me. "No. No can do."

I stopped. "Why not?"

"In trying to protect her, I may neglect my duty to you. I won't make that promise."

Crap. I started forward again, and my two bodyguards trailed behind me. I couldn't keep pushing the insults and ask Wraith not to hurt anyone I cared about. There had to be another solution, at least a temporary one.

"Nina," I waved her up close. She matched my slow shuffle. I squinted at her, hardly able to keep my eyes open. "Can you do me a big favor?" I asked.

"Would," she corrected. "Would I do you a favor. Of course." She paused. "As long as it isn't something that you already know I'm going to hate. Just tell me what it is."

"I need you to go about your day like normal," I said. "Go volunteer wherever you're scheduled today, hit the church and do something, go get groceries. Basically I need you out of the house so I can take a nap."

"Why?" her voice was full of uncertainty.

Both of us looked back at Wraith, who grinned what was most likely supposed to be a reassuring smile. It was not.

"Please."

"But you-"

"I'm perfectly safe. She promised to protect me."

Nina studiously looked forward. "So she doesn't have a choice. She has to."

"Right."

"Okay."

I nearly hugged her in relief. She was so protective, which I appreciated because it meant she loved me, but in situations like this she wasn't going to be able to help anyway. Other than advice. We were beginning to find a balance of what I should call the shots on as the fae in the family, and what she should call the shots on as the mom.

"I'll grab my keys and purse."

She looked like she'd come straight over to the gym from bed. "You can change too, if you want. I'll probably grab something to eat really quick before I go to bed."

She gave me a relieved smile. She wouldn't normally be caught dead in public in her sweats, but apparently the chance of me getting dead out-weighed that.

We made our way up to the apartment together, me nearly passing our door and Nina gently pulling me back. Normally being outside of Sanctuary, I wouldn't be this tired even without a night of sleep. But this night of no sleep came after weeks of being stressed out, and the exhaustion left over from what had happened with Rosie.

Rosie!

"Nina!" I yelled, grabbing her arm as she tried to unlock the apartment door.

"What?" she looked around, eyes wide, waiting to be jumped by something.

"Oh, sorry, I just thought about Rosie! Have you heard anything?"

She rubbed her chest. "Don't do that to me." She checked her watch. "But it's late enough to call Violet. Even with her late night, I think she'll be up by now." She shoved the door open and walked into our front hallway that led to the kitchen. I followed her in, and pulled up a stool to the island while she popped her cell-phone out.

Wraith pulled out another stool and studied me for a second before copying my posture exactly. It looked rather odd in her grandma body.

The call finally connected. "Hey, Violet, it's Nina Inza. I was just calling to check on Rosie. Have you heard anything from the hospital this morning?"

Someone spoke on the other end of the line, but I couldn't hear more than a voice rising and falling. I strained to be able to hear better, leaning out over the island.

Wraith followed suit. She cocked her head to look at me. "The rose woke up. Whatever that means."

My face hit the counter and I turned my head to let the coolness sooth my heated face. Rosie was still alive. And not just alive, awake. I sat up straight. "She's awake, but is she going to be okay? Was there any permanent damage?"

Nina held up a finger, and I groaned.

"A year of rehab," Wraith answered my question. "Can roses be turned into drugs? What's it in rehab for?"

"Ssssh," I said, waiting for Nina to say something. Apparently she couldn't get a word in though, because she just kept saying uh huh, uh huh to whatever Violet was saying on the other side.

The wait until she hung up was probably twenty seconds. It felt like twenty hours.

"Okay then, thank you. Trish will be very relieved to hear that. I'll talk to you later." Nina hit end on her phone and turned to me, a massive smile on her face. "Rosie is going to be fine. She isn't one hundred percent out of the woods yet, but it's looking really good. She's going to have some real struggles over the next few months, but nothing should affect her too badly long term."

I jumped around the counter and grabbed Nina into a tight hug. She pulled away a little after a moment, but I jerked her closer and buried my face in her sweatshirt.

Rosie wasn't dead. Hadn't died because of me. She was going to be fine.

Something cold snuggled up behind me and Nina and I stiffened at the same time. Wraith had turned this into a group hug.

"Hmmm," she said. "I think I understand now why humans are always doing this."

I wriggled free. "I think I'm going to skip the snack. I just need to sleep."

"Of course," Nina said. "If that's what you need. Would you like to go and see Rosie later? Her mom says she's still in the ICU, so we can't actually go into the room, but they're allowing friends to come up to the glass door and wave."

Panic gripped my chest. I gritted my teeth and did my best to smile at Nina, to not let her see under the surface. My hands got clammy and my chest tight. Was this what a panic attack felt like?

Wraith whirled me around to face her. "Yes, Trisha, should we go and visit your roses later?"

I sucked in a breath, keeping my back toward Nina.

"Trish?" Nina asked.

It took me a second, but I took a couple deep breaths. "Later would be good, Nina."

"If you're sure. Just let me know when you want to go. I'll stay within fifteen minutes of the apartment."

"Thanks." I took off down the hallway toward my room. A glimpse of Wraith behind me startled me so bad I almost tripped. Too tired.

Everything startled me when I was tired. I led the way to my room and collapsed on the bed.

The thought of Wraith standing above me and staring down while I slept creeped me out a bit, but it was better than her out in the apartment if Dan came home for some reason. Actually, it would really be better if he didn't come home until I was awake.

"Nina," I yelled down the hallway. "Text Dan."

"Already done." She didn't usually yell, but probably didn't want to be any closer to Wraith than she had to.

I buried my face in my pillow. "Shut the door, please." My voice came out funny, but I knew Wraith would hear me.

The door clicked closed and I felt Wraith walk over to my bed.

"Thank you," I said. "For the assist. How did you know I was freaking out without your ability? I thought I was holding myself together pretty well."

"When you live off of fear, you recognize it instantly, even when you aren't feeding. What is it that made you react like that?"

"My friend." I pulled my face out of the pillow and blinked back tears. There was no point in trying to hide any of this from Wraith. It was almost a relief, to have someone I didn't feel like I had to put a brave front on for. "She's human, from my school. My father had her hurt. As a message to me. I can't go see her."

Anger swept across Wraith's face. "Stupid fae," she hissed. I leaned back away, afraid she meant me. But she didn't. "Involving children in his games. This is one of the reasons I hate the fae." She moved away and started pacing. "And in Sanctuary. The letter of the law doesn't extend to humans, but that doesn't make them fair game."

"I thought she was going to die." My voice came out teary, but I couldn't even bring myself to care. "She could have died, because of me."

"Because of your stupid parents," Wraith corrected. "Did you warn her about the danger?"

"I couldn't find a way without telling her I'm fae."

"Do you trust her?"

That wasn't a question that could be answered lightly. I thought for a moment. "Yes."

"Then you should have told her."

She wanted me to tell a human about the fae? Was she crazy? Oh, yeah, she was, but this was a special crazy. "But we aren't supposed to-"

"Eh, supposed to, smhosed to. You've got a good head about you. From now on you do what you think is right." She came over to pat me on the hand. "Now get some sleep, dear." It was her most convincing grandma voice so far. "I hear it's important for humans and your type of fae."

My smile felt weak, but she didn't seem to notice. She patted my hand again and went back to pacing on the far wall.

I stood and walked over to grab my pjs off the floor where I'd thrown them yesterday morning before walking to the bedroom door. "I'm going to use the restroom and change. Stay in my room." I started to close the door behind me, then thought better of it and stuck my head back in. "Please."

"As you wish." She smiled and even though it was still creepy, it did put me a little more at ease. What a weird feeling.

This time I did close the door. I passed the bathroom and did a quick tour of the apartment to make sure Nina had left. Her keys and purse were gone, sweatsuit she'd been in neatly folded and sitting on her bed.

She must have left in a hurry if it didn't get put completely away. I laughed to myself quietly. I'd know something dire was wrong if ever I found Nina's stuff out of place.

Getting ready for bed just after sunrise felt weird, but I was so tired I shoved that thought to the side. By the time I made it back to my room from the bathroom, Wraith was propped up against a wall, eyes staring into space, mouth hanging open.

I stepped in closer and waved a hand in front of her face. I'd never seen her sleep before, even when we'd spent the night at her place in Faerie.

This was kind of how I would have pictured it. Eerie and yet endearing. I tip-toed to the bed and slid under the covers, eyes going closed instantly. It took quite a while longer for my brain to follow their lead and turn off, but when it did, I was totally out.

CHAPTER SIX

By the time I started to wake up, it was starting to get dark. I blinked to get the sleep out of my eyes, and took a second to figure out if what had happened yesterday was a dream, or was real. Once I figured out that, unfortunately, it had all happened, I checked for Wraith.

She wasn't in my room.

Flinging the blankets off, I rushed out into the hallway. The murmur of voices led me to the kitchen. I ran into the room, skidding on the tile.

"There's our little vampire," Dan said from the sink. Was he doing supper dishes? My stomach rumbled right as I caught sight of Wraith sitting at the counter, sipping from a coffee mug. My human foster dad was doing supper dishes while a hyran sat at his counter?

"Vampire?" Wraith asked. "Where?"

"It was just a joke," Nina said from over at the table. She picked up a plate and sat it on the stack she was carrying. "Vampires only come out at night, and Trish slept until the sun went down. They're a human legend."

Wraith looked amused. "Are they now. Just like the fae?"

That made Dan and Nina both pause and look at me. I shrugged. I had no idea if vampires were real or not. It made sense that there could be a type of fae that the legends were based off of.

"Did you guys eat without me?" It came out more cross than I meant it to. But they knew how much I liked to eat.

Nina sat the dirty dishes next to the sink and went over and pulled me a plate of lasagna out of the fridge. "We gave up on you. Supper has been gone for over an hour, we just got distracted talking." She smiled at Wraith and suddenly my priorities jumped into focus. I probably should be more worried about my parents than my supper.

I took the plate anyway, and pulled the wrap off the top as I walked over to the microwave.

I surveyed the room while my lasagna made the rounds in the microwave. No tension. Everyone looked relaxed. "What did you all even talk about, anyway?" I blurted out.

"You, mostly," Nina said.

"I learned some interesting things." Wraith went over and refilled her coffee cup. "And now I understand better why I like you. These humans have done a good job."

"We can't take much credit for that." Dan pulled the stopper on the sink and grabbed a towel. "She was already pretty amazing when she came to live with us."

A strange mixture of guilt and joy filled me. Guilt, that I wasn't nearly the person Dan and Nina seemed to think I was. There were things they didn't know about me, that maybe even they wouldn't be able to get past. Like how I almost turned Jaden into the Council, just to get myself out of trouble with them.

But the joy... That didn't go away either. Before Dan and Nina, I hadn't known what unconditional love was. And now I thought I did. Even if I wasn't willing to test it, just for testings sake.

"Okay then. I hope they didn't tell you anything too embarrassing." The microwave finally dinged, and I pulled my supper out. The stupid thing had come with the furnished apartment, and took forever to heat anything up.

I took it over to the table and plopped it down, before checking my phone. Four messages from Starren. One from Jaden. And one from Rosie.

Hands trembling, I swiped away the notification so I didn't have to see Rosie's name. Was I a bad friend? Yeah, she would think so. But if she knew the truth of why she'd gotten hurt, she'd know I was a bad friend.

"Everything okay?" Nina asked, and I realized I hadn't even touched my lasagna yet.

I shoveled a bite into my mouth and gave her a thumbs up, keeping my mouth so full that I didn't have to make something up without lying.

I pulled up Starren's voicemail, glad for the visual voicemail on our family plan. That meant I could read what she'd left without the whole room knowing about it.

The kind of crazy that came from Starren sometimes needed to be filtered.

"Trisha. It's important. Call me back."

I deleted that one. No important information.

"Trisha. This is time sensitive. Call me."

Still no information, but that didn't surprise me. Starren didn't trust anyone, and definitely didn't trust me to not lose my phone.

"That's it, Trisha. I'm headed home. Don't leave the apartment."

I checked the time stamp. Eight minutes ago. If she was coming from work, she'd be here any time.

Nina came over and sat at the table with me, followed by Dan. "Trish. I told Dan about our meeting. About what's going on."

Dan nodded, face serious.

"Have we figured out our next steps yet?"

"No. Not yet."

Dan pulled us both in for a quick hug. "We'll get through this, honey. We've done pretty awesome so far. Just keep us in the loop. Do we need to have another meeting? One I can be at?" He paused, and when I didn't answer, continued. "Sorry I missed the last one. There are some things going on at work... I'm not supposed to talk about it."

"That's okay, Dan. You don't have to tell me everything." I was just happy he hadn't pushed the keeping them in the loop thing. If I'd agreed to it, I wouldn't have a choice. I stuffed a forkful of lasagna in my mouth. Where was Starren when I needed her?

On cue, someone started to pound on the door. She must have forgotten her keys again. She did that all the time. I shoveled three bites worth of lasagna into my mouth and jumped up. "I'll get it." Somehow they understood me even around the lasagna, because no one took off for the door.

Sliding to a stop in my socks, I didn't bother looking out the peephole before pulling the door open. "Star, I-" I stopped mid-excuse.

It wasn't Starren.

"Aunt Wren?"

"Is that any way to greet your favorite aunt? Come here." She pulled me into a hug, squeezing me tight. "And I don't have a gun on me this time, promise." She pushed me back out to arm's length and grinned.

"That's good," I mumbled. "Dan won't let me cross the border to heal, even if it's just a step."

"You can heal like the rest of us until this whole parent thing is sorted out," Dan walked into the hallway and gave Wren a quick hug. "Maybe it will teach you to be more careful."

"Ha," Wren said. "That would be the day."

"Out of the way," Nina's voice came from behind Dan. Sometimes I forgot how small she actually was, with her huge personality and all.

Dan shifted sideways, the hallway getting rather crowded as Nina forced her way forward and grabbed Wren, nearly crushing her in a hug. "You're back already! This is amazing!"

"Yeah, I've got some leave time stacked up, so I decided to take it." She squeezed Nina and let her go. "Is that your lasagna I smell?"

"Yes!" Nina turned around and maneuvered through us all toward the kitchen. "Trish just sat down to eat too, so she hasn't had a chance to find the extra in the fridge."

Dan followed Nina. I just stared at Wren for a second, lost as to what I should be feeling right now. She slung an arm around my shoulders and turned me toward the kitchen.

When we turned the corner, she dropped her arm. "Who's this?" she asked, nodding toward Wraith.

"Uh..." I scrambled to come up with the name Wraith had given herself.

Wraith stood and hobbled over in the perfect imitation of a very old woman. "Hazel. Pleased to meet you." She stuck out a hand.

Wren shook it, but I noticed her wiping at her pants when they finished. Hopefully she hadn't noticed how cold Wraith's hand was, but it seemed like she had.

My aunt had learned a lot about the fae last month, when she'd tried to help me get Dan and Nina's memories back. But that didn't mean I wanted her to know it was another fae standing right in front of her.

Thankfully Wren had taken Cumat and some others under her protection and left Starren and me to go into Faerie that time, so she'd never met Wraith.

I'd rather keep it that way. Maybe we could just keep it at Wren meeting "Hazel."

Wren didn't seem too concerned that there was a strange old lady in the apartment. But, it was Dan and Nina's place, and they seemed to attract all kinds of strays. Present company included.

Carefully avoiding looking at Wren, Nina bustled around the kitchen getting Wren's snack ready. "How long are you here?" Nina asked.

"I'm not sure." Wren slid onto a barstool. "I have so much time away sitting on the books, my CO told me to come down here until I got some of it chewed up." She turned and looked me up and down. "Why do you look like crap?"

A key in the front door saved me from trying to come up with an answer. "Sorry, be right back." I left her sitting there and took off down the hallway. In the confusion with Wren, I'd totally forgotten Starren would be arriving at any time.

Before Starren could even get her key out of the lock, I jerked the door a crack, but not enough that she could come in. She tried to push past me, but I kept my arm in place. Starren and Wren together? Disaster. They'd learned to put up with each other when they'd had to, but there was no love lost between them.

"Wren's here," I muttered, shoving her back into the hallway and following her out.

"Wren?" Starren's already grumpy face went stormy. "What's she doing back here? I thought she had some important military job that took up all of her time."

"Yeah. So did I. I hadn't even met her until you did." From the way Nina talked about her little sister, it was a rare gift when they got to see each-other. Odd to have it happen so soon after the last time she'd visited.

"What's going on?" I asked.

"Mother and Father agreed to a meeting. Tonight, under a flag of truce. That means neither of them can do anything to each-other, or to us. I don't feel like we have a choice, but the final decision is yours."

"Mine? Since when do you let me decide anything?"

She shrugged, not really reacting to my hostile accusation. "This affects you most of all. I can only try to protect you."

I sucked in a deep breath and closed my eyes. Seeing either of my parents alone was stressful enough. To see both of them at the same time, when each of them wanted to kidnap me and kill the other? There wasn't a word for that.

"What time, and where?"

"Sunset, at the suggested farmhouse."

Oh good. Back to another wonderful memory. "You aren't going to try and kill me this time, are you?" I asked.

"Haha. Not me. But I'd bring your sword. There are other ways to get into trouble than our parents, and with you along, anything is possible."

I stuck out my tongue at her, and got an almost-smile. It wasn't fully there, but it still made me silly happy. My sister and I were getting closer, so at least there might be one good thing come from our parents being evil.

"Just let me get changed and we can go."

"No," Starren said. "If you go back in there, the hyran will follow us. I don't trust her. Not yet."

I looked down at my pajama-clad body. "I at least need my sword."

"You don't have it on you now?" Starren sighed, knowing the answer. "I have an extra. We can't risk it. Text your Nina without any details, and let's go."

Wow. She really was getting to know me well. She knew I'd never just up and leave Nina without an explanation. There was never any certainty I'd be coming back.

"Seriously? In my pajamas? That doesn't exactly scream that I'm a force to be reckoned with."

She studied me critically for a moment. "That's true. Mother and Father are all about appearances. I've got just the thing." And then she walked away, not even checking to see if I followed or not.

Of course I followed.

When we made it down to the street, she led the way to her bike and rummaged around in the pack strapped to it. She pulled out a full outfit, black leather pants, jacket, and a black shirt to go under it.

Next a pair of knee high lace-up boots made their way out, followed by a sword in a sheath.

"You're ultra-prepared." She gave me a look saying she thought I was ridiculous, which was fair. She was always prepared. And it really helped that her boyfriend could make mini-portals that made storing stuff really easy.

I grabbed the clothes and looked around for somewhere to change. A garbage bin in the alley beside the apartment building provided great cover. I moved over there and waved Starren along behind me to keep guard.

A shiver went through me as I pulled the pants on. The evening air was still chilly. And it smelled like snow. How I knew that after only a short time in the mid-west was anyone's guess, but it was a very distinct smell.

A vehicle coasted up and shut down. I hurried, knowing the sound of that pick-up by heart. "Don't let him come over here," I hissed to Starren while I zipped my pants.

"Over here, Jaden," Starren called.

I growled and rushed through wrestling my 'It's All Good' t-shirt off. "I said tell him not to come over here!"

"Yeah, but this way you'll hurry."

As if I was taking my time in the freezing air while I changed. I pulled on the jacket, which gave me some instant relief, and then pulled on the boots over my now dirty socks. Everything fit perfectly.

Starren must have had this waiting for me, because we were not remotely the same size.

Even though there was no logical reason, the clothes were making me really uncomfortable. I stepped out from behind the trash bin. "Star, I'm not sure-" I stopped mid-sentence because it wasn't Starren standing there. "Where did she go?" I was going to strangle her. Jaden didn't answer, just stared at me with an open mouth. "Jaden?" I snapped.

"To wait in the truck." He stuck a thumb over his shoulder in the general direction of the road, but didn't move. "Did she give you-"

"Yes," I got out between gritted teeth. But the sun was already mostly set, so I didn't have a chance to find anything else. "Let's go."

I stormed past him to the truck. Starren had to know I wouldn't like this. She had to have done this on purpose. I headed toward the back seat where she'd already gotten situated.

"Looks like they fit you," she said, eyeing me critically. "Good thing I had access to your clothes when I commissioned them."

"Commissioned them?" Her words made me lose a little steam, but I still had plenty left.

"Yeah. They're made out of tharif leather. It would take a special blade to cut through those. I know you can heal, but why deal with the pain of the wound if you don't have to?"

Tharif leather? I didn't even know what a tharif was. But she'd had them made for me. To keep me safe. I ran a hand down my thigh. The leather was warm, even in the chilly evening, and soft to the touch. "Thank you," I got out, and went around to the other side of the truck, grateful I hadn't had time to chew her out before she told me what she'd done for me.

"I've never seen tharif in person," Jaden said as he reached for the passenger's door handle. "How did you pay for them? They're crazy expensive."

Crazy expensive? Did the fae have their own currency? It had never come up, and I'd never thought about it.

"No. Someone owed me a favor." Starren didn't expound on anything from there.

Jaden and I exchanged looks as he put on his seat-belt. Owing

Starren a favor would be pretty scary, if she didn't care about the person doing the owing.

The pick-up's engine clunked to life and I settled back, trying to give off a vibe that said I didn't care what we were about to go do. But the closer we got to the line, the more the jitters couldn't be contained.

We were about to see our mom and dad again. In a not-so-great situation. But then, I'd never had anything better than not-so-great with my dad. At least I had a few good memories of my time with my mom.

Jaden glanced over and must have seen my nerves. "Did you get my voicemail?" he asked.

"Oh, yeah, sorry. I didn't get a chance to listen to it before Wren showed up."

"Wren?" he asked.

"Yeah, she has some time off and wanted to visit."

Starren hurmphed in the back seat, and I didn't try to defend Wren. I didn't know if something was up or not, but I'd learned to become suspicious of everything, so I couldn't really argue with Starren.

"So we're pretty sure Mom or Dad won't grab me and take off, right?" I asked. I should be proud at how even I'd kept my voice, but I couldn't feel anything past the dread clawing its way up my throat.

"Even they can't break the terms of a Meeting. There's old magic that holds everyone to their word, and if it's broken, or even attempted to be broken, bad things happen." Starren's voice came across grim, like maybe she had personal experience with this.

"Well. I guess that's something."

I took a deep breath when we crossed the line, keeping my eyes glued to the road ahead. Even though I'd only ever been there once, the way to the farmhouse was burned into my brain.

Funny that the three of us were going back there, under such similar circumstances. And yet, this time we were on the same side.

There was literally no one else in the entire world I'd rather face my parents with. Nina's support would be amazing, but I'd be freaking out that something might happen to her if she were here.

I turned onto the weed-covered driveway to the house, bumping along between the trees until we got to the farmhouse and I put the truck in park.

These trees had helped me once. Had changed the entire direction of my life, had set me on a path to gaining my sister as an ally. A friend, even if she'd never admit that. Did they remember? Would they help me again if I needed it?

Ha. If. More likely would be when I need it.

I got out of the truck, but left it running and the door wide open. Starren's attempt at reassuring me only went so far. I attracted worst-case scenarios, and I always needed to be prepared for that.

Moonlight lit part of the clearing, but the area around the house had too many trees.

Starren and Jaden both got out of the truck also, and came up to guard me from behind. Starren liked being the one in front, so that told me she was more nervous about this whole thing than she wanted to be.

"Hello?" I called. Was the portal inside the old house still functional? I should have come back and burned this place down, but I hadn't thought about that until this moment.

A form stepped out from the shadows of the house. Big and male.

Not my father. Quintin was built on the slim side. All the better to put people at ease before he struck.

Maybe that thought wasn't fair. I didn't even know the man, not really. But he'd hurt Starren in so many ways. And that made him my enemy.

Ouch. I'd never really thought it out that far. But he really was.

"Trish." Oh no. That voice.

"Wade," I hissed. Starren stiffened beside me, and it pulled me out of my own anger. As much as Wade had betrayed me, it had been twice the betrayal to Starren, who he'd been partners with for years.

"What do you want?" I asked. "Where's Father?"

Hello, Trisha. Your mother sends her greetings. The voice in my head nearly made my heart stop before my brain caught on to what was happening. Nara. Wade and Nara.

"Neither of them actually came, did they." I relaxed a little, a confusing mix of anger and disappointment going through me at the same time. Apparently even as their prophesied throne-winner I wasn't important enough for them to come themselves.

"Quintin very much wanted to come, but he had a last minute matter he had to see to himself," Wade said.

"Or he just loves to jerk people around and enjoys the fact that we left Sanctuary to meet him, and he can't even be bothered to be here," Starren answered. Her tone held no inflection. This was the Starren I'd met back in the fall. The one who had all but disappeared over the last couple months.

"Come on, Star. You know it's not like that," Wade said.

"You've lost the right to call me that. Even though Father and I aren't on speaking terms, he is still king, and you will show me respect."

Okay. I needed to get things pointed in the right direction here. Like, now. "What does he want, Wade?"

"You know exactly what he wants." He took a step forward. "Exactly what he's always wanted. His daughter, back at his side."

"Yeah, yeah. If that was ever going to happen before, it isn't going to happen now. Not after Rosie."

Wade took a step closer and Jaden tensed beside me. "You never cared about anyone before. It took me months to even get you to agree to a date. What is it about this Rosie?"

Nah uh. He was not going to think Rosie was something super special to me. As soon as he did, the danger she was in doubled. "It's not about who. It's about what was done. It was despicable, and you are despicable for working for someone who could make an order like that." My voice rose, heat filling my face. I hadn't dealt with all the things that came along with seeing Rosie nearly die yet, and they were starting to leak out.

Jaden bumped me from the side, drawing me back a little. He slid his hand in mine and gave a little squeeze. I squeezed back, but let it go. No use angering Wade.

"You know your father. You know he didn't actually care about being here. Wade must believe he did, but Wade believes many things that aren't true. Your

mother loves you. She wants to be re-united, but it's unsafe while she wars with Quintin."

I held back some not so wonderful thoughts about my mom. Maybe Nara was listening in, maybe not. I didn't need her knowing exactly how I felt. Well, I didn't know exactly how I felt, so there was no way she could, but still.

"I came here to talk to Quintin and Raiena. If they aren't here, this meeting is over." I caught a glimpse of Starren's approving smirk as I turned back to the truck, me facing away from the others, a deliberate choice to show I didn't feel like they were a threat. Everything in the fae world was based on appearances.

"Wait!" Wade called.

I hesitated, but didn't turn back.

"You don't want what happened to your friend to happen to anyone else, do you?"

Now I whipped around. I stalked toward him so fast neither Jaden nor Starren had a chance to grab me. I got up into Wade's face, noticing now that I was so close that he looked rather haggard, eyes dark and tired.

But that didn't stop me. "If something like that ever happens again," I hissed. "All of Faerie is going to feel my wrath." The trees all around us whipped like a tornado barreled down on us. Branches lashed forward, snapping in the non-existent wind.

I didn't need to pretend to be furious right now. I could hardly see straight, my hands shaking.

Wade's gaze flew all around me, checking out the trees. Good. Normally I wouldn't wish PTSD on anyone, but if he remembered what had happened the last time we were here, it could only help me right now.

"He's done so much to you. To your family. He shot Nina. Are you just going to let him get away with that?"

Old anger, never healed, welled up. Nina had forgiven him. I'd tried. I'd thought I was doing fairly well until this moment. Seeing Nina nearly die had wrecked me far worse than I would have thought possible.

"You had better leave," I got out between gritted teeth. "Because

I'm not sure I'm going to be able to hold back much longer. And if Father sends anyone else to town, anyone, he'll regret it. The line is drawn at the border. A line none of you will cross."

As if to back up my statement, a vine crawled around the ground and over to Wade's tall boot. It began to trail its way up his leg. His eyes flashed wild, and he chopped at the vine, cutting it free.

"Your father won't be happy!" his words burst out of him, his voice a little feral.

"You think I'm happy? Does he just expect me to bow down to him in fear?"

One of the larger trees close to the house bent down toward us. It creaked and groaned as it came, the loud pops making Wade jump.

"It's worked rather well for him in the past," Starren said from behind me. I'd been so focused on Wade that I hadn't noticed her and Jaden move up to flank me on either side. "Coercion is his favorite tool. He doesn't understand emotion well enough to manipulate like mother does."

A flash of anger went through me at the accusation against mom, but it was just old habit. She wasn't crazy evil like Quintin, but she definitely had her own problems. Nara's silence on the matter didn't help me feel any differently about the whole thing.

"He understands better than you think," Wade said. "He's got many years of being taught otherwise to retrain, but he wants to work on it. You should give him a chance."

"Like Nina gave you a chance? Repeatedly?" My voice started out deadly quiet, but rose to a pitch so strong my throat ached. In the moments we'd been talking, the woods around us had calmed. That all changed in a moment.

Branches lashed forward, ripping at Wade's hair and clothes. He stumbled back away from us, but none of us bothered to move. A rose vine slapped him across the face, leaving a row of welts. And yet I still couldn't ask the trees to stop.

Without another word, Wade tore through the door into the farmhouse, headed for the portal.

Even after he was gone, I couldn't calm down. With no available target, the trees started in on each other, tearing off bits of bark, severing small branches.

Starren looked around us, uneasy.

I took a deep breath, and closed my eyes. I needed to get this under control, or someone I cared about could get hurt. Maybe staying in Sanctuary wasn't just to keep me safe. Until I could get the anger that had been plaguing me since Nina had gotten hurt and my parents betrayed me under control, maybe I shouldn't be crossing the border.

"You okay?" I heard Jaden ask, and opened my eyes. But he wasn't looking at me. He was checking on Starren.

Her face had lost a shade, standing out in the moonlight. Had I... scared her? Sure, she'd almost been ripped to pieces by the trees before, but we were sisters now.

She shrugged off Jaden's concern. "Well done, Trisha. The only thing either of our parents understand is power. You've shown them you won't back down."

"Or invited them in to see who's stronger," Jaden muttered.

"We can't all stay calm and optimistic," I snapped at Jaden. "I didn't know what else to do. Father can't be reasoned with. He will only stop if he thinks he has a reason to. If that reason is me, so be it."

"We all know what your father is." Nara walked out of the trees, sending Starren into a spin to face her. *"Come back to your mother. She misses you."*

Then why didn't she come?

Nara didn't have an answer. She thought she was telling me the truth, thought that my mom actually loved me. But just because she thought it didn't make it true.

"Tell her if she wants to see me, she can come here herself. And to stop sending people. I don't want anything to do with her or Father." I turned my back to her and started for the truck. *Tell all of the fae to leave me in peace. I'm tired of all of you and all of your stupid games. Don't get me too mad, or I'm coming for you all.*

My gut clenched at the thought. But I'd said it. Somewhere there was a line that would push me over the edge. I just didn't know where it was yet.

The 'meeting' hadn't lasted long. We were only gone an hour. I thought about going back to Jenny's, hiding out for a while, but then I remembered I'd left a hyran with my foster parents. And Wren.

It was Starren who broke the silence. "Father sent Wade for a reason. It's not a coincidence, and he has plenty of other soldiers to send."

"He doesn't understand emotion," Jaden said. "Maybe he truly thought a familiar face would make her more likely to accept what was being said.

Starren shrugged. "He's done far worse to me than Wade did to Trish. I always went back. Until I had a better reason to leave."

I got out of Jaden's truck and slammed the door. Harder than necessary, but it was tough to close sometimes so maybe that helped hide my little burst of temper. I started for the door without remembering to tell Jaden goodnight.

"Trish," he called out the passenger window, leaning across the center console.

"What?" I yelled back.

He gestured up and down and I looked down at myself. Yeah, this get-up would raise a lot of questions if I walked through the front door in it. I waved a hand in thanks and grabbed my PJs out of the bed of his truck to go and change.

Good thing he'd reminded me. I walked in the front door and tried to sneak to my room. There was no getting around Wraith.

Before I even saw her, she had me slammed up against the wall, her grandmotherly hand wrapped around my throat.

"Trisha. Dear Trisha. Why did you leave me behind?" her voice came out in a purr, more scary than I'd ever heard from her before, and that was saying a lot.

"I didn't think I would need you! It was a diplomatic meeting, supposed to be completely safe."

"Meeting? With your parents? You should know by now that there's nothing safe about your parents. Either one of them. I know you feel like your mother isn't as bad as your father, but she is. She just goes about getting what she wants differently than he does. Did you see either of them tonight?"

I deflated, letting my body go limp. If she hadn't been propping me up against the wall, I probably would have fallen. "No. Neither of them came."

Wraith stepped back, made sure I was steady, and then let go of me. "I'm sorry, child."

I blinked at the emotional whiplash, just as Starren walked into the hallway. She raised an eyebrow at us, but just kept walking.

"Trish, is that you?" Nina called from the kitchen.

"Yeah, she's here," Starren answered for me.

"Oh, Starren! I'm so glad you're home, Wren is here!"

"Thanks, Nina." Starren just kept walking toward our room though. She rarely came home except to sleep, and she for sure wasn't going to hang out if Wren was here.

Nina and Wren started talking, but I couldn't hear what they were saying. I scooted toward my room, following Star. Usually we avoided being in there at the same time, but I couldn't face Nina right now.

Actually, what I really needed was to be alone to break down, but that wasn't likely to happen.

"We were thinking about making Mexican for dinner," Nina said. She stepped around the kitchen wall and looked down the hallway. Instantly she paused. "Honey, are you okay?"

"I will be," I said, brushing past her. Stupid fae genes and the no lying thing. I'd really like to be able to say I was fine right now.

"Did something happen with Rosie?"

The worry in her voice made me stop. Crap. I still had a voicemail from Rosie that I hadn't listened to. And crap again. I'd worried Nina for nothing.

Well, kind of nothing. No one had died.

"It isn't Rosie, Nina. I'm not quite ready to talk about it. Rain check?"

"Rain check." She didn't sound very happy, but she was pretty good at respecting my space. Most of the time.

I pulled out my phone as I passed her, more to have something else to focus on than her than me wanting to check my notifications. Another from Rosie. I started to slide it off the screen, but paused, leaving it there. The message was only thirty seconds. I should just listen to it and get the whole thing over with.

She wouldn't be mad at me. Because she didn't know she had gotten hurt because of me. It was probably some normal Rosie thing, like checking in on me when she was the one in the hospital. I should totally just listen to it, text her some excuse about how I'd been busy, glad she was going to be okay, and then ghost her.

Internally I winced. I used to be able to ghost people without a thought. Every time I switched foster homes or got moved to a different group home, everyone in my life reset. But this life... It felt more permanent. It had to be. I'd die if I lost all of the people who'd just kept battering at my walls until I let them in.

Which meant Rosie was here to stay, if I could get rid of the fae problem. So I needed to handle this carefully.

I walked toward my room. "Wraith, you're with me." She followed me into my room and watched as I threw my phone on the bed without listening to the message. Maybe in the morning. It was late again.

Not late enough that I'd usually think anything of it, but Rosie might be asleep. Yeah, of course she would be, after something traumatic like that, she'd need a lot of rest.

Bed time. Because sleep would come so easily, and I wouldn't have to worry at all about bad dreams.

Right.

CHAPTER SEVEN

The sound of pots and pans made me groan. I'd slept about as much as I'd expected, which really wasn't great. And yet, it was morning already.

I shuffled through getting ready for the day, and remembered half way through that there was a granny/monster I was somewhat responsible for somewhere in the apartment.

The leg of my jeans didn't cooperate as I jerked them on, stumbling out into the hallway. Wraith hadn't shown anything even near aggression since she'd arrived, but I didn't know her well enough to know if she had any triggers I should be worried about.

That was something even a human could have, let alone a huge snake monster who fed on fear.

The smell of pancakes hit me. My stomach rumbled, and nausea hit me. When had I truly eaten last?

Eh, it didn't matter. I just knew it was time to eat. And pancakes were a good sign that Wraith hadn't gone on some type of rampage.

Three heads swung my way when I walked into the kitchen. No Starren or Dan. Starren had probably slipped out while everyone else was asleep.

Nina saw me look around. "Dan got called into work."

That was unusual. I still didn't really know exactly what he did. At first I'd never cared, then I'd cared a bit because I cared about him and he hadn't been able to answer many of my questions, and then I'd been back to too much on my mind to care.

Wren was wearing one of Nina's nice sun-dresses. The ones she wore to... Ah. Sunday. She was going to church with Nina.

"Hungry?" Nina asked. Without waiting for an answer, she handed me a plate of pancakes.

I took it and went over to sit by Wraith, who had an empty plate in front of her. I'd grabbed my phone out of habit when I'd left my room, and the notifications lit up when I sat it on the counter by my plate.

Two missed calls, both from Rosie.

Nah. I wasn't going to deal with that this morning. I flipped the phone over, face down, so I couldn't see the screen mocking me.

"You could come too, if you want," Wren said, and the room went quiet.

"Ah, what?" I asked, after I figured out she was talking to me.

"To church. With Nina and me. We'll make it a girls' day out since Dan is busy."

"Sure, why not."

Nina's pan clattered into the sink, and she turned to stare at me. Wow, okay, she didn't have to make a big deal out of it. Sure, I didn't normally go, but today I needed a distraction. Of any kind.

"I'll just go get changed." I took off, leaving my plate of pancakes untouched. I wasn't hungry anymore.

Wraith followed me.

I grabbed clothes out of my room and nearly ran into her standing in the doorway.

"I don't like her," Wraith said.

"What?" She couldn't mean Wren. Wren was Nina's sister, everyone had to like her, because everyone had to like Nina.

"Something..." Wraith trailed off, staring into space. "I don't know. Something doesn't feel quite right."

"Think about it, and when you come up with something, you let me know." I left her standing there and headed for the bathroom to change. When I came out, Nina and Wren were talking as they waited for me. Apparently they never stopped talking, something I'd thought was just because of the situation last time Wren had stayed with us.

Nina threw an arm around my shoulders and shepherded me out the door. "I'm so excited you're going with us. It's going to be an awesome girls' day out."

Sure. Like going to church was my version of a good time. Well, actually, I didn't really know. I'd only gone to church with Dan and Nina once, and that had been back in D.C. They'd always asked me if I wanted to go with them, but never pushed, so I'd always said no.

Today, sitting at the apartment alone, thinking about what had happened this week, wondering what would happen in the future...

Nah. Even church had to be better than that.

I closed the door behind me, and followed Wren and Nina, who pretended to not notice that I was dragging my feet. I only made it three steps before the door behind me opened and Wraith came out, closing it behind her.

"You're going to church?" I asked her.

"Why not?" she flounced by me in a nice shirt she must have stolen from Nina and a very poorly fitting pair of jeans.

Why not, indeed.

I sighed and followed her. We made it downstairs and headed for Nina's van.

There was literally not one moment of silence on the six minute drive. Maybe this distraction hadn't been a great choice.

Nina parked and I drug my feet as we walked toward the open front doors. It was a smallish church, compared to the one she'd attended in D.C. Small, and uncomplicated.

People waved to Nina as we walked, and she waved back, in her element. It was nice to see her so happy. She wouldn't be if she knew more about what was going on right now with my parents, or knew about the fact that the grandma trailing us and taking everything wasn't at all what she seemed.

"Nina!" the man at the door said.

"Hello, Pastor." Nina shook his hand and gestured toward her entourage. "This is my sister Wren, my daughter Trish, and..." she studied Wraith. "A friend of Trisha's." Wraith pushed forward and shook the pastor's hand, making him wince. Yeah, we were going to have to work on grip strength apparently.

I nodded, but didn't say anything. This guy didn't look like what I thought a pastor should look like. One of the foster families I'd lived with for a few weeks had taken me to church with them, but it was nothing like this place. Formal and stuffy, which worked for some people I guess, but had made me uncomfortable as a kid in hand-me-downs.

"So nice to meet you all!" the pastor said. He gestured toward the church. "Grab a seat."

Nina led the way again, the three of us following like ducklings. Wren didn't seem particularly comfortable either, but Wraith didn't have a care in the world.

Being stronger than everyone else and nearly indestructible probably helped with that.

Nina took us straight up to the front and ushered Wren into a bench first before following her, leaving room for me to sit by Nina, and then Wraith beside me. When I sat down, she patted my knee and smiled, that smile that I'd hated at first because I'd thought it was fake. I knew better now.

"So glad you came," Nina mouthed, as the music started.

I settled back into the bench. This wasn't so bad. Maybe even peaceful. At least the atmosphere was nice. I shouldn't have waited this long to come. If I'd know it would make Nina this happy, I wouldn't have.

Ouch. That was a lie to myself. Not spoken out loud, or I wouldn't have been able to say it. No, this was one I'd kept deep down. I didn't belong in a place like this. I wasn't like Dan or Nina. Kind, caring, good. I was a mess. And I caused messes for everyone else.

I fiddled in my seat. A glance at Wraith showed her having absolutely no problems. She swayed to the music, looking almost as joyous as the people around us. She was so weird. But that was probably why we got along so well.

The band finished their song and the projector at the front that had words to the songs changed to a beautiful mountain scene. The pastor got up, carried his Bible to the pulpit and smiled out over everyone.

"Good morning to you all. I'm so glad you're here."

He kept on, but my attention wandered. Had the church with the foster parents before really been stuffy, or had I just been scared and hadn't wanted to admit it? Eh, it didn't really matter. I didn't belong at either place.

I glanced around the room to avoid looking at the pastor.

I missed the man on the first pass, but the second time I scanned people's faces, I saw him. Dressed like any of the other church goers, he just sat there. One of the guys from Jennys, sitting in a back pew.

Was he here for me? My pulse rate picked up and my hands got clammy. What if he'd followed us here? What if he had orders to hurt someone I cared about?

I had to get out of here.

Squeezing past Wraith, I rushed right up the aisle toward the main doors in the back. But now what? I couldn't just leave the man here. What if he did something even though I'd left?

All eyes were on me as I kept going. The guy I was worried about caught my eye, and the shock on his face made me slow down. He didn't know I was here either.

When he recovered, he stood and bolted for the door. I chased him out of the church and into the parking lot.

"Wait!" I yelled.

He didn't listen.

I tore after him, glad I was wearing tennis shoes and not the sandals Nina always wore to church.

"I'll get him for you." Wraith's voice was full of glee as she easily passed me and took off down an alley in pursuit.

By the time I turned the corner, she had him lifted up against a wall, waiting. We'd left Nina and Wren far enough behind that I had a quick chance to get a couple questions in.

I shoved in close and Wraith brought him down to face level. "Who are you? What are you doing at my parent's church?"

"Your parent's church?" His face went white. "Your parents go to church?"

Oh. "Wrong parents." Maybe he didn't even know. It seemed like a pretty big coincidence...

His face cleared up a little. "I didn't know. I swear. I'm just here for Sanctuary, and have been visiting different human places, that's all."

I studied him for a moment, then nodded for Wraith to drop him. Just in time too, because Wren and Nina came around the corner about then. It wouldn't do for them to see this grandma hauling a two-hundred pound man around.

"Why are you in Sanctuary? What did you do?"

He kept his hands up, but his body language said he was calming down a bit. "Things are starting to heat up." He inclined his head toward Wren and Nina. "You know. At home."

"They know everything. You can talk freely in front of them."

Now his eyes bugged out again. "You told humans?"

"Not willingly. My hand was forced, both times. Now tell me more about why you're here."

"There are lots of us here. We're just looking for somewhere safe to remain neutral." He snapped his jacket, getting the wrinkles out that Wraith had put there. "We figured the best place to be was somewhere we know they aren't going to destroy. Which is basically here."

"And why's that?" Wren asked, moving in closer. She had her soldier face on.

"Because both of them still want Trish. They can't come into Sanctuary conscripting because of the old laws, and they won't do anything to make Trish join the other side." He looked back over to me. "There are lots of us here now. We've been avoiding you because... well. You know." Now he actually looked apologetic.

Because my family was crazy.

"But you don't seem so bad!" he added hastily.

Wow. Wonderful. At least he wasn't putting me on the same level as my parents anymore. "What's your name?" I asked.

"Guj," he said. "But humans can't seem to say that, so I've been going by Gus."

"Do you have a pen and paper?" I asked Nina.

She pulled her purse over her shoulder and rooted around for a second, but of course she did. She handed it to me and I wrote down my number.

"This is in case any of you see anything to do with my parents. Call me right away. I'll get it handled." Hopefully. Probably not, but I'd certainly try.

Gus took the paper from me and looked down at it. "Can I go now?" He was asking Wraith, not me, but when I nodded she stepped out of the way.

Wren waited until he was out of earshot. "What was that about?"

"I knew he was fae, and I was afraid he was following me. But I don't think he was. My bad." I turned and started back toward the church parking lot. I'd rather get out of here before the service ended. Nina was going to be embarrassed enough coming back next week, I didn't need to make it any worse.

"How did you know he was fae? Is there some way to tell?"

Wren's question was innocent enough. But it came after Wraith talking to me about her at home. Was she up to something? Surely not. She was Nina's sister. Anyone related to Nina had to be a good person, right?

"No," Wraith answered for me, minus her normal grin. "There's no way to tell the difference between the fae and a human." She smiled then, but it wasn't good natured at all. "Unless it's one of the lower fae and they don't have a pass inside Sanctuary. Then you know right away."

Great. Now there was some weird thing going on between them. Nina came over and slung an arm over my shoulders. How she wasn't mad that I'd made a scene in front of all of her friends, I didn't know. But I really appreciated it.

"Hey," she said.

"Hey," I answered. "Sorry about all that."

"Eh." She hugged me to her. "It's about what I'd expect from anything you do out of your normal routine."

"Hey!" I laughed though, because it was so sadly true.

Her eyes sparkled and I hugged her back.

"Thank you. I don't think church is for me though. I'm a little too far gone." We reached the car and Nina let me go to hit the locks.

"Uh huh," Nina said. Wraith and Wren piled into the back of the car before I could get in and away from Nina.

"Seriously, Nina. I don't fit in with all you perfect people, in your perfect families. It's awkward."

"Who needs a doctor?" Nina asked.

I stared at her. How was I supposed to know? Maybe she did, with how random the question was.

"Not a specific who, but in general. Who goes to a doctor?"

Was this a trick question? "Someone who's hurt or sick?"

She smiled. "Exactly. I don't go to church because I'm perfect, Trish. I go because I'm not. Because I can't be. You know?"

I'm sure I had a dumbfounded look on my face at this point. Why hadn't anyone ever made it that easy to understand in the past?

"Well I think you're pretty perfect," Wren said through her open door. "Now get in. I'm ready to eat again."

Nina just laughed. "We both know that's not how you saw it when we were teens."

"Hey, being a teen mom isn't easy. Especially when your 'kid' is almost as old as you are." She leaned over toward Wraith and continued in a fake whisper. "Especially when that kid was me."

Wraith grumbled something, but I couldn't make out what she said. I walked around and got in the front seat, Nina just beating me into hers.

"So," Wren said. "Where are we getting lunch?"

CHAPTER EIGHT

After sushi for lunch, we headed back to the apartment. Wren and Nina went upstairs, while I said I was going to visit Jaden.

Which I had to do, because I said I would, but I mostly just wanted a chat with Wraith.

We walked in silence for a bit, me making sure we were far away from Nina, and her just staring off into space. Who knew what was going on in that head.

Once we'd gone far enough that I knew for certain Nina wasn't going to accidentally interrupt us, I asked what had been on my mind. "Have you figured out why you don't like Wren?"

She eyed me for a few steps. "Have you?"

"What? I like her fine."

"Sure. But you're also worried. Or we wouldn't be having this talk."

"I just... I don't have anything, really. Just a gut feeling. It's weird that she came to visit, right? Poor Nina can't get her to visit for years at a time, and then she finds out about me and she's here twice in a couple months? That seems weird."

"Maybe she just realized what she had to lose," Wraith said.

I glared at her. She was supposed to be on my side of all of this. Of everything. That's what she'd told me, basically.

"I think we should keep an eye on her. I have a bad feeling too. But is a bad feeling worth you risking your relationship with your mother over?"

Risking my relationship with Nina? Of course, how could I be so stupid. Wren was her actual flesh and blood. She'd raised her little sister from when they were kids. They'd known each other their whole lives. I couldn't go on just a gut feeling.

"You're right."

"I know. I always am."

"No one is always right."

"I don't say anything unless I'm sure. And I'm not sure unless I can base something on facts. Therefore, I'm always right."

I sighed. She must believe it to be true, and who was I to argue. We paused outside Jaden's building. His truck wasn't here. He didn't work on Sundays, so where was he?

"I should have texted him first," I said, pulling out my phone.

I barely hit the send button before I got a message back. "He's at Jenny's. What's he doing spending so much time there?"

"Maybe he likes Jenny?" Wraith's face twitched as she tried to keep it straight. "What? You can't expect him to wait around forever."

That was so... true. He hadn't dated anyone that I knew of since we'd met. Of course, the circumstances hadn't been great, and now that I thought about it, I wasn't sure how he felt about dating a human. Which left Starren and me as the other fae options in town. That I knew of.

Stupid. Of course Jaden wouldn't think anything of dating a human. He probably liked them better than he liked the fae, after all he'd been through.

"Wraith. We're going to Jenny's."

Apparently no one cared that they'd seen me here before. As soon as I stepped inside the door, the room went quiet. A much larger feat today, as the room was packed.

Jaden stood up from where he was sitting in the corner and came over. "Trish! I didn't think you'd come."

Probably because I hadn't answered his text. "What ya doing back here?" Ouch. My casual voice needed some work.

"I'm here about you, actually."

"Uh, me?" The room still sat in near silence, all eyes on me.

"Yeah. Everyone here wants to know what you're like. I've been convincing them that you're nothing like your parents."

"Good luck with that. People believe what they want to."

Jaden led us back toward his table. A guy who'd been sitting with him scrambled out of our way, leaving his food on the table. I sat down and swiped two of his onion rings and handed one to Wraith. She sniffed it and then popped it in her mouth.

"They were suspicious at first. It's hard to see you in a different light than your parents when they are destroying Faerie right now. But now I think they're starting to believe me. And I think we can help them."

The waitress who'd served us last time we were here, Martha, walked by and slung a piece of chicken club pizza in front of me.

"Thanks?" I called after her.

"They all know who you are. And what the prophecy says. We're starting to think..."

My mouth stuffed full of pizza, I just lifted an eyebrow.

He didn't continue.

"Yes?" I got out around a mouthful of cheese.

"Maybe..."

"Spit it out, kid." Wraith grabbed another onion ring. "Some of us aren't so patient."

"What if the prophecy is being typically fae and is super vague for a reason? What if you're not only the one that the prophecy was spoken about, but also the one to fulfill it?"

"What the heck is that supposed to mean?" I asked.

Wraith took a seat beside me, studying me to the point it was uncomfortable. "He might be right," she said finally.

"Right about what? I really don't get what you're trying to say."

Jaden waved over three men from the bar. I hadn't noticed them before, but the way they started over instantly said they'd been watching us. One was the guy whose onion rings were now gone.

"This is Goiut," Jaden said, nodding toward the man obviously in charge.

I nodded, just to be polite.

"He's been helping me with the refugees coming in."

Ah. Jaden had asked me to help with that, but I'd basically ignored him. I wasn't a fan of the fae. I didn't have any reason to help them.

"Most of the people in this room don't have homes right now," Jaden answered.

Ouch. He knew exactly where to hit me. I took another glance around the room and noticed some other teens for the first time. Were there kids too? Most likely. Kids needed stability. Look how I'd turned out growing up without a place to call home. A jaded misfit who had to be taught that I was lovable.

That thought was still weird. I had people who loved me.

"Because of you," Goiut said quietly enough that I wasn't sure I'd heard him correctly.

"Excuse you?" Wraith said, which made me think I had heard what he said.

"If it wasn't for you and that stupid prophecy, we'd all be home right now. Enjoying what a world is actually supposed to be like. Not this dirty, unkempt place."

Technically, he may be right. But it wasn't like I'd had a choice in the matter. The entire bar watched us now. Intently. Unlike humans, apparently fae didn't care if you noticed them eavesdropping.

"Leave her alone," a voice said from another table. Gus, from earlier at the church, stood up, pushing his chair back. "It's not her fault her parents are insane. Who here doesn't have someone in their family that they don't want anyone to know they're related to?"

He gestured around the room and got a few strained smiles.

"I think she's different."

Not that I cared too much what a random guy thought of me, but this was kind of a relief. Being compared to my parents was brutal.

"I think we should see what she's offering."

Excuse me? "What I'm offering?" My gaze swung from Gus to Jaden.

"Uh, give us a sec," Jaden said. He grabbed my arm and tugged me toward the door to the back room. Wraith grabbed the half sandwich he'd left on the table and followed.

After walking me through the door and waiting for Wraith to meander in, Jaden checked for people close by and then shut it. He reached back and rubbed his neck, looking somehow sheepish and nervous at the same time.

"People... they want to talk. To you."

"Talk to me? Why?"

"You know how I'm always asking for your help with settling in refugees?"

"Yeah?"

"Well, for some reason they think I'm one of your people and I'm doing it because you told me to." He held his hands up. "I've told them that's not the case, like a hundred times. But they heard how you and Starren took out the Council, and the Council has caused a lot of pain over the years. A lot."

"I didn't have anything to do with that!" That had been all Starren and Quintin. My dad had used her to take out the Council, so he could take over ruling Faerie and not have to share power with anyone. Look how well that had worked out for him, with many of the fae flooding over to Mom's side.

"We both know that. But no one can convince them otherwise. Even with the no lying thing, they think I'm just finding a way around it. Fae don't trust anyone."

He was right. The fae weren't a great race, and they didn't even have confidence in each other, let alone humans. Things in Faerie must be getting really bad for this many to be moving to Sanctuary.

"The humans are going to notice. Enough weird stuff has been happening that everyone is on edge. They're watching for weird, Jaden, and we're all weird. Your vision is going to come true if we aren't careful."

"I won't let it. We're slowly integrating people into life here. I've got people on basic training about Earth, people homing refugees with other fae who have been here longer, people working on getting us IDs for everyone. We don't know how long this war will last. This might just be the beginning."

He was right. It would last until one of my parents was dead. And I was expected to choose between them.

"I'm not going to get involved with either of my parents."

Jaden blinked at me, at a loss for words for a second. "Of course not. The people here are thinking maybe there's a third option. Maybe that prophecy wasn't about you helping someone else. Maybe it was just about you."

"Uh, me?"

"Yeah. Whoever has the girl will rule or whatever. What if you don't let anyone have you, and you just handle things yourself?"

Ah, what? Me? In charge of anything but myself? I didn't even do well with that. "No way. Huh uh. Not happening." I tried to charge out the door and back into the bar, but Wraith stood in the way. I shoved against her, but apparently she weighed the same in any body, because she didn't even shift her weight.

"Maybe you should listen to the boy," she said.

"Maybe I don't want to listen to the boy," I fired back.

"Maybe you will even if you don't want to. Because otherwise maybe you won't be able to leave the room." She stayed solidly in front of me.

I spun around, checking the room for another exit. There. On the far wall. I stormed over and tried the door, but it was locked. Shoot.

"I'm not trying to make you do something you don't want to, Trish," Jaden said. "I'm just pointing something out. Something that could thwart all of your parent's plans. End this war."

"How? You want me to just declare myself the winner and ignore them and their armies?" This was insane. Literally insane. And something I would have never expected from peace-loving Jaden.

"Not some declaration of war or anything. Just that Sanctuary is yours, and they'd better not come here again. So something like Rosie doesn't get repeated."

Okay, now my blood was boiling. I stalked back over and got in Jaden's face. "Just make statements like that, huh? With nothing to back them up? I don't even have powers here."

"No. But neither do they. And you could have the humans on your side. If the humans and the fae here teamed up, there's nothing Quintin or Raiena could do against us."

That was it. This wasn't a discussion. If this was the reason he'd been actually trying to get me down here, I was done with him. He had been fae, manipulated me. A small section of my heart yelled at me to calm down and consider all of the things he'd done for me in the past, but the defensive side won out.

I left him and went back to Wraith.

"There is another option," Wraith said quietly.

"Oh yeah?" I asked, afraid I already knew what she was going to say.

"Neither of them would be able to rule if they were in the grave."

I ground my teeth, doing my best not to snap something I'd regret. "Ratheothen, get out of my way." Either my tone or my use of her full name did the trick. She silently stepped aside.

I stopped in the doorway, but didn't turn around. "Jaden. We've been through a lot together. But don't bring this up again. I will not be responsible for anyone else."

The bar was completely quiet when I walked through. I slammed the door behind me when I stepped back out into the sunlight. I only made it a few steps before Wraith came out behind me. She didn't try to catch up, just trailed behind.

At least she was far enough away that she couldn't see the angry tears about to spill. I couldn't be responsible for any more people. Look what had happened to Nina on my watch. To Rosie. No. I had enough to take care of right now, the fae without a faction were just going to have to find someone else to be their hero.

Two days went by with nothing of note happening. At this point that felt like a record, so I counted it as a win.

I'd never been thankful that Rosie went to a different school than I did before, but I was now. She tried calling once more, and texted to ask me what was going on, but I still hadn't even listened to her voicemail.

Things felt almost normal. Other than the times I caught someone watching me out of the corner of my eye. Now I weighed every glance a stranger took in my direction, every slight interaction. Not only did I have my mom and dad's people here, but all the refugee fae.

Maybe someone had passed around a picture. Maybe somehow they just all could sense it. But I knew when I bumped into a fae woman at a convenience store on the way home from school, just because of her reaction. And all I'd wanted was a Snickers.

Wraith had followed me to school Monday and Tuesday, making a bit of a nuisance of herself as she figured out what role to play. Until she'd offered to volunteer to help with the lunch clean-up, something 'every grandma should do.'

Wait. She might be a grandma. I didn't even know. She'd definitely be old enough, if the things she'd implied when I'd seen her in Faerie were true. Apparently hyran lived extremely long lives.

Actually pretending to be a human had put an annoying extra bounce in her step. Being at the top of the food chain came with certain perks, such as not worrying about something or someone killing you at any time. She sure seemed good with life right now, following me home from school.

"That van," Wraith interrupted my thoughts, all the normal levity gone from her tone. "It's watching you."

I looked up in the direction she'd nodded, and my stomach sank. I knew that van. It had carted me around when I'd been without parents for a bit.

"Let's go," I spun around to make a break for it, and nearly tripped right over Rosie in a wheelchair. I turned back to the van, and watched her mom climb out and lean against it, crossing her arms in front of her chest. Oh boy. She'd known I would run and did not look happy.

"You haven't answered any of my calls," Rosie said from behind me.

I did a slow turn, trying to come up with an explanation. Anything that I'd actually be able to get out without lying.

Nothing came to mind, so I kept my mouth shut.

"Who's this?" Wraith asked.

"Who are you?" Rosie challenged back.

"I'm... Trish's...." Wraith just stopped there.

"Friend." I said. "Hazel. This is Rosie. Rosie, Hazel."

"Yes, her friend," Wraith said, gleeful.

Hey. How many people could say they were friends with a hyran? Not many, from how I took what other people had said.

"Can we have a minute?" Rosie asked Wraith. It sounded more like a command than a question, which would have been comical if she'd known she was ordering around a several century old being from another world.

We waited around awkwardly for Wraith to move out of earshot. Or at least, out of what earshot would be for how she looked at the moment. I didn't know what actually earshot for a hyran was. Starren probably would.

Rosie clearing her throat brought me out of my procrastination. Might as well get this over with.

"How are you?" I asked. It felt stupid, with her sitting there in a wheelchair, but I truly wanted to know.

"I've been better."

Her face didn't reveal what she was thinking, making me twitch as I stood there, looking anywhere but at her.

"You know, it's not even the pain that makes me say that." Now she had my attention. I looked her in the eye. "It's the fact that my best friend, and the only person who was there with me when this happened, won't answer me. Is ignoring me. And I have no idea why."

Saying it was for her own good probably wouldn't go over well. "Are you going to be okay?" I nodded toward the chair.

Her eyes filled with tears. "The doctors aren't hopeful. There was a lot of damage."

I'd asked to be polite, when I didn't really want the answer. She was in that chair because of me. She'd been hurt because she was my friend. I stood up straight. I had to fix this.

"Would you come with me somewhere?" I asked.

She gave me a weird look, and I couldn't blame her. I wanted her to just trust me, after I hadn't been very trust-worthy over the last week.

"Can I get there in the chair?" she asked.

I nodded.

She waved to her mom, and Violet waved back before getting in her mini-van and pulling away.

I motioned Wraith over. "Stay with her for a minute. I need to get Nina's keys."

At first I took my time going up the stairs to get a moment to think, but once I realized I'd left Wraith alone with Rosie, I doubled my speed. I opened the apartment door and grabbed Nina's spare key off the wall. She would be volunteering today, and one of the other women always picked her up, leaving me free to take her car without an explanation.

Did I feel bad about it? Oh yeah. But I also knew that if Dan or Nina found out what I was about to do, I'd be in serious trouble and wouldn't be allowed to do what I was about to do. Even I thought it was crazy. I was totally in a rush to do it because if I let myself think about it, I wouldn't.

And I had to. For my own sake, if not for Rosie's.

I rushed back downstairs, slightly afraid of what I'd find when I got there, but Rosie and Wraith were just both staring at the entranceway waiting for me in silence.

"I need to show you something," I said. I moved around behind Rosie and pushed her chair toward Nina's car parked on the side road.

I helped her into the back seat and went around to put the chair in the trunk, then stopped to take a deep breath before getting in the driver's seat. Wraith got in the front passenger seat, and I pulled away from the curb.

How did I explain what I was hoping to do? Especially if it didn't work. She'd think I was crazy. And if it did work...

Things would change. Hopefully Rosie would still want to be my friend. Hopefully she wouldn't tell the world how she was healed. But if she did, so be it.

I parked the car at the city limits. I was about to out myself, but today was not the day for a granny to turn into an eight-foot tall monster right in front of Rosie's eyes.

Since I couldn't get her back over the line quickly if she was in a chair, we were just going to have to stay in the car. I motioned for Wraith to get out of the vehicle. She stared me down for a second, and I could feel her threat in her look. I'd better not take off.

As soon as she was out, I nosed the car just over the line until I could feel the rush of my powers returning. I put the car in park, just to the side of the road, opened the windows so I could hear Wraith if I needed to, and turned to look at Rosie in the back seat.

"Rosie. I... I don't know how to tell you any of this. I don't know if you'll still trust me, if you'll still want to be my friend. But there's something I have to do for you." I paused. "Or, at least try, I guess. I've never done it on command."

"Trish, there's nothing you can do to make me not want to be your friend. I don't know why you'd even think that." Her face was drawn in pain, but she still smiled at me. "I mean, not talking to me this week wasn't great, but..."

"Don't say that unless you know everything. I won't believe you."

"Then tell me everything, Trish."

"I can't. Literally. But I can show you." Mom had planned way ahead when I was a kid and had made me promise not to tell anyone that I was fae without them having seen something that needed an explanation. Of course, there were ways around that.

I held out my hand. "I'm not being weird. Trust me."

She lifted an eyebrow, but held her hand out anyway. "I think the you not being weird is debatable, but that's okay. Weird doesn't mean bad."

I took her hand and closed my eyes. The first part I was better at. I'd been able to make it happen on purpose with Starren back in Faerie. It was the second part that I couldn't seem to control.

It took me just a second, but when it hit, it hit. The pain in my leg made me drop down in the seat to get the pressure off of it. Somehow I kept hold of Rosie's hand though.

She gasped. "What just happened?"

I took a deep breath through my nose. Did the half of her pain I just took come before or after the pain meds? I gritted my teeth for a second to adjust.

"Why doesn't my leg hurt as bad anymore?"

Oh great. Now that she wasn't hurting as much, she was a lot more demanding. But she was adjusting to hurting less, and I was adjusting to hurting a lot. "It's something I can do. Now be quiet."

She snapped her mouth closed, apparently understanding my need to concentrate, but she watched me closely.

I had her pain. Now I just needed to take her injury. Outside of Sanctuary, I would heal in minutes, where it could take her a year, and may never be the same.

We sat there for a full minute.

Nothing happened.

I forced my eyes tightly closed, grinding my teeth. I wasn't risking outing myself just to help her with her pain for a few minutes. This had to work.

A tear slid down my cheek. Something wiped it away and I opened my eyes. A branch had reached through the open car window to caress my hair and then moved back to the tree it belonged to.

Rosie watched it, face white. "Trish? Would you please tell me what's going on?"

I ignored the pain, slapping the seat with my free hand. "It's supposed to work!"

"What's supposed to work? I don't understand what's going on."

I wanted to pace. To punch something. But to do that, I'd have to let go of Rosie's hand, letting her deal with one hundred percent of the pain on her own again.

"What good is being like this if I can't help the people I care about?" I yelled out the window, not sure who to even ask.

There was no answer.

"Trish, are you okay?" Rosie asked.

I slid back into the seat, my leg hurting enough that it couldn't bear my weight even without a real injury. Was she actually asking if I was okay when she was sitting there with a crushed leg because of me?

"I'm..." I couldn't say fine. It wouldn't come out. "It was my fault you got hurt, Rosie," I said instead. "Someone wanted to send me a message, and they did that using you."

"Send you a message? About what?"

So far so good, she didn't sound mad. She sounded confused, which she had every right to be.

"My real parents... they're a bit crazy. And they're trying to get me to leave Dan and Nina and go back to them. But I don't want to, so they started threatening me. I never..." I choked on the words. I had thought there was a possibility she could get hurt. I couldn't say that I hadn't. Which made this even worse. "I didn't want you to get in the middle, that's why I'd been avoiding you."

"And then I made you go get pizza with me."

"You didn't make me. And I should have known better. But I went with you anyway, risked you getting hurt, because I needed a friend." That was more honest than I'd meant for it to be. But it was out there now.

"Your parents must be insane."

"Basically." She hadn't run away yet, but that wasn't much of a win considering what shape she was in. But I could hold a little hope, since she was still talking to me.

"I would have still wanted to hang out with you, even though I might be in danger," Rosie said. "If you'd have told me what was going on. I might have been able to help somehow."

"I didn't think they'd go that far. Not really. Sure, the thought crossed my mind, but I can be kind of paranoid sometimes."

She chuckled. It wasn't anywhere close to the full, strong laugh she normally put out, but I'd take it.

We smiled at each other for a second, and then Rosie nodded at our hands. "So you explained the hit and run. Now what about this?"

This. This was more complicated. This was more of who I was, the part of me I hadn't chosen, and couldn't change. No matter how much I wished I could.

"How are you making my pain better?"

"I wanted to make it go away," I blurted out. "But I don't know how to control it. I can't control anything!" An angry tear slipped free and I almost lost Rosie's hand as I turned away from her so she didn't see it.

"How were you going to do that, Trish?" Her voice had lost all humor. She was more serious than I'd ever seen her, even when we'd been talking about aliens that fateful day she'd been hurt.

What should I tell her? Nothing but the truth was a given, but how much of the truth?

She deserved it all.

"There are aliens around, Rosie. Just not the type you think of when you hear the word. And I'm one of them. I'm from another world." She tugged on her hand and I let it go. "We come to Earth through portals though, not on spaceships."

"Not cool, Trish," Rosie hissed. "Making fun of me after the week I've had. Seriously, I thought you believed me."

I held up my hands. "I believe everything you thought you saw! Seriously! I'm telling you the truth. I wouldn't be able to lie to you, even if I wanted to."

"Because of some weird alien rule?"

"Close enough, I guess."

She closed her eyes and rubbed her face. "I don't know what to believe. What were you trying to do?"

"Sometimes, well, at least one time, I took someone else's injury. I heal, like, really quick. So I can take an injury or wound from someone who doesn't, and then I just get better."

She perked up. She believed me. "So how long does it take? I've been freaking out, I wasn't completely honest with you earlier. The doc says there's a good chance I'll never walk correctly again. That I'll be in pain for the rest of my life. I'm so done with hurting this bad, when will it go away?"

"Uh…" I didn't have an answer. I didn't know why it worked sometimes and sometimes didn't. "I don't know, Rosie. The one time I did it, it happened right away. The wound moved almost as soon as I touched her."

"So what's the difference this time?"

"I don't know. I've tried it since, and I've never been able to get it to work again."

"That's okay," she grabbed my hand. "We'll figure it out. Come on, try again."

Just try again. Like I was learning how to swim, or hit a baseball. But I couldn't tell her no. Her eyes, so hopeful behind the pain. I squeezed her hand back and closed my eyes, concentrating.

Nothing happened. "I can't make it happen, Rosie. I thought maybe... I thought it would work."

"It has to work." Rosie's voice had a hysterical note. "I can't live with not being able to walk. I can't!"

She shouldn't have to. I should be able to fix this.

"Trisha?" Wraith called from somewhere outside the car.

"Busy," I yelled back. I gritted my teeth, doing my best to funnel everything I had through my hand. I opened my eyes to check on the progress, but there was no glowing light, no anything.

"I don't care. Get back here. Now."

"Who is that lady?" Rosie asked.

I ignored her, letting go of her hand and wildly reached for the ignition. Wraith wasn't the type to get excited for nothing. I slammed the car in reverse and started backing up without taking the time to check the rearview mirror.

The car jolted to a stop. I shivered, and slowly looked up. Dark eyes stared back at me, at the level of the mirror. It was covered in dirt. Or more accurately, made of dirt.

A golem. Like the lava one we'd fought in the fae tunnels earlier this year.

"Wraith?" I asked.

She didn't move. "I'll take care of it. Get out of here."

"What is that thing?" Rosie asked from the back, panic in her voice.

I ignored her and slammed the car into drive, mashing down the pedal.

The car spurted forward. As we tore onward, the mud lifted in front of us, coagulating into a monster. I hit it at thirty miles an hour. In the back, Rosie screeched.

The thing exploded, bursting across the windshield. I hit the wipers, but didn't take my foot off the gas at all.

Farther ahead, another popped up. I hit this one going even faster, but the car bounced off sideways, the sound of crumpling metal filling the air. The only difference between them was that this one had extra time to harden. Hitting one that had been together for more than thirty seconds would probably be bad. Really bad.

The road bubbled ahead, and I jerked the wheel sideways, turning at the intersection. If these things started to form out of asphalt...

The car skidded through the turn, but stuck to the road. I mashed the accelerator to the floor, pushing the engine until the needle started flying higher and higher. Thankfully Indiana roads were straight and I could see for like, a mile.

I glanced in the mirror. Somehow even though they looked like they were just clumps of mud, the things were keeping up. And there were six of them behind us now, working in a semi-circle.

Two popped up in the road ahead.

"Hold on!" I yelled to Rosie before yanking the wheel and going off road. We tore across the edge of a field and bounced back onto another road.

There. Right ahead of us. The Sanctuary line. Safety.

The engine strained and we shot forward toward the line. We were ten feet away when a monster popped up in front of us. I yanked the wheel and the car went sideways. We slid around the creature and across the border. The monsters behind us couldn't stop in time and hit the Sanctuary line, disintegrating on impact.

I took a deep breath, quivering, before I remembered that I had a passenger. I spun around in my seat. "Are you okay?"

"Don't stop!" Rosie did her best to twist around in her seat, but grimaced in pain. "What were those things?"

"They can't get us here," I said. "Anywhere inside the city limits is safe."

"Are you sure? I still got hit by a car."

"Abilities don't work here. But fae can still harm people in regular ways, I guess." Abilities didn't work in Sanctuary. Which most likely meant that the creatures attacking us were part of a fae ability.

"Fae?"

"Yeah, that's what we're called. Those old Celtic legends."

Rosie's eyes bugged out a bit and I sighed. Apparently alien to fae was a bigger leap than I'd thought.

A knock on the passenger side window almost sent me flying through the door. Wraith's face peered in, covered in streaks of mud.

I hit the unlock button and she climbed in.

"All good?" I asked her, keeping my voice neutral for Rosie's sake.

"You think a mud golem is going to slow me down?" She grinned, showing her teeth far too much for just a regular smile.

I got a better look at her now that she was inside, and cringed. "You're getting mud all over Nina's car."

"Kid, that's the least of your worries."

Oh crap. We'd bounced off that one golem pretty hard. I ripped off my seatbelt and jumped out of the car. I pulled my hair as soon as I saw the damages. Dents all down the driver's side, and a crumpled front bumper.

"Nina's going to kill me," I whispered.

Wraith stuck her head out the window. "I wouldn't worry about that. With the things I've seen you take on, a human shouldn't deserve a thought. Besides, you have me."

I ignored Rosie's strange look at the granny in my front seat announcing to the world that she could defend me.

"I'm not talking literally. She's going to be so mad I crossed the border."

"Why?" Rosie called.

I got back in the car and dropped my forehead to the steering wheel for a second. "The people who are out to get me can't when I'm inside the city limits. But I can't use my ability here, so I couldn't heal you."

"You couldn't anyway," Wraith inserted helpfully.

"You risked dying to help me heal my leg?" Rosie asked.

"Worse than dying," Wraith announced. "She risked getting captured by one of her parents."

Unpacking that right now was beyond me. "Let's just get you home," I said. "Your mom has to be worried." If her mom knew why she'd gotten hurt, she'd probably never let Rosie come around me again.

The car made a slight grinding noise when I put it into drive, but coasted forward without anything too unusual. Maybe it was fine. Maybe Jaden could pull out the dents, and Nina would never be the wiser.

Yeah. And maybe my parents would just go back to Faerie and leave me in peace.

After getting Rosie into her house and situated, I texted Jaden. I was still mad at him, but I didn't know anyone else who could possibly help me, or at least know someone who could.

Rosie had fallen asleep on the short trip back to her house, a testament to how much pain she was in, and how much strain I'd put on her. But it had saved me from answering a ton of questions that I wasn't yet prepared to answer, so I wouldn't complain.

Per usual, he was at the bar. If I'd ever seen him drinking, I'd be concerned that he was spending so much time there for an entirely different reason than I actually was.

We clunked to a stop outside Jenny's just as he was coming out. My need to not have Nina mad at me outweighed my extreme urge to get out of here before I had another unpleasant encounter with some fae here, but not by much.

Nina would be mad about the car, sure. That I could handle. But she'd also be really mad when she heard how the damage had happened, and that I wasn't as prepared for.

The car door creaked when it opened. A bad sign. I jumped out and ran over to Jaden. "Tell me you can knock out those dents. They aren't that bad, right?"

"Not that bad if you ran into an elephant." He walked around the car and whistled when he saw the driver's side. "What exactly did you hit? You didn't say in your text."

No way I was going to tell him. He'd probably freak as much as Nina would, and I didn't have any reason to give him an explanation.

"She ran over a golem. Several actually, but I think most of the damage is from the first one."

I really needed to ditch this granny. Sure, she'd helped me out today, but I wasn't sure that was enough for all of the stuff she put me through.

"A golem?" Jaden's voice went hard. "In Sanctuary?"

"Not exactly..."

"Your girl went over the line today," Wraith cackled. "And we had loads of fun. Didn't we, Trisha?"

Fun? Not what I'd call today, but we were all still alive, so I wouldn't complain too much. "Can you fix it or not?" I asked Jaden.

"I can't on my own, but I have a friend who could help. It'll take us at least a day though. Not sure how you're going to hide this from Nina for that long."

A strange mix of dread and relief went through me. "When can you start?"

"He gets off work in a couple hours. But unlike me, he doesn't work for free. I can't see him getting started without the cash."

And I didn't have any money. But I did have an aunt in town, one that also liked to keep Nina happy. And who had caused a lot of trouble when she was younger, if Nina's innuendoes were accurate. Maybe Wren would help me.

I reached in and turned the car off, grabbing the keys and tossing them to Jaden. "Thank you. A ton. I'll get some money. How much are you thinking?"

"Well the bumper itself is going to be at least two hundred, and that's if I can find one the right model at the scrapyard. It'll probably be five hundred or so, more if we have to paint the bumper to match."

Five hundred dollars? Man, this attempt to fix Rosie had come with a hefty price. One I'd have no problem paying, if it had worked.

But it hadn't. I still didn't have any idea how to control that part of my ability. Not only had it not worked, but I could have gotten Rosie killed just for being with me today. Taking her across the border had been stupid. More than stupid.

I should have gone across on my own. Found a way to practice, and gotten this thing under control before taking her into danger without a plan. But I couldn't help myself when I'd seen her in so much pain.

"I'll get you the money," I said. "You just get started."

"Not until you tell me why you'd do something as stupid as leave Sanctuary."

I stiffened and turned to march away.

He grabbed my arm gently. "Trish. Talk to me."

"It was for Rosie." That was all he was going to get. I pulled my arm free, but not forcefully. He didn't deserve that.

He sighed behind me. "Please ask for help next time."

I gestured toward Wraith. "I had it covered."

"We don't know her motives. We don't know what she's capable of. You can't just trust her to have your back like that. Even though she's promised not to hurt you or any of your people, that doesn't mean she couldn't abandon you at the perfect moment and let you get killed."

Technically he was right. But it didn't feel like it. I had to go with my gut on this one, because not trusting her in a dangerous situation could also get me killed.

"I'll see you as soon as I get the money around," I said.

I walked off, and my shadow followed. She gave me space for the first block and a half, and then slowly closed the distance between us.

After walking beside me in silence for another block, she broke it. "He's right you know. You shouldn't trust me. Really, you should trust no one."

I considered her words. "I lived like that for a long time. It's lonely. I won't live like that again."

"Wise words for one so young. Maybe I can learn something from you."

We walked some more before she spoke again.

"Thank you. For trusting me. I haven't had that bond in quite some time."

It was me that smiled at her this time. A little tentative, but it was there. "We all need someone, right? Besides. I might need you to save my life very soon, if I can't find a way to get this car fixed and paid for."

"A joke?" she asked.

I nodded.

She laughed, and I grinned along with her.

When we got home, the apartment was empty except for Starren, sitting at the table. It was unusual to catch her home. I went over and pulled out the chair beside her, taking a seat. Wraith opting for the couch.

"Hey. Nina here?"

"No. She took her sister to the gym."

Ah. That explained why Starren was here. Wren wasn't.

Starren just kept eating her banana and playing on her phone.

"How's..." I didn't even know what to ask, really. When we didn't have a common enemy or a situation to figure out, my sister and I had nothing in common. "everything?"

"Fine." She didn't even look up.

I sighed and stood.

"How's everything with you?"

My heart leapt a little. It wasn't often that she made an effort to be social. I tried to tamp down the excitement. If she felt it, she'd be weirded out, and then this would be over.

"Interesting," I said, after trying fine and not being able to get it out.

Now she looked up. "More interesting than before?"

Oh great. Of course I couldn't just have a conversation with my sister. "I may have damaged Nina's car." The answer spilled out before I could stop it. I shouldn't tell her what was going on, she wouldn't understand, but I wanted to. I wanted us to have a relationship beyond just hey, how are you. "You wouldn't happen to have five hundred dollars I could borrow, would you?"

"And how'd you do that?" She seemed vaguely interested now, and I'd take it, because it was more than I usually got unless someone was trying to kill me.

"She hit a golem," Wraith cackled. "Full speed! It hadn't fully hardened yet, or there wouldn't have been much of the vehicle left."

I'd almost forgotten she was there. I shouldn't have, since she was always there anymore, but I had. And here she was, being more honest than I appreciated. I could have just told Starren I'd hit some dirt.

"So? If you don't have the full five hundred, you can just chip in. If I can get enough people-" I got up and paced the small space.

"I'm not giving you the money." She sat back on two legs in her chair. "You need to tell your Nina what happened. She can make you work it off or whatever, but you shouldn't be hiding this from her."

"She'll freak out if she hears what happened. And then she might do something that gets her hurt. I'm not going to let that happen."

Starren dropped back down on four legs, grabbed my forearm and gently pushed me back into my chair. Once we were the same height, she stared into my eyes. "That isn't your decision, Trisha. Nina can make that choice for herself. You can't control what's around you. You can't control other people. You can only control yourself."

"You control everything," I muttered.

"Father taught me how to manipulate every situation. To make sure everything happened in exactly the manner I want it to." Now she leaned in close, her voice going to a hiss. "Do you think I want to be like Father?"

I leaned away from her. It had been a while since I'd been on this end of her intenseness.

"Every thought I have, I mull over. Is this how Father made me? And if it is, then I do the opposite of my instinct. Only when someone's life is at stake will I ever treat the world as I did before. Don't make me remember what I was made to be. Just help me be better."

Her eyes looked suspiciously damp, but since I'd never seen her cry, I couldn't say for sure that's what was happening.

"I need to learn to be more like you," I said. "I need to figure out how to control this, how to get the whole thing to happen in the right way."

"More like me? You idiot. I'm trying to figure out how to be more like you. You're the first person who truly cared about me for me, instead of caring that I didn't die because they needed me for something. If I hear one more word about you trying to be someone you're not, I'm going to kick you into next week."

She wanted to be more like me? Even though she was fae, I wanted to call her a liar. Why would anyone want to be like me? I wanted to beg for the money, and was about to at least insist a little more when the key turned in the lock.

Nina and Wren walked in, laughing. Apparently they'd taken Wren's car to the gym, and Nina didn't know hers was missing yet.

An odd sense of both relief and disappointment hit me. It would have been nice to have the decision made for me.

"We do need to talk though," Starren said. She'd lost a bit of the intensity, but not of the serious. "Information came to light today..." she nodded at Wren who walked around the hallway wall into the kitchen.

Information came to light today. That in and of itself wasn't enough information to mean anything.

"What has you two laughing like that?" I asked, plastering a fake smile across my face.

Nina swatted Wren in the shoulder. "No telling tales," she said.

"Things that happened way before you were born," Wren said. "I'll tell you when we're alone." She ducked Nina's mock attempt at throwing a pillow in her face, laughing.

Why was Wren still here? It was really starting to bug me. Not that I didn't like her. And I really liked how she made Nina feel like everything was going to be okay, even when nothing was right with my world at the moment.

Scratch that. Everyone I cared about was still alive. I'd never take that for granted again, after seeing Nina, lifeless.

Starren stood up without saying anything. She started toward our room, then pointedly waited for me to follow.

Wraith got up to come too, but I motioned for her to sit down. Her presence was probably why Starren hadn't gotten straight to whatever she wanted as soon as I walked in.

"Everything okay, honey?" Nina called after me.

I waved, but didn't answer. Things weren't okay at all, and I had the sinking feeling that whatever Starren wanted to talk about would only make it worse.

CHAPTER NINE

"We've got a problem." There was the real Starren. Jumping right into what was important. She handed me a newspaper from off the dresser.

I scanned the front page. The first headline caught my attention instantly. 'Three More Missing' it read in bold letters, the article taking up most of the front page. I scanned it quickly. In a town this size, it wasn't crazy for someone to go missing. Usually someone hiding from paying child support or escaping abuse. But the article listed the names of the people who had disappeared in the last month.

Nine. Nine names.

"What's going on?" I asked Starren, even though I thought I knew.

"Something is preying on the humans here," Starren said. She started to pace. "We need to stop it." She saw the look on my face and stopped, her expression going cross. "It's not that I care about them. It's that the fae are going to be discovered."

Sure. But I didn't say that out loud. She had changed far more than she thought.

She started the pacing back up. "Either we have one monster to deal with," she jerked her head in the direction of the kitchen. "Or the fae presence is getting large enough in the area that humans are noticing, and the fae aren't ready for anyone to know yet."

"She was with me." Okay, I didn't know the specific times these people had gone missing. But Wraith was always with me.

"Then, and I can't believe I'm about to say this, we have a bigger problem than a hyran."

Considering how much she feared hyran, and for a long time I thought she wasn't afraid of anything, a bigger problem than a hyran was scary. Really scary.

Starren leaned in close. "Our parents are here."

I crossed my arms in front of my chest. "That's a big leap, Star."

"What's your explanation?"

I took a full minute to come up with one, but couldn't. Starren was the one I came to for problems like this. I should take her statement seriously. But I really didn't want to.

"It could be anything," I said lamely.

"It's them, and you know it," she answered.

Deep down, I did. They'd said they would come. And now they were. "What do we do?" I asked.

"Give me a day. I'm going to find them. And I'll come up with a plan to take care of things. You don't have to get involved if you don't want to, but I needed you to know. In case I fail."

In case she failed? What was she actually going to do? And Starren, fail? That seemed impossible. But going up against the king and queen of the fae, even when they were fighting each other as well, was a bad idea.

"You know I'm with you, Starren. Just tell me what to do."

Her face went hard. "I don't think you're going to like the answer to what needs done."

My whole body went cold. "What does that mean?"

"I think you know. Are you still with me?"

"You can't just kill them!" Whoops, that came out way too loud. I dialed it back down, so Nina and Wren didn't hear me. There was no stopping Wraith from eavesdropping.

"I see no other option." She didn't sound like the person she'd been growing into. She sounded like the old Starren, where everyone was a means to an end.

"I'll find one. You get whatever information you can, and I'll work on what to do with it." I had no idea where to even start, but I couldn't just let her try to kill our parents. For one, it would be nearly impossible and there was a good chance she'd be the one who ended up dead. For two, I'd seen what killing the Council had done to her. She couldn't have our parents on her conscience. "Now. Money, please."

Starren lifted an eyebrow, turned around and grabbed her backpack off the other bed and headed for the door. "Tell Nina." She left, shutting the door behind her.

Tell Nina. Sure. Nina, I smashed your car hitting a monster. Oh, how did I run into one in Sanctuary? About that...

Nah. She'd make me promise not to leave the city limits, and then I'd be stuck, unable to cross and see if I could figure out how to heal on purpose, instead of just by accident.

I walked out of the bedroom and into the kitchen. Wren was there, playing on her phone. She looked up and smiled when I walked in.

"Where's Nina?" I asked.

"Getting ready for a grocery run. We ran out of wine last night."

No, no, no. A grocery run involved a car. No.

"What's wrong?" Wren asked. "You look a little freaked out."

"I, ah," didn't know what to say. "I borrowed Nina's car earlier, and might have... bumped something." She didn't need to know the magical side of things.

Wren laughed, surprising me.

"What's so funny?" My voice was grumpy, but I couldn't help it. I was about to disappoint Nina, and Wren, who was my aunt and should therefore be on my side, was laughing at me.

"Sorry, sorry. But that totally sounds like something I would have done at your age. In fact, I think I did." She squinted for a second. "Some of that time is a bit blurry. I really wasn't a great teen." She patted the seat beside her. "So. What you going to do about it?"

"Jaden thinks he can fix it. If I can come up with the money to get another bumper at the scrap yard. I just have to keep her from trying to drive until tomorrow."

Wren touched her nose, eyes still laughing. "I got you. How much money do you need?"

"Seriously?"

"Seriously. You'll owe me, of course, but I'll loan you some cash."

"You're a life-saver." I hugged her, surprising myself. Being suspicious of her was stupid. She was an awesome person. I leaned back. "I know it's a lot, but Jaden is thinking five hundred dollars."

"Let's run to the ATM. I'll give you six, just to make sure. And you can make payments."

I almost hugged her again, but I kept it together. "How can we get Nina to stay home?"

"Hey, Nina?" Wren called.

"Yeah?" Nina yelled back from the direction of her room.

"Trish and I are going to do your store trip for you."

Nina came out of the bedroom, hair wet. She must have showered after the gym. "Are you sure?"

"Of course I'm sure." Wren pulled me in for a half hug. "I haven't hardly seen this girl since I got here. We could use a little time together. You can't hog me my whole visit."

Nina beamed at us. "Of course." She shooed us toward the door. "You girls have fun. Seriously."

A pang hit me, but I ignored it. Nina didn't know the real reason we were going out. If she did, she'd be devastated that I'd completely disregarded her and Dan's wishes and gone over the line. She couldn't find out.

"Thanks, Nina. We'll be back soon," I said. I held in the urge to hug her. It wasn't something I did a lot, even though we had a great relationship at this point, and she caught on to how I was feeling about things way too easily.

Wren led the way downstairs, me right behind her, and Wraith right behind me. "Just a second, Wren," I said. When she nodded and walked farther down the hall, I pulled Wraith over. "I need you to do something for me."

She smiled. "Of course."

"I need you to follow Starren. Keep her safe."

That smile turned into a frown really quick. "I'm here to protect you, not her."

"Protecting her is protecting me. I'm perfectly safe right now, and she might be able to get us some good information. That won't help us if she's dead."

Wraith cocked her head, considering. I crossed my fingers that she wouldn't ask if I was just trying to get rid of her, because I couldn't come up with a creative way to say no without lying.

"Fine. But I'll be back soon."

I nodded. "Thank you. Seriously."

She stormed off in a huff, obviously not happy, but giving me a chance to breathe. I caught up to Wren, and we walked out of the building together. We got into her car, and it took me a second to get out of my thoughts and see her staring at me.

"Sorry, what?"

"What area of town are we going to drop the money off in? So I know what ATM to head to."

"Oh, sorry." I stopped myself right before 'Jenny's' slipped out of my mouth. She was helping me now, but did I really want to tell her where an entire group of fae refugees were staying? I didn't have a single solid reason not to trust her with their location, she'd even helped some fae get here when the Fae Distribution Center had been attacked. But it just didn't feel right. "Jaden's apartment."

She looked at me oddly, like she noticed my long pause while my brain did all its calculations, but she put the car in drive and pulled away from the curb.

My phone buzzed in my pocket. I pulled it out, in case it was Jaden, but it was a text from Rosie.

'Figure out how to do it yet?'

At least she'd thought enough to not say what it was I should be figuring out.

'Not yet. Still on it.'

Still on it? Apparently I was going to try again, because I couldn't have told her I was if I wasn't. My grip on the door handle tightened, and I took a couple big breaths. What if I never figured it out? What if I couldn't fix her?

"Everything okay over there?" Wren asked. "This isn't exactly what I expected we'd do when we hung out, me driving in silence and you having a panic attack."

It would feel pretty good right now to let out everything that had happened in the last few days. Wren wouldn't be upset like Nina would be. She knew I could handle myself, and she trusted me to get a job done.

But in telling her, I'd risk everyone else. To make her understand the pressure I was under right now, I'd have to tell her about the fae at Jenny's, and Jaden's expectations.

"Have you seen Cray?" I asked instead of answering her.

She gave me a look that said she knew what I was doing, but let it slide. "He was going to the movies. He didn't say anything more than that."

I almost smiled. A small bright spot. Cray never went anywhere by himself, and he'd been with a girl the last several times he'd gone out.

"I hope that by now, you know you can trust me. That you know you can tell me anything, and I only have your best interests at heart. Even though we don't share blood, we're family. I truly think of you as my niece."

It was a nice sentiment. And I appreciated that she said we didn't share blood, instead of saying we weren't even from the same world. But humans could lie. I had to keep telling myself that, before I spilled my guts to someone I shouldn't.

"Thank you, Wren. Really. I wanted to see Rosie without Nina making a big deal out of it or trying to come along and support me, so I took the car without asking." All true. Just without the extra details.

"Nina can be a bit over the top," Wren said, her voice sympathetic. "Hopefully Jaden deserves your trust on this, and we can get it all figured out."

"Jaden deserves my trust in everything," I clarified.

"Of course," Wren took her eyes off the road to look at me. "I wasn't implying otherwise."

We drove through the ATM in silence, then cruised back onto the road, heading for Jaden's apartment. It was only a minute up the road, but no matter how much I wracked my brain, I couldn't find a safe topic, so the trip felt like an hour.

Wren pulled up in front of the building and threw the car in park.

"Thank you, Wren. Seriously. I didn't have anyone left to ask."

She squeezed my hand. "That's what family is for, Trish. I'm here for you. You just need to ask. After D.C., you know I'm up for anything."

She had handled herself well with the whole D.C. thing. I'd been worried, since she got introduced to the fae and thrown into a whole mess on the same day, but she'd come through for me, and the fae who'd nearly been killed in the tunnels. I needed to remember that.

"Well..." I really wasn't good at asking for favors. And I'd already asked for a lot. But I seriously needed her help. "If you could keep Nina busy today, I would appreciate it more than you know. The car will be back in the morning."

Wren tapped the side of her nose. "I got you."

I let out a breath in relief. Another crisis averted. As long as Dan didn't want to drive Nina's car for some weird reason. Okay, now I was just freaking myself out. He never drove her car. And he'd been gone so much lately for work, I'd hardly seen him anyway.

"I'll get this to Jaden, then," I said, patting my pocket where I'd put the money. I got out of the car and shut the door, leaning in the open window.

"Want me to wait? I can give you a ride home."

"No. He won't mind running me home if I decide I don't want to walk."

She grinned. "I got ya. Okay. Go get some Jaden time." She put the car in drive and took off.

"It's not like that!" I yelled after her. But there was no way she heard me.

I waited until she was out of sight, and then started hiking back to Jenny's. Wonderful. Not. I was so tired of that place.

I stopped outside of Jenny's. I didn't want to go in. Every time I stepped through that door, people had expectations for me. Some were good, some not.

Many of them didn't seem to care about me one way or another. But some thought I was my parents, and I didn't know how to show them I wasn't.

I texted Jaden that I was waiting outside. That way I didn't have to see anyone.

People passed me while I waited. And every single one, I studied. Was that man fae? The woman in the purple coat? What about the kid, walking his dog?

He was probably okay. As far as I knew, fae didn't really have pets.

Finally Jaden stepped outside to meet me. "You got the money?" he asked, unusually to the point. Was he just tired, or was he getting tired of me? Of me, and all of the trouble I always brought with me. There had once been a time when I refused asking for help. Recently, it seemed like that was all that happened.

"Yes, here." I handed him Wren's money. "And if there's any extra, keep it. I owe you."

He huddled into his coat a bit. I hadn't noticed the wind picking up until that moment. "You don't owe me anything, Trish. That's not how friends work."

Sometimes I forget that he grew up on Earth, with a fairly normal childhood. He knew what it was like to have friends. Real friends. I was getting there, but it still felt weird.

A group of men ducked around us, headed for Jenny's front door. One of them noticed me, and bumped one of the others, whispering to him.

The second guy made his way over to us. Now that he was closer, I remembered him. Jaden had introduced him the last time I was here. His name escaped me though. Go something. I was hoping he just pass on by, but he didn't. He stopped a short distance away and nodded.

"Trisha." It was just my first name, but the way he said it sounded so formal. "I hear you prefer that name to your fae-given name?"

I nodded. The other name only made me think of my father, which was very unpleasant.

"I wanted to formally thank you. I am in your debt."

I should have answered him, but I was too blown away. Fae never admitted then they owed something. It gave the other person power over them. The surprise was followed quickly by confusion. What had I ever done for him?

"You don't recognize me."

I stared him in the face, trying to figure it out.

"No no, it's fine, I didn't expect you to. I was in the tunnel that day. When the golem attacked. You and your sister saved me. I won't forget who actually want to help the fae, and who don't care harming anyone in their way. That's why I'm helping Jaden. Wren got us here like she told you she would, and then she left us to fend for ourselves. To figure out this world, with little help. Jaden stepped in. A friend of yours. We won't forget."

"Jaden did that on his own," I said. "That had nothing to do with me."

"But you saved him too, didn't you," another one of the refugees said, sidling in beside the first man. "And because of your kindness to him and his family, he was here to help us. Your ways are not the ways of the fae. We like your ways better."

Me? Kind? I opened my mouth to say something back to her, but then found I didn't have an answer. I didn't care for the ways of the fae either. At all. Which was what had started this whole thing in the first place, when I'd agreed to hunt down Jaden to be allowed to stay on Earth.

"How's Cumat doing?" I asked instead. Starren would never answer me when I asked, so I'd stopped.

"He is well, and his loyalties have shifted." The woman raised her eyebrows, like I should know what that meant.

I didn't.

"When the time is right, he'll come forward. And he won't be alone."

Okay, I did not like where this was going. "Okay then." It came out really lame, but they all pretended not to notice. "I'd better get going then."

"We'll be ready," the first man said. "When the time comes."

"Stop saying that," I whispered under my breath. It wasn't loud enough for them to hear, so they just kept staring at me. I needed out of here, now. "When's your friend off work now?" I asked Jaden.

"He should be to the scrapyard in twenty minutes. Nina's car isn't an unusual model, so he should have the bumper here within an hour. Or so I hope."

"Want to go get ice cream or something?" I asked. I didn't really want ice cream, but I also didn't want to go home and try to keep a secret from Nina.

"No, but thanks." He nodded toward the other fae. "We have a lot to talk about. You could stay, if you want." His eyes asked me to be the person he wanted me to be, but his body language said he already knew my answer.

"Thanks, but I gotta go." I could say it even though I didn't have anywhere to be, because I wanted to be almost anywhere but here. I spun around and took off at a fast walk, not looking behind me. I didn't need to see Jaden's face to know he was disappointed.

My phone buzzed, and I pulled it out, glad for the distraction.

'Want to come over?' the text from Rosie said. 'I'm bored out of my mind and my mom won't leave me alone.'

Bored out of her mind I could understand. But if I went over, would she grill me? Ask me to try to heal her again? I owed it to her. She was stuck in a chair because of me right now. And I really didn't have anywhere else to go at the moment.

'I'll be over. Give me 15.'

Then I texted Nina to let her know I was going to Rosie's and started walking.

It was a ways. At least two miles. But I didn't even care. In fact, I didn't particularly want to be there, but my need not to be anywhere else was worse.

The sun had mostly set by the time I hit Rosie's doorbell.

It was a minute before I heard something weird on the other side of the door. Finally it flung open and I stared over Rosie's head for a second before looking down to catch her eyes. Her chair caught me by surprise, even though it shouldn't have.

"Hi," I said, and then just stood there awkwardly.

"Hi," she said back, and rolled her chair out of the way. "Come on in."

I followed her in and closed the door behind us. She led the way into her familiar living room, and parked by the couch.

After I didn't follow for a moment, she patted the couch beside her. "Come on. I'm bored out of my mind right now. I only have so many friends to take shifts visiting me."

I did as she asked. "Where's your mom?"

"She's picking up some overtime. Apparently our insurance wasn't as good as she'd hoped."

Ouch. It had been long enough since Rosie had gotten hurt for the bills to start coming in. Another thing that I was responsible for. Her mom had to feel guilty about leaving her, but what other choice did she have?

"Has Mason been out to see you?"

She grimaced. "He tried. I told him no, but he won't stop calling."

"Maybe you should give him another chance."

"Maybe. But I don't think so."

We sat there in awkward silence. Things had never been awkward before, in our entire friendship. Even when I couldn't tell her why I wasn't living with my foster parents and needed to crash somewhere. She'd made me feel at home.

"So," Rosie said. "Now that I'm not in shock and nothing is trying to kill us, would you like to elaborate on... you?"

Well. At least she hadn't asked if I'd figured out how to heal her yet. Because I hadn't even had a chance to try to figure it out. Really, it was an amazing gift, and I needed to know how to do it on command. But every time I tried, I saw Nina's pale face, the life leaving her, and I freaked out.

"I'm not sure exactly what you'd like to know." Or how much to tell her. Or how honest to be.

"Everything." She leaned forward, and though her face was still somewhat tight from pain, the eager happiness I saw there was the Rosie from before the accident. "Starting with more about what you are, exactly. Are you an alien? I wasn't really sure what you meant earlier."

"As far as I know, there aren't space aliens. But that's not out of the realm of possibility. But if you want to say I'm an alien because I'm from a different world, I guess that's okay." Weird, but okay. Who knew, people might be more accepting of spaceships than portals. They were in pop culture a lot more, and weren't as likely to be hiding in your back yard.

Her grin somehow got bigger. "That's epic. So you can heal people. What else can you do?"

"I can talk to plants." Sure, that was downplaying it a bit, but I didn't really want to tell her that plants obeyed me and I could rip a person to pieces if I wanted to. Or even by accident, if I was mad enough.

"That's neat, but the healing is way more practical. What do plants have to say, really." Apparently it was rhetorical, because she kept going. "How long have you been on Earth? Do your foster parents know? Is Starren your real sister, because that means there are more fae. That's a question, how many fae are there? Are there lots on Earth?"

I just blinked at her for a moment, figuring out what to answer first.

She suddenly looked devastated. "Don't answer anything you don't want to! I don't want you to think this changes our friendship. I'm not going to suddenly be scared of you because I learned something I didn't know before. You're still my best friend."

Best friend? I'd never been anyone's best friend before. She deserved to know everything. Correction. Everything that wouldn't get her in any more trouble than she already was.

"I've been on Earth as long as I can remember. I don't actually know when that happened, but I grew up with humans. My foster parents do know, long story. Starren is very much my sister, surprise, right? Now you know two fae. Well, more than that. But I'll let them choose if they want you to know or not. I don't really know how many fae are around. I avoided them until last fall."

"Last fall, when you moved here? And how many 'other' fae do I know but not know they're fae?"

Whoops. Shouldn't have let that slip. I needed to consider my answers better. I wasn't going to hide anything about me. The fae did that. But I shouldn't be making that choice for others. "Yeah. I moved here because I got in trouble in D.C. Fort Wayne is a safe space for fae, at least safe from other fae. We call it Sanctuary."

"Sanctuary. I like that." She studied me for a moment. "Don't think I didn't notice you not answering the other question. But I'm not going to push. I just want you to know that. What kind of trouble were you in? Is it resolved now?"

"Not exactly. The problem that started all this, yeah, but it just created a bunch more problems."

"Tell me everything."

I nodded. "But first. You hungry? I could order in."

She laughed. "You and your stomach. Yeah, I could eat."

I smiled back, partially relieved, with a side of freaking out. Part of me had hoped she would react, that she would decide we weren't friends anymore so she could be safe. But apparently that wasn't going to happen, and I also couldn't be more happy.

Over the next hour, I laid out a large chunk of the story of my life, with some edits, of course. After I stopped talking, Rosie had questions.

"So. Your mom and dad are evil?"

"Not my mom so much. I think she's just... I don't know." I wiped crumbs off my pants, focusing on something other than my mom.

"What are you going to do about them? Should I try to get my mom to leave the city? What powers do your parents have?"

"I don't know the extent of my parents powers," I answered. The fact made me uncomfortable. Going into a situation with such limited knowledge...

"And the plan?" Rosie asked.

I jumped up from the couch and collected all of our Chinese takeout containers.

"Trish?"

"Stop pushing," I said. But apparently she didn't get it.

"But I need to know if something big is going to happen. If you could just tell me the plan I–"

"I don't have a plan!" It burst out, angry. "I'm doing all I can, but how am I supposed to stop the fae? What am I supposed to do? Pick a side? I don't like either side! Both of them are terrible people at times, both of them selfish. What am I supposed to do, Rosie?"

She didn't say anything. Just stared at me with an open mouth.

"That wasn't a rhetorical question. I don't have an answer. The answer everyone keeps giving me is terrible. I can't... I don't want to hurt them." I marched into the attached kitchen and stuffed the trash inside the can. I marched right back out and past Rosie, sick to my stomach that the anger I'd been carrying was coming out now, at her of all people. But I couldn't stay. "Thanks for supper." I started for the front door.

"Trish, wait!" She wheeled after me. "I'm sorry! This is all really new, and I'm freaking out a little bit. If there are armies gathering around the city, I just want to make sure everyone I love stays safe."

Of course she did. That was what most people wanted. Me included. But how to go about that... That was something else.

I paused in the doorway to go outside, the cold wind making my eyes tear up and yet soothing me at the same time.

"You don't have to pick a side," Rosie said. "You have your own people. And I'm sure you'll all be able to come up with something. When you do, could you let me know? So I can stop worrying?"

Why had I told her anything? To make me feel better. How selfish. I shouldn't have freaked her out so bad. It wasn't like she could do anything to help.

"Will do," I said, without looking back. "Goodnight."

I walked out and gently closed the door behind me. There was an answer to this mess out there somewhere. An answer that didn't end up with me being a pawn, or everyone I cared about getting killed. And I was going to find it.

CHAPTER TEN

I wandered the city most of the night, until I was too cold. Nina must have thought I was still at Rosie's, or she'd have been grabbing Dan and going out on the city to track me down.

I thought about texting Jaden, asking him where he was on the car and if I could help, but I didn't need him accidentally guilting me all of the time. He never meant to, but when he somehow always made the right choices, it automatically made me feel like a screw up.

Here I was again, with nowhere to go. I'd thought those days were over. Carver would let me land at his place, but then I'd probably see Starren, and I wasn't up for that.

So I roamed the alleys of Fort Wayne, hoping to run into Storm. I missed that doggy dragon.

No luck though. Long after dark, I gave up. The temperature had dropped, and I couldn't take the cold much longer.

I'd pushed every thought about what to do about my parents out of my head the entire march around the city. My brain needed a bit of time to think about something else.

Shuffling into the apartment, I paused in the entranceway to work on my face. Dan, Nina, and Wren were chatting in the living room. I worked up a smile, the closest thing I could do to lying, and walked in.

"Trish!" Nina waved me over. "How's Rosie doing? You were over there a lot longer than I expected."

I gave them all a weak wave. "She's in pain but seems like she's handling things well." I didn't add that we'd had a fight and I'd left hours ago, trying to cover up my insecurities. "I'm really tired though. I'm headed to bed."

"Get everything handled with your day?" Wren asked.

"Yeah, all good."

"Night, Trish," Dan said. "I feel like I've hardly seen you."

"Whose fault is that?" I fired back, with more venom than I'd intended. It was supposed to come out as a joke, but it really didn't.

"Yeah, I'm sorry. We've had a lot of stuff come up lately, and I've been swamped. I'll make it up to you. Maybe we can take a trip to the zoo this weekend."

Yay, a trip to the zoo, where there would be bunches of families with little kids, people out on dates, and me and my parents. "We'll see how it all works out," I answered without committing, and started back to my room.

"Trish," Dan said, making me pause. "You know I'll always be there for you, right? You know that I'm in your corner, no matter what?"

His tone was heartbreakingly sincere. Enough that I turned back to look at him. The seriousness of his voice was matched by the look in his eyes.

"Yeah, Dan. Of course." It sounded casual, but I believed it. Far stronger than I would have thought possible.

"Good. I love you."

I knew how much he loved me. But the verbal version? That didn't happen a lot. Why was he being weird tonight? I didn't have the energy to worry about it. "Love you too, Dan."

He smiled, the wrinkles beside his eyes more pronounced than usual. He seemed really tired. I answered his smile with one of my own, and then continued back toward my room.

The light was on under Cray's door. I stopped and almost knocked. I was in a weird place, where I didn't want to be alone, but didn't have the energy to deal with another person right now, so I passed by and walked into my room.

Starren wasn't there, which didn't surprise me. She'd most likely sneak in way after midnight, if she came home at all. I'd given up worrying about her two weeks into us living together, and that had been back when we'd shared that crappy apartment.

I didn't even bother with my pajamas. I fell onto my bed, staring at the ceiling. Stopping my parents never truly went out of my head. And I couldn't push it to the back of my thoughts at the moment. Different scenarios went through my brain, but nothing that would actually work.

I pulled out my phone to distract myself. I hadn't checked it in hours, while I'd been wandering around town.

A text from Jaden. The car would be finished early in the morning. Perfect. I'd sneak away and grab it early, before Nina got up. She liked sleeping in, and even with Wren here hadn't changed her schedule about that.

"Your errand was worthless." Wraith's hiss nearly sent me flying out of my bed. I flipped over to face her, and my stomach churned. Her face, while still human, had such an inhuman expression on it that no one would mistake her for a little old grandma if they saw her.

She slid out from under Starren's bed, and I pulled my knees up to my chest, trying not to let her feel my fear.

Stupid. Fear was literally her thing.

"I'm sorry," I said. "I needed to take care of some stuff, and it would have been hard to do with you there. Some people are uncomfortable with a hyran around, and others who don't know what that is would be uncomfortable with a grandma around while they were trying to talk. It's not personal, seriously."

"Starren was in no danger. How am I to protect you if I don't know where you are?" She rose to her full height of like four feet going on twelve. It would have looked ridiculous if it was anyone else. "You must stop with this, Trisha. Things are getting more dangerous. While I was looking for you tonight..." she trailed off, then gave me a grin that didn't reach her eyes. "More people have infiltrated the city. Fae I know. Fae I do not like. You must be more careful, lest one of your parents decide it's worth the risk and snatches you from Sanctuary."

"Worth the risk?" I asked. "What would they be risking?"

"Your parents have been around quite some time. But there are things far older than they are. Things that shouldn't be messed with. And if they do... It could prove disastrous."

This was the first I'd really heard about this. I hadn't spent much time considering what would happen if Sanctuary was broken, only if it could be, back in the beginning when I'd wanted to believe we were safe here, but was having a hard time trusting anything the fae said.

"It's fine, Wraith. I appreciate you wanting to take care of me, but I've been looking after myself for quite a while. It feels strange, not getting any alone time." Though strange as it felt, that had changed in the last year. Without Starren, Nina, and Dan, I'd have been in a lot of trouble. But then, maybe I wouldn't have fought the fae so hard about Jaden if I'd never known Nina, and I'd have just accepted my fate without a fight.

"Fine, then," Wraith gave an angry sniff. "I'll give you more space. But if I'm not there when you need me, that's on you."

I stopped a sigh of relief, so it didn't tip her off. While I truly did appreciate what she wanted to do for me, I was a pretty private person, and all of this together time had started to get old days ago.

"Thank you. Truly. For being my friend."

Wraith smiled, not her usual beaming smile, but not the sly one either. She slid into Starren's bed. "I'm tired of the floor." She rolled over, and started snoring. What? How did she do that so easily?

I fell back against my pillow again, staring at the ceiling. My mind raced. I had a bad feeling about the amount of sleep I'd be getting tonight.

The amount of sleep, or lack thereof, was about what I'd expected. But that meant I was up and out of the apartment before anyone else even woke.

A message on my phone said Cray had gone to talk to Cumat about the situation. Starren had finally told him where to find the dwarf, and without any other ideas, he was going to ask for help. I didn't see how, but I didn't have any better ideas so I just said thanks.

I'd texted Jaden before slipping out, asking if the car was ready. He'd sent a one word answer, almost, which made me worry a bit. He was never short with me. But then, everyone had their limit. Maybe I'd found his. Maybe he was tired of all of the trouble I brought on him all of the time.

I walked around the outside of Jenny's to the alley out back. The place was probably locked this early in the day, but I would have taken the same route even if it wasn't. The fae needed to stop including me in things, and maybe if I stopped coming around they'd forget about me.

Right.

Just off the alley was an open garage door. Nina's car sat inside, looking like new. Jaden was under the front, checking something.

"It looks great," I said.

He thunked his head on the bottom of the bumper before rolling out from under the car. "You startled me! Phillip was supposed to be keeping watch."

I leaned back and checked both ways down the alley. "Don't see him."

"He probably got hungry. But he could have at least warned me."

It went quiet. I watched Jaden for a moment. I hated having anything strained between us, but I just couldn't be what he wanted me to be. So things were going to have to change on his end, because it wasn't happening on mine.

"There's someone who wants to see you," Jaden finally said.

"Wonderful. That's always a highlight, when 'someone' wants to see me."

He didn't even crack a smile. "It's Ferid. He wants to meet."

Ferid? As in ogre Ferid? As in the guy I tricked into letting Starren, Carver, and me go in Faerie, therefore sealing my fate that he'd hunt me forever?

"Really?" My voice squeaked a little, but I didn't even blame myself this time.

"He has intel, and he'll only give it to you."

Intel. Most likely against my parents. Which meant he had no problem pitting us all against each-other. "I don't want his intel. I want to be left alone."

Jaden looked down at his hands, covered in grime. He'd probably stayed up all night to get the car put back together. "I know you don't. And if I could help it, I'd keep you out of everything. But he'll only talk to you, so I thought I'd throw it out there. Let you decide." He looked up at me again. "It doesn't matter how much you don't want to get involved. It's going to happen. The only thing you can change is how."

"Don't say that!" I yelled. "I don't have any control over my life! Everyone is always making all of the important decisions for me. Taking me from my father and sister. Leaving me in a group home. Forcing me to hunt you down or lose Dan and Nina. I had to move here to keep them safe. I never wanted to go to Faerie, and now I've been there twice. I'm tired of this!"

Jaden took a step closer. "None of us truly have control of our lives. Everyone wants to think they do, but it isn't true. Who you are is made up of what you do with the control that you do have. You chose to save me and my family, even when it made your life more difficult. You chose to face some of your deepest fears and go to Faerie to save people you love. You can't control what happens to you in life, you can only control what you do with it."

I felt my body start to crumble, but couldn't stop it. Jaden pulled me in for a hug, and I snuggled into him a bit. He was right. And it was a relief. A person could only do their best. If that wasn't enough, it didn't matter. It was still the best they could do.

"Jaden?" Martha the waitress yelled out a small window behind the bar. "Call for you."

We pulled apart and I looked up at him. "Who would be calling you on the bar phone?"

"I have no idea."

I followed him inside. He walked over to an old phone behind the counter and held it up to his ear. "Hello?"

A voice started speaking on the other side of the line, but I couldn't hear what the man said. I motioned for Jaden to put it on speakerphone, but he ignored me.

"No. Unacceptable. We tried that once, and neither of the people who called the meeting showed."

He was quiet for a second, listening while I freaked out. The last meeting we'd been to had been with Wade, and not my parents. For someone to call the bar phone... It was a power play. Telling everyone that whoever was on the other side of that phone knew exactly where to find the refugees Jaden had been helping.

Jaden listened a moment longer, then slowly hung up the phone.

"What did he say?" I demanded. "I know what they want. But what did they threaten this time?"

"We have until noon to meet your father at the farmhouse. He didn't give me a specific threat, but he said we would be highly motivated."

"Highly motivated. Highly motivated? What does that even mean?"

Jaden looked to Martha, who'd been listening to the whole conversation. "Warn people not to come here. It isn't safe anymore. Meeting spot H at nine p.m."

She nodded and grabbed the phone.

Jaden walked toward the back door. I followed.

"Whoever it was didn't give you anything else? Just that we would be highly motivated?"

"That was it." He shoved the door open and stepped out into the sunshine. Today actually felt like spring, which I was told was rare in the Midwest.

"So what do we do now?" I asked.

"I don't know. I need some time to think. And check on some things."

Those 'things' were probably his family. Oh shoot, highly motivated could mean my family too. "I need to go," I told Jaden, and spun around, about to take off at a run.

"Wait," he said. He sounded tired. I looked back at him, and he managed a small smile. "Aren't you forgetting something?" He nodded toward Nina's car.

"Oh," I said. "Duh." I walked over to the car and opened the driver door. "Thank you. For everything."

He nodded. "Get going. Let me know when you've checked on everyone."

Of course he knew what I needed to do. "You too."

I jumped into the car and started it up, throwing it in drive before I was even fully settled in the seat. It was a short trip back to the apartment, even shorter because of how quickly I was driving. I kept an eye out for cops. Not only could I not afford a ticket, but I wouldn't be able to handle the time it would take to get it.

Thankfully the morning traffic hadn't really gotten started. About a block from home, I noticed someone dressed funny, like they were going to a con or something. Or like they were from a different world.

I pressed on the gas pedal, passing three more odd looking people walking in the direction of my apartment. The light in front of me went red and I barely had the chance to stop. People crowded the crosswalk, starting toward the front of the car.

Oh no they weren't. I checked for traffic and gunned the car through the red light, sick to my stomach at running it, but more freaked out about the chance of getting trapped and having to decide if to run someone over or not.

I skidded into a parking spot at the apartment, not even caring that it wasn't the same one I'd taken the car from yesterday. Nina was about to have a lot more on her mind than her car being one over from where she remembered parking it.

Three more fae watched me run past them, and I berated myself for leaving this morning without my sword.

Not that I would have needed it. None of them tried to stop me. None even tried to interact with me. They just stared as I raced past them, with no expressions on their faces.

The apartment door was locked, and I let out a small breath of relief, composing myself. I unlocked it and let myself in, hanging the car key on the key rack by the door.

"Nina?" I called, my need to make sure they were okay stronger than my sense of self-preservation.

"In the kitchen," Nina called back.

I sucked in a breath and closed my eyes for just a second. She didn't sound upset. She sounded a little weird, but not like anyone was about to die or anything. Though this was really early for her to be up.

I walked down the hall toward the living room. "We need to talk. I'm-" I stopped dead in my tracks. There was someone sitting at the counter, drinking tea. Someone I knew all too well. Someone who didn't belong here. "Mother?"

CHAPTER ELEVEN

"What are you doing here?" the question came out strangled, upset.

"I had to check on you. I've been getting more and more reports about your father moving troops into place around the city, and I was worried. I had to see that you're okay for myself." She stood and walked over to me, looking slightly down into my face.

"So all those people out there? They're yours?"

She nodded. "I can't travel anywhere without an escort. It isn't safe with your father trying to destroy me."

Father truly was evil. I'd seen that first hand, when he'd had the Council slaughtered. Something Starren still had nightmares about, though I only knew it because we shared a room.

We needed help. Though father hadn't said what he was going to do to us if we didn't meet with him by the deadline, my imagination was filling in the blanks.

And whatever my imagination could come up with, he would do something worse.

My phone buzzed at the same time as Nina's. Unusual, so I pulled it out even though it was probably rude when my mom had come so far.

The message was from Dan. 'Turn on the news.'

Nina must have gotten the same message, because she went for the remote. Apparently it didn't matter which channel.

"Where is Dan?" I asked while Nina scrolled.

"He got called into work. Some emergency."

Wraith moved out of the shadows of the bedroom hallway and came to stand beside me, making my mom pale slightly. It was the only reaction she had, but it told me a lot. How she knew who, or what, Wraith was when she looked like a human, I didn't know.

"I was watching. For you." Wraith said.

"Thank you," I answered, and meant it. I wouldn't put it past my mom to try and force my compliance by using Nina. She wasn't as bad as Quintin, but I didn't trust her either.

If I had to choose, she would be the lesser of two evils. But even though it was lesser, it was still scary.

The news flashed across the screen, and a fae I didn't know filled the space behind the reporter. I knew he was fae by the fact that he was floating in mid-air.

"Give us the one your world calls Trisha Penchant by noon. If you do so, your city will be safe. If not, face the consequences." He disappeared in a flash of light.

I sat down heavily, the stool I'd aimed for barely supporting me. This was it. He'd just outed me to the whole world. Yeah, sure, no one knew why he wanted me or that I was fae, but it was only a matter of time.

A knock on the apartment door snapped me out of my panic. My phone rang, but I ignored it. "Nina?" I asked. I didn't even know exactly what I was asking.

She swooped over and pulled me into a tight hug. "It's going to be fine, honey. We're going to get through this." She leaned back, keeping her hands on my shoulders. "We've got you, Trish." She turned to my mom. "How do we get her out of town?"

The knocking on the front door grew more insistent. "Trisha Penchant?" a male voice asked from the other side. Of course they could find me instantly. I was in all the foster system software.

"I can get her out. We'll have to take care of the men at the door first." Mom looked to Wraith. "Ready for a fight?"

Wraith ignored her and moved over to me. "Quintin is serious when he says anything. The consequences of leaving town will be dire. I have seen how you tortured yourself over your friend who was injured. Is running what you truly wish to do? Maybe it's time to fight back."

I thought of the man hitting Rosie. Of Jaden's grin, back before this latest rash of crazy had started. I looked over at Nina, who would never again have a normal life. Jaden's little sisters would be in danger. His mom, who he adored. Cray. Carver. Starren. Oh, Starren, who father already hated.

"You have thirty seconds before the door is broken through," the man in the hallway said.

Wraith bristled, my mom drew a sword, and Nina stepped between me and the hallway. But I couldn't do it to them. Couldn't let this happen.

"I'm coming!" I yelled, and moved around Nina. I squeezed her hand as I walked by.

She tried to grab my arm, but I dodged and ran forward to fling the door open.

Five men in full tactical gear stood on the other side. Five men, and Wren.

To her credit, she looked almost sick. She'd probably been the reason they hadn't just busted in the door when they'd first gotten here. But it didn't matter. I'd been right about her this whole time.

"Trish," Wren said. "Everything is going to be okay. We're here to help."

I cocked my head and looked around at the men with large rifles, then back to her. "It doesn't feel that way."

"It's just protective custody until we get this all figured out," Wren answered. "Phone, please."

"So I haven't done anything wrong?" I asked.

"Of course not."

"Then I don't think legally you can take me."

"Under the Patriot Act, we can do anything we need to if it's to protect the country," one of the men said. "A strange flying man is demanding us to turn you over. I think this qualifies. Phone. Now."

I didn't see arguing with the phone thing helping, so I silently fished it out of my pocket and handed it to Wren.

"Wren," Nina said behind me, her voice broken. It hurt to hear the pain in her voice, but at least I wasn't the one causing it.

"We're just keeping her safe, Nina."

Wraith moved up beside me.

I looked her in the eye and shook my head no. "Protect Nina," I whispered so quietly no one else would be able to understand.

She stared for a moment, but then reluctantly nodded.

Nina pulled her cell-phone out. "I'm calling Dan."

"He already knows," Wren said. "He's meeting us... where we're going."

Dan knew? Dan was in on this?

"Then I'm going too," Nina insisted.

I tried to meet her eyes, but she was too busy staring down Wren. Wren walked in close and pulled Nina over a few steps, whispering to her.

Nina pulled her arm back, forcefully, and crossed both her arms in front of her chest. "Non-negotiable, Wren."

"Then you'll be arrested," the rude man said. He stepped forward and grabbed my wrist. "This is taking too long. It isn't safe for you to be out of our protection."

Nina was only going to get herself in trouble. There was nothing she could do to help at this point, and the more she fought, the worse it would get.

"It's okay, Nina. Really." The fact that I could say it should have been reassuring to both of us, but it wasn't. Right at this moment it was okay, because I didn't want her getting in trouble. But that could change very fast, and I wouldn't have her.

"Not for you to decide, Trisha. You're my under-age daughter. These people can't take you without taking me."

A woman I hadn't noticed standing behind everyone else shoved her way forward, her heels tapping on the tile floor. "Actually, we can." She held up a paper. "Trisha isn't your daughter. She's only a foster-child. The state is her legal guardian."

Nina wilted for just a second before straightening back up. "She's my daughter, no matter what the paperwork says."

The man started to tug me away and Nina's face went white with fury.

"Hazel," I said loudly. I had to get this handled before Nina ended up incarcerated because of me. That wouldn't help anyone. Wraith didn't seem to notice me saying her name, so I tried again. "Hazel!"

"Oh!" Wraith said. "What?"

I nodded and Nina, and Wraith nodded back. She moved over and wrapped an arm around her shoulders. Nina struggled a little, but with the distinct lack of effort holding her back on Wraith's part, it didn't look like it.

"I'll get ahold of you as soon as I can," I yelled to Nina as the man tugged me away. "Promise!"

"Trish!" Nina yelled, but it was too late. Wraith pulled her back into the apartment while we got on the elevator.

I bit my lip, trying to hide tears. It was going to be a lot more difficult keeping a brave face now that Nina wasn't here.

Wren crowded in close beside me. "It's going to be okay. This is to keep you safe."

I stared at the floor, not answering.

"Someone wants you Trish, we had to do this. I couldn't help you at the apartment."

Now I did look up at her. "It's best at the moment. But what happens when they can't stop the person who wants me? When they want to turn me over to protect human life?"

The woman in the pantsuit gave me an odd look when I said human life, like I'd confirmed something for her. I got the feeling that there was no reason to hide who I really was from these people. The horror stories my mom had convinced me would come true if humans found out about me? Yeah, I was about to learn if those would happen or not. They had to know something, and if I let anyone help me, it would confirm things to them that I really didn't want confirmed about my friends and family.

"What's Dan's part in all this?" I asked. The other members of the team probably already knew what was going on. No reason to hide the dirty laundry.

I dreaded her answer, but needed it. Needed it badly. If Dan had betrayed me... It would hurt. Worse even than my parents being crazy. He'd come to Faerie for me. He'd moved to Fort Wayne. Or had he done those things for Nina?

"He's been a part of the whole fae thing since I got here earlier this week," Wren said.

The elevator stopped moving and dinged as the door slid open. The slight movement nearly unbalanced me as I swayed. For Dan to betray me... nearly unthinkable. For him to betray Nina? Impossible. Which meant either she knew, which I couldn't believe, or there was more going on here than I could see.

Wait a second. That weird conversation we'd had in the hallway of the apartment. He'd told me I could trust him, no matter what, and I'd said I did. Was that actually true? I'd believed it at the time, or I couldn't have said it.

Did I believe it now?

The woman gently pushed me out of the elevator. On the ground level, more people dressed in riot gear waited.

Apparently they didn't believe in trying to do this subtly.

I shoved down the fear working its way up my throat. They were trying to protect me. Dan would never have let them come for me if they weren't. That automatic thought made up my mind. If Nina knew about this, she would have stopped it. And Dan would never hurt Nina. Even if he didn't actually love me like a daughter, he wouldn't do this to his wife.

He had asked me to trust him, knowing something like this might happen. Which left me with a choice right now.

And I was going to choose to believe in my family.

CHAPTER TWELVE

The SUV I'd been shoved into about twenty minutes ago skidded to a stop in front of a gate. I leaned around the soldier to my left to try and get a better look at where we were, but I didn't recognize the place.

No one had talked to me, even a word along the drive. I could see them listening to voices through their earpieces, but they didn't have anything to say to those people either.

By the time Wren had untangled herself from Nina, the SUV I was in had taken off, so I didn't know if to hope she was in the one behind us or not.

At least they hadn't cuffed me. Sitting here left way too much time for thinking. What was Mom doing here? Did she actually care about me, or did she just want me to join her, like the last time we'd seen each other? Where was Father?

The gate opened enough for the SUV to gun its way through before making it to an unimposing concrete building. A sign out front finally told me where I was. Firehawk Army Reserve Base. Wherever that was.

Two men dressed in military uniforms stood behind a man who looked like he was in charge. One of them reached forward and opened the door. The man sitting beside me climbed out and then looked back in at me expectantly. I took a deep breath and then followed him.

The man in charge stuck his hand out. "Major Benjamin Kormann, at your service. You can call me Kormann."

I reluctantly shook his hand, my self-preservation biting my tongue for me.

"Let's get you inside, shall we?"

As if I had a choice. I didn't know if to appreciate his diplomacy or to be insulted.

I planted myself in place. "Where's Dan?"

"You'll be able to see Dan soon." His tone was soothing, but I found that insulting also. I wasn't a child or a scared kitten. It was interesting that he didn't ask who Dan was or pretend he wasn't here.

"I'm not going anywhere until you tell me where Dan is." I crossed my arms in front of my chest and stiffened to the point that if they wanted me to move, someone was going to have to pick me up.

"He's answering some questions at the moment. It won't be long until you can see him."

"What kind of questions?"

Wren came up from behind and put an arm over my shoulder. I shoved it off. "Just about why that guy wants you, Trish. You have nothing to worry about." She gave me a weird look, eyes wide, like she was trying to tell me something.

"Yes, about that," Kormann said. "Any ideas why a strange floating man would specifically ask for you? Seems kind of odd that he's looking for a teenage foster girl. Possibly a lost relation?"

Touchy ground here. Without being able to lie, I could get myself backed into a corner real quick. "I doubt we're related." Very true. But Kormann didn't know that. Did Wren know I couldn't lie? How much had she told people?

I had no doubt that she told them all about the fae at this point. She would be worried that whoever Floating Man was, he was about to cause trouble. Heck, I was too. But had she told them I was fae?

Now that I thought about it, they probably didn't know. Surely they would be a bit more cautious with me if they knew I wasn't of this world.

Kormann squinted at me, like he noticed my evasion, but he didn't push. "Dan will be to see you as soon as he can. Until then, we have some questions for you." He turned and walked away without checking over his shoulder, like he knew I didn't really have options.

Soldiers, or officers, or whatever the official term for the people surrounding me, herded me inside. They weren't rough, but I knew I wouldn't be getting away with anything.

Two on the outskirts of our little circle kept a close eye on our surroundings. If they knew what the actual threat was, they'd have a whole squadron more of these people here.

If a squadron was the amount I thought it was.

I held back a hysterical chuckle. No way a human prison could compete with the prison I'd spent a little time in when I had visited Faerie. It would go against all human ethics stuff. At least here in the U.S., anyway. I couldn't speak for anywhere else, I'd never even had a passport.

The doors we went through opened up into a hallway. The sparse and nearly sterile look almost reminded me of the hallway at the Fae Distribution Center. Before it had been decimated by a gooey monster made of tar.

We marched four doors down, and Kormann gestured for me to go through the open doorway. Wren tried to follow, but he stopped her.

"Sir?" she asked, her tone sharp.

"You're to head back to the CO's office for a debrief with Thomas," Kormann answered.

"I was told I would be able to stay with my niece until my brother-in-law arrived. She's under age." Her tone was clipped, angry. Not the aunt I knew at all. "Sir," she added at the end, after enough time had passed that she clearly hadn't wanted to.

"You do as you're told, Soldier, or we'll be having a very different conversation."

Okay, now I did feel a little bad for her. What if she hadn't betrayed us, and it was just my paranoia talking when I'd assumed she had? "It's okay, Wren. I'm fine."

She spun around on one heel and marched away. Whew. I wouldn't want to be the person asking her questions.

I passed Kormann and walked into the room. A small table and three chairs were the only thing inside. Apparently this wasn't the nice meeting room. I walked over and took a seat, doing my best to act relaxed and in control of the situation.

Kormann took a file someone passed him through the door and shut the door behind him, so it was just the two of us in the room. He walked over and sat the file on the table, loosening his tie. I studied him, trying to decide if it was an act or not.

I couldn't tell.

"So. You've been in the system since you were nine. Moved through a few homes, a few group homes, ended up with the Inzas almost two years ago. What made you move from D.C. to Fort Wayne?"

Okay, an easy one first. I'd already had to answer this when other people had asked. "Fort Wayne feels a lot safer than D.C. Just wanted that ability to walk the streets without fear, you know?"

He raised an eyebrow but kept looking at the papers in his file. What else did he have on me?

"Is there a specific reason you didn't feel safe in D.C.?"

Oh, shoot. No one had ever asked me that before. In general people were just proud that they had a nice city, and left it at of course anyone would want to live here rather than D.C.

"I had a problem with an ex-boyfriend. Staying in D.C. wasn't an option anymore."

He shuffled through the papers. "There wasn't a police report filed?"

"No." Short and sweet. Made it harder to catch me. Maybe he'd get tired of this. I had really impressed myself though, the story about Wade had popped right up.

"Strange. I'll have to ask Mr. Inza about that."

Oh shoot. I'd congratulated myself too soon. Dan could lie, and might come up with something completely different. "Sure, maybe he would have something helpful to add."

Now he did look up, staring me down for a moment. All of the nice guy act was gone. He put his elbows on the table and steepled his fingers. "Do you know who the man threatening the city is? What he is capable of? And why he asked for you?"

"I don't." I didn't specify which question I was answering. Which kept me from having to tell the truth about the last one. I did know why he'd asked for me, and I didn't want to tell Kormann that it was because he was trying to force me back to my bio dad.

He studied me in silence for a full minute. I gripped my fingers tightly, forcing them not to fiddle with anything. A thought hit me. Father had offered an out for the city, but not just to them. He'd offered it to me. He'd had that guy say that if I was turned over by the humans, the city would be safe. That meant he'd not only not be able to attack the city himself, but he'd have to defend it.

"You know what I think?" Kormann's voice brought me back to the present.

I didn't answer. I didn't really want to know. Did I?

"I think that most teenage girls would be freaking out right now, if some strange, possibly alien, life-form was asking for them by name. Was threatening the city they lived in. You seem very calm. Can you tell me why you're so calm?"

Oh crap. Here I'd been worried about spilling something I shouldn't, when I should have figured he would be assessing everything, not just my answers.

"Lots of childhood trauma," I said. "It makes one better able to deal with things. There were reasons I was in foster care."

Now I had to think about reacting enough, but at the same time, not reacting differently than I had been, because he'd probably notice. And that made me in my head way too much. There was no way this wasn't going to go badly for me if I didn't get things together.

"What were your parents like?"

"What does that have to do with some weirdo asking about me?" How many questions could I avoid before he got mad? I wasn't going to lie to myself and say before he caught on. Pretty sure we were already there.

"We don't know. We don't know why he asked for you, and so we need to go through every piece of your life until we find out. You have never seen that man before?"

"No. I've never seen that man before."

He stared me down, like he was going to force a confession. In this one moment, it would be nice that he knew I couldn't lie, because he didn't look convinced.

If the fae were coming for me here, it would be better for the humans to know what was about to hit them. But if they weren't, I didn't want to be the one to spill the beans about a whole new world and all that. Was there some way I could warn him without sounding crazy, and not causing the war Jaden had seen?

Kormann just stared at me, like he could watch the wheels turning in my brain. Good thing he couldn't read those wheels, or he'd come out of this conversation knowing far more than he or I wanted him to.

A knock on the door interrupted us. Kormann didn't have time to say anything before Dan burst into the room. He looked disheveled, completely different than his normal put together self. I had to physically hold onto the chair I was sitting on to not jump up and run to him.

"Kormann," he snapped. "I have permission to speak to my daughter alone. Please check your phone, and then give us space."

Storm cloud covering his normally cool face, Kormann did as asked. Apparently the message Dan expected to be there was, because Kormann stood and straightened his suit. "I'll give you a few moments, but then I'm going to need to continue our conversation."

He should have called it an interrogation, but I was just happy to have a couple minutes with him gone to catch my thoughts.

As soon as the door closed behind him, I jumped out of the chair and launched myself at Dan. He caught me mid-air and pulled me into a bear hug, his stubble tickling my head.

"I was so afraid you'd be mad at me," Dan admitted into my hair.

I leaned back to look at him, surprised that he'd share that. "Of course not. I know I can trust you."

He beamed, his expression not matching the exhaustion on his face. "You don't know how much that means to me. You have a lot of people you can trust." He made a weird face that didn't match his happy tone. "People that will be there for you. No matter the consequences." He mouthed 'microphone,' finally clearing up the weirdness. "You don't have to worry. You're just here to stay safe." At that he shook his head no, and a shiver went through me. He didn't think I was safe.

I let go of him and moved back toward the table, checking the room over better. No signs of a camera, but of course an interrogation room like this would have recording equipment.

"Not to worry. You won't be here long. You'll see the stars again soon."

I cocked my head, confused again.

"You love the stars. It's a recent thing, but you spend so much time with the stars now."

Okay, anybody listening to this wouldn't be fooled at all if he kept going. What kind of stars had I recently started caring about? Not celestial ones. Or celebrity ones. Oh! Starren! Starren was on her way to break me out.

"Oh no, that's okay. I don't need to see the stars tonight. I'll probably be here a while, and I wouldn't want to be in any hurry." Starren didn't need to come break me out. In fact, I was starting to think that the only way out of this for everyone else was for the humans to turn me over.

I closed my eyes, taking my deep breaths. If I let them turn me over, that meant my dad would have me. That my dad could possibly win the war against my mom, and start his foray into Earth.

Or... My mom was here. She wasn't an option I'd wanted to consider, but it was starting to look like she was my only option. If I let the others break me out, they'd be on the run for life. Dan and Nina included. There was no way Kormann and Co. wouldn't figure out that they had helped.

Even if he didn't, I would never be able to see them again.

My mom was the only answer. The only one who could help right now.

"Dan." I reached forward and gave his hand a squeeze. "Could you tell my mother something for me?"

Now it was his turn to look confused. I never called Nina mother, and he didn't know my bio mom was in town. But he'd figure it out.

"Please tell her that I'd like to help, when I get out of here."

Now he got it, if the sick feeling going through me was what I was reading on his face.

"Are you sure? Helping her could be... a big deal."

"I don't see a better way right now." I couldn't say that my father had threatened... something, without giving away everything to whoever was listening. But I feared my father far more than my mom, and if he said something bad was about to happen, I believed him.

"So no stars? Are you sure?"

A great question. "I'm sure." Wow. I hadn't thought I was until that moment, but apparently I was sure enough.

The door flew open and Kormann walked back in. "Time's up, Inza." He pointed his thumb over his shoulder. "I need to talk to your kid. We're on a timeline here."

We were indeed. And the scary thing was, we knew the timeframe, but not the consequences. Apparently Kormann here was taking the flying man seriously. What would he think if he knew what I could do?

Dan gave me another quick hug and walked to the door. He paused at the opening and looked back at me. "Everything is going to be okay. We're going to fix this."

"Thank you, Dan." I wanted to say that I knew he could fix it, but I didn't. One of my parents was crazy. The other one was evil. Both were extremely powerful. Where did that leave room for me?

Time passed, with Ben grilling me. He was never too rude, and they fed me, but the clock was running down. No matter what I said, I couldn't convince him to turn me over.

By the time eleven came and went, I was starting to sweat. Kormann had left me alone in the room about twenty minutes ago. I'd been glad at the time, because it was the first chance I'd had to be by myself since early this morning.

But then the thoughts started coming.

They needed to take me to the meeting spot. They needed to turn me over. They didn't know it, but my father would do anything it took to get what he wanted, and what he happened to want right now was me. And mother, showing up now? Was that a coincidence? How could it be? What did she want from me?

Ha. I knew what she wanted.

I walked over and tried the door handle. Locked, of course.

I moved back to the table and paced along it. No windows in the room. One door. I'd gone over it fifteen times, just in case I felt like I needed to leave without their permission. But there was no way out. Not that it mattered. It needed to be the humans who turned me over, not myself.

The door handle jiggled and the door swung in. Instead of Kormann who I expected, Wren walked through.

She walked over and tried to give me a hug. I didn't return it. She wasn't getting any of that until I figured out what her whole involvement in this had been.

"Sit, Trish," she said, moving over to the table and watching me expectantly.

"I've sat enough today, thank you," I answered. "What's going on? Why am I not on the way to the meeting place?"

She put her elbows on the table, leaning forward. She looked tired. Really tired. "They've decided no negotiating with terrorists. And Kormann doesn't want a kid turned over. Fair when he doesn't know what you can do."

"He doesn't?" I shifted in closer to her. "Because I would have thought you'd have told him by now."

Her lips tightened, but she kept a calm expression on her face. "I told them about the fae. I had to. They could possibly be the biggest threat the world has ever seen. The stuff down in that tunnel... Trish, it scared me. Scared me bad."

I loosened up a bit. It had scared me too, and I had already known about the fae.

"They thought I was crazy. That's why I was down here visiting. They put me on medical leave."

"Medical leave?" So she hadn't just been down here to spy on us. The heaviness in my stomach lifted a little.

"Now they actually want to listen to me, and I don't have any answers. Is there anything you know that can help?"

Even if I did completely trust her, which I didn't, there were mics in the room. I couldn't say anything that wouldn't be on file forever. "No. You need to convince them to turn me over. It's what's best."

"Is it your dad?" she asked.

"That wasn't him," I answered. I didn't mention that he was behind it though. I moved over to her and bent down to whisper. I didn't care if the mic heard the sound of my voice. It didn't matter at this point if they knew that I knew about the mics. "You need to get them to turn me over. If you don't, bad stuff is going to happen. I don't know what, but bad. And I can't just turn myself over. It's a fae thing. He said that if you turn me over the city will be safe. If it isn't humans that turn me over, his fae won't have anything to hold them back if he decides to go that route."

Her face whitened, and I almost felt bad that I'd been mad at her. She had betrayed us, but she thought she was keeping us safe.

She stood. "Not a chance. We're not turning a teenager over to a psychopath when we have no evidence he actually intends to do anything."

"He does intend to do something, or he wouldn't have made the threat. I'm done with just hanging out here, waiting for someone to understand the severity of the situation. I told everyone to stand down, but that's going to change if one of your people doesn't take me out to the farmhouse. Right now."

"Trish. It's time for you to be a teenager. Let other people figure out the problems in the world. People trained in diplomacy and war."

I cocked an eyebrow at her. "No human in the world is prepared for diplomacy with the fae. Everything that comes out of their mouths is measured, studied, scrutinized until they can twist their words to mean whatever they want." I frowned. "Except for me. I didn't grow up with them, so I'm really bad at all that."

"That's a relief." Wren gave me a wry grin. "But seriously. I know you're worried, of course you are, but I truly don't believe there is anything I can say that will make Kormann advise the higher ups to throw you to the wolves."

I'd rather be thrown to the wolves than given to my father, but I didn't say that out loud. Maybe Wren did really care about me. If so, then telling her how very much I didn't want to go would only make things worse.

"I need to see this through. They want me. And I can't let anyone else get hurt because of me."

The door opened again, and Kormann was back. "Nearly show-time." He handed me my phone. "No calls for now, but I'll let you hang onto this. Let's go." His tone was much more gentle now that he wasn't trying to trick me into giving something away.

Following him seemed like the best idea, and he wasn't waiting for me, so I hurried to catch up without waiting on Wren. "Where are we going? Are you going to turn me over? Please, you need to just take me out there, drop me off, and everything will be fine."

Kormann eyed me for a second, but then answered. "To the control room. To see what we're dealing with when noon hits. Soldier," he said to Wren. "Return to your post."

"But-" she started to argue with him, which even I knew was a big no-no.

He lifted an eyebrow.

Her shoulders crumbled, but she did as she was told, turning and heading back down the hall. I didn't know where her post was or what she did, but if I had to guess I would say Kormann didn't trust her right now, with her loyalties split in two directions.

The moment of truth. I turned on my phone screen to check the time. 11:52, and lots of notifications. People I didn't even talk to anymore from my old school to one of the foster homes lit up my screen. Apparently the entire world knew that Trisha Penchant was a person of interest.

I ignored all of the extra names, looking for ones I knew. Jaden, of course. Cray. Starren. Dan and Nina, Rosie. Even Rebecca, Jaden's mom. It felt kind of weird having so many people check in on me, when not that long ago I'd had no one.

Somehow it made me extremely uncomfortable and extremely happy at the same time.

Kormann led me down the hallway farther into the base until we walked through two large sliding glass doors and into a large room full of people and computer screens. Every angle of the place the man had appeared before covered the screens, as well as random pieces of town. Dot's. The gym. I shivered. Mostly places I spent time at.

Thankfully, no Jenny's.

"Trish!" Nina's voice snapped me back to checking out the room. She rushed over from a small sitting area to one side, Dan close on her heels. She swept me into a tight hug as soon as she was in arms reach. "Are you okay?"

"Yeah, all good. They've been treating me fine."

She sent a very non-Nina glare over my shoulder, so frosty I couldn't help but feel sorry for whoever was on the receiving end. I turned to look. Wren.

Did she deserve it? Yeah. But I sure wouldn't want to be on the receiving end of a look like that from Nina, so I almost felt sorry for her. Almost.

"Time's nearly up," Kormann said from beside Dan. He left us standing there, like he just expected us to follow. Which made sense, since no one else had as much skin in the game as I did.

I made it about thirty seconds before I popped out my phone and started checking messages to pass the few minutes we had left before all chaos broke free. We didn't have enough time for me to get to the farmhouse now, even if I could convince everyone, which I obviously couldn't.

I shot off I'm fine messages to Jaden, Cray, and Rebecca. Starren was asking if I wanted a visit from my mother, phrased so it could be taken as Nina. 'Too late for that,' I answered her.

Rosie had left a voicemail. I pulled up the visual voicemail so no one else could listen in. 'Trish. I found the answer. I have something that will solve all your problems. It will be here tonight. Just hold on.'

Interesting, but I couldn't really believe that someone who'd just found out about the fae had the answer to all of my problems. I'd see what happened in the next five minutes, then answer her.

A giant digital clock ticked down on one of the large screens in front, like this was some TV show and a bomb was about to go off somewhere important.

Three. Two. One. Noon.

And there he was. The floating man from earlier had appeared in exactly the same field he'd been in earlier. The entire room went deathly quiet, everyone's eyes glued to the screen. Should I make a break for it? Run to the farmhouse, beg Father not to do whatever it was he wanted to do?

No. He'd had all of this planned. He'd known I wouldn't be there. Whatever happened next, it was what he wanted.

Military vehicles flooded out of the trees, surrounding him. I didn't recognize the spot, but it almost had to be outside of Sanctuary. There were a few parks in town with that much nature, but the guy was using his powers, so he couldn't be inside the border.

"You were given fair warning," the man said, and then disappeared. Short and sweet. I could respect that, if I wasn't about to faint waiting to find out what the exact punishment was that my father would mete out.

As soon as the man winked out, a strange haze seeped up from the ground. It was odd, like watching water flow up a hill. It climbed its way into the sky, forming a dome. The sound of a massive gong or something like it echoed out across the city. The room around me erupted with people doing different jobs I didn't understand.

People on screen at the different places I loved started to flip out. First looking at the sky, and then covering their ears and dropping to the ground when the sound flowed through.

It took a second to register Nina's tight grip on my arm, but I didn't acknowledge it. Down to my soul I knew something bad was about to happen, and I hadn't stopped it. Just like I hadn't stopped Rosie from being hurt.

I turned around to Kormann. "You need to let me out. Now."

Kormann looked down at me, and a small part of me was surprised that even with everything going on, he was taking the time to speak with me. "What are you going to do?"

That was a great question. I didn't have an answer. It was too late to turn myself over, but I couldn't just let the apocalypse start here. I tried to shove my way past him, but he put out an arm and stopped me.

Dan growled a little behind me, but Kormann didn't even look up. "You're just a teenage girl, right? What are you going to do about this?"

"What the–" an exclamation across the room interrupted our little moment. People all started shouting, and I turned back to the TV screens to see why.

A column of rock slowly rose from the ground, pieces smashing into place, interlocking. A golem. To its right, mud sloughed together, flowing into a vaguely human form, and to its left, a swirl of wind picked up debris, sucking it in and not letting it escape.

No. No one was allowed to attack Sanctuary. It was right in the name. Surely not even Father would break one of the old laws.

Who was I kidding. He craved power so badly that he'd murdered the Fae Council, people he'd known for centuries. If there were no serious consequences to attacking Sanctuary, what was truly stopping him?

"This," I waved my hand at the TV screens. "This is because of me. You have to let me go." I was talking to Kormann, but keeping my eyes on the screen. The golems were fully formed now, but hadn't moved forward, like they were waiting for a command.

One had nearly gotten the best of Starren and me, fighting together, back at the Fae Distribution Center. It had only stopped because a human showed up, or it would have killed her and drug me away.

Obviously the whole not get revealed to humans thing wasn't going to help us today.

"What are those things capable of?" Kormann asked.

"We're about to find out," one of the other women in the room said.

The rock golem took the lead, ripping a boulder from the ground and hurling it toward the closest military vehicle, a small truck used to haul personnel. The truck rocked sideways, the door crushed in.

"Return fire," Kormann said, and one of the men relayed his message.

The sound of gunfire filled the room from all of the speakers, every TV screen filled with the scene outside of town now.

Bullets pinged off the rock golem, ricocheting in every direction. The mud golem absorbed each shot without a care, and the rounds went straight through the wind. All of the golems attention went from the large military vehicles, straight to the soldiers. This wasn't going to go well.

A tornado of wind blasted through the ranks, sending soldiers flying. Rocks rolled across the ground like some macabre bowling match, crushing anyone and anything in the way. Screams echoed through the speakers.

"Get them inside the city limits," I told Kormann, eyes glued to the screen.

"What?" he snapped.

"Get all your people inside the city limits!"

Now his attention swung to me. He met my eyes for a second, and must have seen how serious I was about this. "Get all units inside the city limits, and hit them with a rocket launcher," he growled to his assistant, who moved away to relay his messages to the correct people.

I watched in horror as men and women responded to the order to get back over the border, pulling along their unmoving comrades.

The golems shambled along behind them, herding them across the border. The rock golem tossed a head sized boulder at the line, and it disintegrated at the city limits.

I breathed out in relief. Sanctuary held against even these creatures, apparently. This was the evidence I needed though. I'd always believed my father had been behind the attack on The Fae Distribution Center, but I hadn't had any way of proving it.

I no longer needed to.

"What just happened?" Kormann demanded.

"They shouldn't be able to cross the city limits." I was giving away the fact that I had some knowledge in this area, but it was too important not to.

This was a nice reprieve, but I did need to find Father. These magical beings couldn't exist inside Sanctuary, which meant another fae created and controlled them. It was amazing at the moment, but as Starren had proven with Jaime last year, humans didn't have the same protections as fae here. If my father decided to send his army in, there wouldn't be anything stopping him.

There was no way I could handle this on my own.

A wave of soldiers made room for two men carrying a large piece of equipment. They stayed just inside the city limits as they prepared. No problem. Human weapons would work fine there.

Once ready, one of the men lifted the giant gun thing to his shoulder and set it off.

A small projectile burst forward, slamming into the mud golem. It exploded into a pile of goo, and the entire room cheered. I didn't let myself get excited yet. I'd fought one of these things before. It wasn't that easy to kill. The soldiers with the weapon worked to re-load it.

"Wait," one of the analysts in the room said. "Look."

Sure enough, the mud started to flow back up into the golem's form.

By now the launcher was ready to go again, and the soldier wielding it took aim and fired. Chips of stone flew off the rock golem, but then quivered on the ground and flew back into place.

The golems renewed their attack on the city limits, hitting it with debris.

"Call an air-strike," Kormann said. "Even those things can't withstand a missile."

Nina squeezed my hand. I'd almost forgotten she was here, so wrapped up in what was going on. People were going to die because of me. Maybe already had died. But I couldn't help Father win a war. Couldn't fulfill the prophecy for him, even if all it did was make the numbers swell.

The sound of jets rumbled by overhead. They must have been nearby, ready just in case. They were there and gone on the screen in less than a second, dropping something.

The bombs hit the hazy dome covering the city and slipped down the side, exploding in a fiery roar about halfway to the ground. The grass on one side of the barrier charred, and on the other remained untouched.

"They didn't get through, Sir," one of the soldiers said.

"I can see that," Kormann snapped.

"What does this mean, Kormann?" Dan asked. Apparently they knew each other.

"I think we should ask her." He turned and faced me. "Care to enlighten us?"

"Just let me go. I can stop all this, but I need to do it my way."

"That's not happening. You're the only insurance policy we've got."

"It's too late for that," I said. The room had gone silent again. Everyone pretended to watch the screens, but I could tell their attention was on us. I needed to be careful, or I might get locked up until this was all over, and who knew how it would end. "You didn't turn me over by noon. The only way this is going to stop is if you let me go."

Kormann turned to his assistant. "What news from Washington?"

"None, Sir." The man's voice broke a little. "Nothing is getting through the dome."

"Someone is going to have to make a break for it," Kormann said. "Get to the other side, and get a message through from there. Tell Lieutenant Hights to pick a soldier."

"You'll just sending them to die!" I shouted. "Even if the golems weren't there, it looks like the dome won't let anything through!"

"Looks like?" Kormann asked.

"I don't know anything about that," I answered. "I just know it's an insane risk."

The assistant had paused at my outburst. Kormann nodded to him, and he relayed the order.

Just as a man broke free of the other soldiers to carry out the new orders, a portal opened beside the rock golem. Fae poured out. Not like any human army, they were of all shapes and sizes, dressed in all types of clothes.

"Who are those people?" Kormann roared, but no one had an answer for him.

Oh shoot. I really didn't want humans to know about me. I really didn't want to lose my home with Dan and Nina. But if this wasn't settled correctly, I might lose everything.

I grabbed Dan's hand and tugged him a few steps away while Kormann was distracted. Nina watched us go, and slid between us and Kormann. "Okay. Now's the time."

Dan nodded and pulled out his phone. "No service. They're waiting just outside. I couldn't get them to leave." He squeezed my hand and took off for the exit.

No one tried to stop him. It was me they wanted.

The fae on screen lined up, filling the space between the dome's edge and the city limit, with just a small section of field between them and the human soldiers. A smaller version of the dome created a barrier between the two groups. The soldier's weapons wouldn't do them any good until the fae were within close range.

And the fae in close range were past deadly.

An alarm blared, and red lights began to flash. This was it. The rescue I'd put off in hope of keeping things from escalating. That had worked so well.

I inched toward the exit, Nina close behind but keeping herself between me and the rest of the room.

"What now?" Kormann asked no one.

"The base has been breached," someone from up front said.

"How?" Kormann's assistant asked.

"Ninety percent of the base is there right now," Kormann swung an arm at the TVs. "This is the perfect time for an attack." We'd almost made it to the door when he noticed us leaving. "Where do you think you're going?"

"This isn't going to stop without me getting involved," I said. "I'm sorry, but I have to go." I turned and moved in front of the door, ready to break into a dead run. But the door didn't open.

"The base is locked down," Kormann said. "You aren't going anywhere. Find a seat. Nina. Keep your daughter under control."

Freedom. So close, and so far away. I could see the entire path to the door that led outside through the glass.

"This isn't like you, Kormann," Nina said. "Be reasonable. You can't hold a teenage girl hostage just because you think you may need her."

"Be quiet, Nina. We haven't known each other long enough for you to make that kind of judgment."

"Come on," I whispered. "Where are you?"

I barely got the words out of my mouth before the door at the end of the hallway was ripped from its hinges, taking bricks and mortar with it.

A rather angry grandma face poked in, and then my friends streamed around her to flood the hallway. They were all dressed in non-descript clothes and wearing masks, but that didn't mean I couldn't tell who each person was. No Dan though, which actually was a relief.

Kormann looked at me, then looked at them. "Who are these people?"

"I think it would be best if you let me go now."

They advanced up the hallway with Starren and my mom at the front. Carver and Cray were behind them, with Wraith taking up the rear. No Jaden. Where was Jaden? Was he okay? Father had threatened us both, he had better be okay.

"Come on, Trish. You know I can't do that."

I waited until I had his full attention. "If you don't want anyone to get hurt, I suggest you let me go. I don't want to do this. Trust me, I seriously don't. But I have to if we want the crazy outside the city limits to stop."

"Listen to her, Kormann," Nina added.

He leaned in over me, ignoring Nina. "You aren't going anywhere."

I pointed a thumb over my shoulder at my family, who was now nearly to the glass sliding doors, the angry granny shoving her way to the front. "They would beg to differ."

"Even if they could get through those doors, which they can't, they're still outnumbered and out-gunned." He waved a hand and six soldiers left their posts, pulling rifles from the wall and lining up in front of the door.

The four who stayed in place to watch the screens weren't doing a very good job at the moment.

My gut clinched. Why did everything have to be so tough? But the others just kept on coming, stopping right at the glass like there wasn't about to be a massacre.

"How do you know?" I bluffed. "You saw a man fly today. Saw strange monsters made out of mud and rock. You don't know what those people can do."

He studied me for a moment. "You're right. But since you so conveniently told me about the town line, I'm not too worried. I'm assuming none of them can do anything here either?"

Crap. "I never said any of them were anything but human. But you'll be surprised by what they can do without powers."

The half-hearted denial was barely out of my mouth before Wraith leaned back, and then flung herself full-force in a head butt. The glass doors shattered into dust, the metal hinges creaking and popping, ripping out of the walls.

I jumped in front of Nina, shielding her. Well shoot. Wraith was even stronger than I'd thought.

The soldiers held it together far better than I would have if I had just learned about the fae today and an old granny came in and destroyed a military base, keeping their rifles trained and ready to fire on order.

"We're here for Trisha," Wraith announced.

My mom shoved her way around her. "And you'd better give her to us without a fight."

Wraith maneuvered herself past Mom and nearly into the barrel of a gun. "Or you'll deeply regret it."

"Sir!" one of the soldiers left watching the screens said.

"What?" Kormann snapped. Poor man. As if he didn't have enough on his mind.

We all turned to see why she'd tried to get Kormann's attention, and I got a bit dizzy. There, pouring out of the woods around the golems, were ogres, led by the king of the ogres, Ferid, dressed in full armor. We'd met, and it hadn't gone great. Who was he here for?

The fae who'd come through the portal a few minutes ago all started to chant something loudly in a different language.

Ferid let the tip of his massive sword rest on the ground, his body tense. "Send out the Penchant," he shouted, and I could almost hear the roar from outside the building as well as through the speakers.

I swung back to Kormann, who was staring at the TV, looking completely at a loss.

"It's okay. We've got this." I reached out and squeezed his arm. Mistake, that was so awkward. How did Nina always make it seem so natural?

"Why do you think we don't have this?" Kormann snapped back. "I still haven't seen one good reason to let you go free."

Wraith stepped forward and grabbed one of the soldiers, lifting her high into the air. The rest of my family stepped back out of the way, and the soldier in the air opened fire. The bullets pinged off of Wraith, ricocheting around the room and embedding themselves into various points around the room.

"Stop!" I yelled. "No one gets hurt unless we let this escalate!" I inched toward Wraith, taking it slow to make sure no one took a shot at me. Wraith's strength and impenetrable skin were part of her physical makeup, which even Sanctuary couldn't take away. That wasn't the case for me.

"Who are these people?" Kormann asked, face white, lips tight.

"People who are trying to stop a war," Mom said from behind Wraith. "You know what's best. Now get over your pride and let us go."

I didn't dare take my eyes off Wraith to see what the rest of the room thought about this whole exchange.

"You don't want to see what happens next if you don't."

I tore my eyes from Wraith to stare down Mom. She had to mean what she said, and that didn't bode well for anyone.

"Kormann," Nina said. "You know Dan. You don't know me as well, but you need to trust us. If we don't get Trish out there, bad things are going to happen. Really bad things."

The chanting through the speakers stopped, and the fae on screen looked like they were forming ranks. They were going to charge the line.

"Fine," Kormann said. He waved a hand and the soldiers hesitantly lowered their weapons. "But I'm going with you. You will report to me at all times." He signaled his assistant forward. "Get cars ready. We're moving out." When the assistant hurried away, he looked at my family. "You cowards can remove your masks now."

Starren jerked in anger, but Carver grabbed her arm. "We're fine, thank you," Carver said.

"We'll need transportation also," Wraith said sweetly, dropping the woman she'd had in the air this whole time. "Please."

Kormann nodded curtly and marched through the shattered door.

Finally. This was it. We all flowed behind him, Carver patting me on the back and Cray pulling me in for a squeeze. He must have come back from trying to talk with Cumat after he saw the news. Which meant Cumat was hiding somewhere in town, which I'd suspected all along.

We moved out into the sunlight. Four SUVs waited, and a ton of other cars and jeeps. Apparently what was left of the base was coming with us.

Good. We were going to need all the help we could get.

CHAPTER THIRTEEN

When I opened the door, Dan was already inside the SUV. He pulled me into a hug, and then nearly crushed Nina in another.

We all piled into vehicles, with Nina and my mom jockeying over who sat next to me. Finally I scooted into the middle, and they each took a side. Kormann tried to block Wraith as she moved through the door, but she shouldered him out of the way like she didn't even see him. The other set of seats in the SUV faced ours, like some fancy limo. Wraith and Kormann took those, followed by Kormann's assistant.

"We're going to have to go around the outside of town," Kormann said. "It would take us hours to get through the mess in the city right now. People are panicking. But the route will put us outside the city limits. Is that going to be a problem?"

"No," Mom answered for me. "Not a problem."

Sure she was a queen in Faerie, but here she was no one. She really shouldn't just be making decisions for us all like that. But it was the right decision, so I couldn't argue.

"Nina?" Kormann asked.

I could practically feel my mom quiver in fury at the insult. Asking the human for her opinion, how insulting.

"Just get us there as fast as possible."

I nodded in agreement. Ferid wasn't the patient type. Even if it was only him I had to worry about, I'd be in a hurry.

And he definitely wasn't the only thing I had to worry about.

"So. We're alone now," Kormann said. "Spill."

I didn't want to spill. I didn't know how much to spill. And I didn't really trust the man. Right now I just wanted to know that Jaden was okay, and save the world, in that order.

The SUV rolled forward, wasting no time.

"The fae have decided they want your world for themselves," Mom said from beside me. I kneed her, hard. She hadn't even asked how I was doing.

"I see," Kormann said. He didn't ask what the fae were, which made me think Wren had been a little too open about some things. "How many are there? What are their abilities? How do we get the dome dropped?"

Did I let my mom answer? What if she told him something I didn't want him to know? Ha. Like there would really be any coming back from today, the way things were. I snuck my phone out of my pocket and let them talk.

A message from Rosie, but nothing from Jaden. I texted him real quick. 'Are you okay? What's going on?'

I felt the light tingle of my ability entering my body. Apparently the city line hadn't been far from the base. We kept on for another couple minutes before the SUV screeched to a halt.

"Report!" Kormann yelled toward the front.

"I don't know what's going on," the driver answered. "Traffic is stopped."

Kormann flung the door open and stuck his head out to look.

I climbed over Nina and followed his lead. Car doors ahead of us flung open, and people started to scream.

A big rumble shook the ground. A golem began to form out of broken asphalt, this one huge. Maybe the others were as big, but they sure hadn't looked like it on the TV screen.

It was too big of a coincidence that it was forming here, now, when I was here trying to get to the soon-to-be battlefield. It was after me.

I jumped out of the car and shielded my eyes, looking up at it towering above me. I had to get out of here. There wasn't anything any of us could do against this thing, and Dan and Nina were here.

"Wraith," I yelled. "Protect Dan and Nina!" I started running. I didn't know exactly how to get to farm house, but I knew the general direction. The ground shook as the golem pursued.

Thankful that I had my abilities at the moment, I cursed the cars in the way as I dodged around them, taking way too long to get anywhere.

A shadow blocked out the sun, soaring in front of me. A shadow in the shape of a...

Bam. Something grabbed me from above. I let my body hang loose, not fighting. "Storm!" He was so much bigger than the last time I'd seen him as a dragon. Was he a baby?

He craned his long neck around to grin at me in dragon form.

"Where have you been?" Of course he wasn't able to answer me.

Even if he could he wouldn't have had the chance. The golem was on us. It swung, nearly making contact with Storm. He barrel rolled sideways, and it missed, the turbulence making us fling to the right so hard I felt my shoulder separate.

I bit my lip to stop the scream, the pain already starting to go away.

The golem took another swing, and we nose-dived toward the ground, skimming the top of the cars. We got close enough to the SUV that I got a good look at Dan and Nina's horrified faces, followed by Kormann looking like he was about to have a heart attack.

"Get me to Ferid," I shouted against the wind. I didn't really know how much he understood, but his flight picked up speed and he seemed to pick a direction.

Dragon flight was so much faster than travel by car. We banked over the edge of the city, suburbs that weren't actually in the city limits. People scattered below us, terrified of the new horror the day had brought.

Storm let go of me about two glorious minutes later, sending me tumbling across the grass to land right at Ferid's feet.

Well. Maybe I should have been a bit more specific for my dragon.

In the time it had taken Storm to get me here, a full-on battle had erupted. Bodies littered the grass, some humanoid fae, many not.

I retched as I stumbled away from Ferid, my stomach turning at the smell of blood.

"Penchant." Ferid's voice rumbled through the loud chaos around me. He lifted the huge sword, blood streaming down the blade.

Oh no. This was it. The end. Even I wouldn't be able to recover from losing my head. Would I? I closed my eyes. There was no chance of ducking out of the way of a sword that long.

The whistle of the blade falling made me cringe, but there wasn't any pain. I opened one eye to see a not very human fae lying beside me, cleaved in two.

"We need to talk," Ferid said.

"So you said in your message. But the last time we talked, it didn't go very well."

"I'm here to help you." He lifted his sword again, redirecting a thrust from another fae. It only took a second for him to dispatch that one as well, making me gag. "Invite us into your Sanctuary so your people do not slaughter us. And then we will talk about how to return all of this to peace."

"I'll see if I can convince the humans not to do anything, but it's going to be a tough sell."

"Get it done if you wish the ogres on your side."

Okay, yes, I very much wanted the ogres on my side. And he was bound to his word as fae, even though he was low fae.

"Swear to me that you intend to fight with me," I said.

He grunted and bashed a fae coming at him with his shield. "I swear."

Good enough. He'd been on Mom's side when I'd visited Faerie. It was unlikely he'd switched to Quintin's side in this short a period of time.

I took off for the city limits. My phone buzzed in my pocket, but I ignored it. Now was not the time.

Then I remembered that I still didn't know where Jaden was. Crap. I would have to check it as soon as I could.

I reached the city limits, hands raised, and didn't cross the line just in case someone got trigger happy and shot me. "Who's in charge here?" I yelled.

The woman from the apartment building earlier shoved her way to the front. "Trisha?"

"Oh, hey. I'm about to bring some ogres in, and I need your people to not shoot them."

Her eyes bulged. "Bring them in here? I thought they couldn't cross the line."

"They can totally cross the line. They just don't want to because their powers won't work. But we need these guys, so tell me you won't shoot them."

"I'm not authorized–"

"Then get authorized! We don't have time for this."

She nodded and pulled out a radio. I waited impatiently while she conferred with someone I assumed was Kormann. The questions went on too long, the sound of battle behind me getting more and more fierce. Why hadn't I brought my sword with me?

"Bring them in," the woman said.

Storm flapped by overhead, and the soldiers ducked for cover. He was keeping an eye on me, but I didn't know how or where to direct him. Or if I truly wanted deaths on my hands.

I waved to Ferid and he put a horn to his mouth. The ogres all heard and looked to him for orders. "To the Penchant!"

As one the ogres roared and charged toward the city limits, crashing over the fae in the way like a wave. If it was just the fae they fought, they would have no problems. If it was just the golems, they would probably be evenly matched. But even with their extreme plates of armor and gigantic swords, they were clearly losing.

"Hold," the woman behind me said.

I didn't look back, trusting her to control her people.

"Hold."

The first ogre burst across the line. As soon as he hit it, his body changed like Wraith's had. Now he looked like a forty-year old man who spent every moment of his day at the gym, and was dressed in a sweatsuit.

The rest of the ogres piled across the line, all of them looking nearly identical as humans, just with different colored sweats. Well that was weird.

"Major Kormann will be here momentarily," the woman in charge said.

I turned to her for a second, impressed that she hadn't flipped out. I was weirded out, and I knew about this stuff. "What's your name? You know mine, but I don't know yours."

"Sergeant Halder," she answered.

I was strangely proud of how strong her voice was. All of these humans had just watched ogres turn into humans, and hadn't blinked an eye.

"Okay, Sergeant. I need you to hold the line until I talk with these guys. Can you do that?" I threw every speck of authority I had into the statement, hoping against hope she didn't know how old I actually was.

"The Major said to follow your orders. We'll hold the line." She looked up, and her face went tight. I followed her line of sight to see what had finally freaked her out. "The dragon is back."

"Yeah, he's on our side. Don't worry about him." Hopefully. Sure, I knew he loved me, but just how smart was he really? And were dragons bloodthirsty, or fun and playful? Pop culture was very confusing on all that.

But it did give me an idea.

The fae outside the line looked like they were forming ranks again. Not typical ranks, but at least preparing for something.

I stepped outside of the line and whistled as loudly as I could. "Storm. Come here, boy."

The dragon wheeled in the sky and floated toward me.

"Did you just call that thing *boy*? Like it's a dog?" Halder asked from behind me.

"Yeah, he kind of is my dog." I didn't explain more than that. I didn't need anyone to know he stayed in dog form while inside Sanctuary, and go looking for other dragons.

I waved at him to make sure I had his attention, and then swept my arm in a line, trying to communicate with him. The fae paused. Even they were nervous about a dragon.

Storm swept past me at full speed, right along the line I'd shown him. Ugh. No. Not what I'd wanted, but maybe enough to keep the fae back.

Two SUVs screeched to a halt behind me. Dan and Nina were the first ones out. Nina was yelling something as she ran toward me, but I couldn't hear her over all the noise. Right behind her, my mom got out.

"You." Ferid didn't sound so friendly now. Not that he really had before, but now he sounded like he'd like to kill me. "You've sided with your mother?" He watched her walk our way, his hand clenching the sword that looked very out of place with his sweat suit.

Behind him the other ogres growled among themselves, the noise making the soldiers obviously uneasy. This was about to turn into a bad situation, fast.

"Didn't you?" I asked without confirming either way. "Side with my mother?" By now Nina was jerking me into a hug, and Mom was close behind.

"I was allied with her. But no longer. At this point I wish to see both her and your father burn. It's what I wanted to talk with you about. I'm surprised you would even listen to what she has to say after she attacked the human city you claim to love."

Um, what? "What are you talking about?"

"Don't listen to him, love," Mom said, swooping over and putting an arm around me, crowding Nina out.

I shrugged her arm off. "What are you talking about, Ferid?"

"The golems. She is the only fae I know with the ability to create them. The strongest of those who control nature."

A wave of nausea flooded me. She wouldn't. She couldn't have. I spun around toward Mom. "What? This was you the whole time? And back at the Fae Distribution Center? You killed all those people?"

"Now, let's talk-"

"You set Quintin up! You were behind all of this, so I'd side with you! And it almost worked!"

She looked coy, like she was proud of herself. "Almost?"

My whole body shook with rage. I'd always believed Father to be evil, and Mom just a little crazy. But it was obvious now, that wasn't the case. She was just as bad as him, if not worse. Just so much more fae about it.

The fae army on the other side of the line paused, apparently waiting for orders from their queen.

Starren had warned me. So many, many times. But I'd thought maybe Mom was just misunderstood. That maybe she just didn't quite know how to love.

Every illusion about that shattered the moment I knew how many deaths were on her hands.

"Go to your people," I got out, but barely.

"What, honey? Speak up." Had she heard Nina call me honey? It felt wrong when she said it.

"Go to your people before I let these ogres rip you to pieces."

Starren walked up beside me. She stopped with her shoulder nearly touching mine, and planted her feet, showing her support.

"But honey, I-"

"No more of your poison!" I shouted. "I'm tired of hearing excuses! Reasons for why you left Starren. Why you left me! I'm tired of everything being about you and your plans!"

"I thought you cared more about your friends, Trisha. About your sister. Are you really going to risk all of their lives? Are you going to let them die?" She played with her sword in its sheath, driving home her point.

"Let them die?" one of the soldiers asked the others.

Her threat sounded familiar. And I didn't know what or who to believe anymore. "Rosie?" I croaked out. "Was that you?"

"What's Rosie?" Mom asked. She looked genuinely confused. Wonderful. Then I really was fighting both parents.

I didn't get a chance to answer her question. Behind me, Kormann loudly said, "What now?" distracting me. I turned to see what he was talking about and almost shouted in frustration. Another portal had opened.

"Father," Starren snarled.

How she knew was anyone's guess, but she was right. Unlike Raiena, Quintin liked to be at the front of everything. He was first through the portal, dressed in bright white armor, long hair flowing around his shoulders and sword in hand.

"Are you kidding me?" Nina muttered beside me. I couldn't help but agree with her.

Behind Quintin, fae marched out of the portal, these far more in sync. Apparently father had been studying human fighting styles, because fae didn't usually work so well together.

The area they'd chosen to start all this in was very tactical on their part. The trees ended before the line, and there was very little other vegetation in the empty field. I wouldn't be able to fight anything like I normally would.

"Get out of here," Starren growled at Raiena.

Raiena looked to me for support, but I didn't give her any.

"You'll still choose me," she said. "Your father is a bloodthirsty tyrant who wants to rule all of Faerie and Earth. You'll come to me, when you need me."

And then she walked away, not even checking over her shoulder. As soon as she stepped over the city limits, her flowy mom clothes flashed away and turned into black armor with shoulder spikes, with two hand-axes strapped to her back on top of the sword.

Quintin's army just kept coming. They lined up outside the portal, standing in perfect form. He walked forward to meet Raiena, and they stood there for a moment, staring into each other's eyes.

What was I supposed to do about this? Kormann and Dan kept checking my reaction every time anything happened. Nina was internally freaking out. Sure, she was hiding it well, but I could still tell. I moved closer to the line, and Dan grabbed Nina's hand when she tried to follow.

Starren came after me.

"Mareena," Quintin called. "Won't you join us for a family discussion?"

"I am not a part of any family you two are part of," I yelled back.

"He doesn't even know what a family is," Starren whispered to me. "He's just manipulating. He knows how much family means to you." She leaned in closer. "Here's our chance. The two of us can take them." Something bumped my hand. It looked like empty air, which meant it was my sword in its invisible sheath. Starren must have been carrying it for me this whole time. I took it and strapped it to my back. "The ranks will fall apart without leaders. Tell your dragon to cause a distraction."

"I can't just order Storm around," I argued, like that was the part of her statement I had a problem with.

"Well then. It's just us." She started forward.

I grabbed her arm. "Star. Wait. You're really okay with killing our parents?"

"Yes." She said it with no thought, no emotion. But she said it. She could kill either, or both, of them, without any qualms.

I wasn't there yet. "Let's try talking first. Plus, I'm not going to be a lot of help in a fight. There aren't any trees around."

"You're still good with a sword." She studied our parents for a moment. "Never mind. Not that good."

I took a deep breath and marched over the line to stand a few feet away from my parents. Both of them smiled, and I had a fleeting moment of not being able to decide which was more creepy.

"We've been talking, Trisha," Raiena said. Somewhere in the last five minutes, I'd transitioned from calling her Mom in my head, to calling her by name. She was not the person I'd always hoped she was. My mom was dead to me.

"The two of you?" Starren asked.

"Yes," Quintin said. "We've been in negotiations for some time now. We've decided. It's time to stop the in-fighting."

"Okay?" I didn't mean for it to come out as a question, but it did.

Raiena took a step forward, longing on her face. Just a short time ago, I would have thought that the longing was for us to be a family. Now I knew better. "Together, our family would be unstoppable. Perhaps that's what the prophecy meant all along. I can teach you, guide you in your ability. The humans won't stand a chance."

"You've given up on deciding on which one of you will rule everything?" Starren asked.

"For now," Quintin answered.

"She just tried to frame you! To get me to side with her and fight against you!" I shouted.

"Yes," Quintin said. "That's very typical for your mother. Nothing we haven't worked through in the past."

"You know I would never help you kill humans," I said.

Raiena nodded toward where Dan and Nina were standing, watching the exchange anxiously. "We'll let you keep your pets, of course."

They seriously believed the only reason I didn't want them to try and take over the world was that I was afraid they'd take Dan and Nina from me? "Why do you want Earth so bad anyway?"

"You'll learn the answer to that after a few centuries of life," Quintin answered.

"Wait a minute. You want to start a war with the humans because you're bored?" I was going to kill them. Okay, I wasn't ready for literally yet, but they were about to push me over that edge. "Seriously?"

"This is your last chance, Mareena. Stand with us, or fall with them," Quintin said.

How they expected to take over the entire world, I didn't know. But they had both traveled the planet for long enough that if they thought they could, they probably could. I looked back to Dan and Nina, holding hands. Knowing my parents, if I defied them, those I loved would be first to die. Dan and Nina. Maybe Starren. Cray, Rosie, even Wren.

"Come on, honey. We aren't going to kill all the humans. Just enough to make a statement. We need some of them. But more will die in your little rebellion than need to."

Her callousness had the exact opposite impact than what she'd wanted. "Don't call me honey," I hissed. "You don't have the right."

As if he felt my distress, Storm flew by low overhead.

"As you wish," Quintin said. He lifted a hand, and the front row of his fae lifted bows. Magic may not work in Sanctuary, but an arrow certainly would.

"Prepare to fire!" Kormann yelled behind me.

"Council," Starren said.

"What?" Raiena asked, her voice angry.

"I call council," Starren repeated.

I had no idea what that meant, but it was making my parents mad, so it had to be something good.

"That's what we're doing right now!" It was unusual to hear

anything Raiena's voice, but apparently she was mad enough she couldn't control it.

"We will take your terms and speak to the other leaders of the land. Please lay out your terms." How Starren kept it together so well, I'd never understand. I just wanted to slap someone. And at the moment I was extremely grateful to have her. I had always disliked the fae, and didn't know any of their customs. Maybe this one would by us some time.

"Our terms are surrender of all human lands. Mareena chooses one of us as the sole ruler," Quintin said.

Starren snorted. "Not asking for much, are you?"

Quintin smirked.

"You know the humans will never accept those terms," Starren said.

"So be it. Then there will be war."

"We will relay your message," Starren said.

"And meet us here in one hour." She must have not expected a discussion on this, because Raiena turned and walked toward her troops without waiting for an answer.

"We'll see you in one hour. And don't even think about turning your dragon on us. We came prepared." Quintin laughed, and then left to join his own fae.

Starren and I stood and watched them walk away. "Well," I said. "You bought us a little time."

"A whole lot of good that's going to do us," Starren answered. We turned and started back toward the rest. "Now we all get to die in an hour."

CHAPTER FOURTEEN

We didn't make it all the way back to the people we'd left before Nina broke free from Dan's half-hearted hold and rushed us. She jerked us both in for a group hug. An oomph of surprise came out of Starren, but she didn't resist, which said a lot.

"What do they want?" Nina asked after she finally loosened up her hold.

By now Kormann, Ferid, and Wraith had joined us, Kormann keeping a wary eye on Ferid.

"Report," Kormann ordered, like I was one of his subordinates.

Starren stiffened beside me, but I grabbed her arm. I didn't get to Wraith in time.

"You be careful who you speak to like that. I don't hold much with titles, but this girl's father is the king of Faerie."

Kormann blanched. "I was holding the princess of Faerie..." he trailed off, looking around like he hoped none of us caught onto his thought.

We all did.

"It doesn't matter," I said. "What we need to do is figure out now."

"What do they want?" Kormann asked.

"To kill the humans and take Earth as their own," Starren answered.

I frowned at her. She didn't have to be so glib while giving bad news.

She shrugged.

I pulled my phone out of my pocket.

"Highness?" Kormann asked.

Wraith started laughing hysterically.

"Don't call me that," I said, not looking up from my phone. "I just need to see if someone is okay."

"We need to come up with a plan," Kormann said.

"We need to figure out a way to kill them," Ferid answered. "There is no other way to stop them."

Under seven messages from Rosie, who was probably watching all of this on the news, there was a text from Jaden. 'On my way. Don't die.'

Wow. Very informative. But at least he was alive, and his family was probably fine or he wouldn't be coming here.

The adults started arguing around me, and I ignored them while I opened Rosie's text chain. 'Have solution. Call me.' 'Whoa, is that dragon real?' 'Call me, Trish.'

I stopped reading there. She thought she was helping, but if no one who'd known about the fae for their entire lives had a solution other than murder, she wouldn't be able to come up with one.

There it was. I bit my lip, fighting a sting of tears. It had come down to the human race, or my parents. Could I really put their lives above so many others, especially when it was them causing the problem?

No. They had made this decision for me.

"Are the participants protected under council?" I asked Starren. The whole group around me quieted.

"Yes," Starren answered. "No ill-intent allowed."

I snorted. "No ill-intent? Then how can Quintin and Raiena go to any?"

Nina looked like she was about to pull me into another hug, but she controlled herself. Which was probably better with everyone watching, but I wouldn't have minded.

"We should move back," Starren said. "Even without an ability, some fae have hearing that you wouldn't believe."

"Why even call a council?" Ferid grumbled. "It just delays the inevitable. We should have attacked before giving them time to plan on their end."

"All of their plans are already made," Starren argued. "You should know that."

I sighed. I'd had to keep them from killing each other in Faerie. Literally. Hopefully now that we were on the same side, they could keep it together.

"You can't start your rule out looking weak," Ferid said in my direction.

"Who, me?" I asked, pointing at myself.

"Of course." He hefted his sword. "We've decided the prophecy could mean anything. And that everyone would be better off without Quintin and Raiena."

Oh wonderful. He was here, expecting me to become queen. "I'm not taking any throne."

He stopped and leaned into me, his squinty eyes demanding my attention. "Then you'll lose the support of the ogre. We're not here to save humans."

More fae with an ulterior motive. How original.

"We'll discuss all this if we survive," Starren said. "There's no point fighting about it when we're all likely to die."

The whoosh of wings behind us caught my attention. Storm was coming in hot and low. He skimmed the ground, just touching it as he crossed the Sanctuary line. Without any kind of changing period, instead of my dragon, it was my dog running toward us.

My dog, and yet not. He was bigger, his coat shining, no ribs showing. He looked glorious all filled out. "Storm?" I asked. He ran at me and jumped, knocking me to the ground. I grabbed him in a tight hug and buried my face in his coat for a second of comfort. "Where have you been?"

"Looks like he's been molting," Wraith answered for him. "Somewhere around here there's a pile of extremely rare dragon scales."

"Molting?" I looked him over more carefully. Dogs obviously didn't molt, but apparently dragons did. "I guess you're forgiven."

"Can all fae look like creatures from the human world?" Kormann asked me. He was basically ignoring everyone else, but I couldn't blame him. He probably just didn't know how to deal. "How many of these things are there hiding in Fort Wayne?"

"I have no idea," I answered honestly.

We walked in silence back to the line of our soldiers. Someone had thrown up a small command tent, basically a cover with two walls, and had started setting out equipment.

"Tell your people to have some loud conversations," Starren told Kormann. "It doesn't matter about what."

Halder had come over as soon as we got closer. When Kormann nodded, she hurried off to spread the news.

En masse we moved into the tent. Around me, the people I needed to figure this all out started to talk over each-other until everyone was just shouting their opinions.

None of them were about how to go about this without bloodshed. Each person had a different plan on how to lure my parents away from their armies, and kill them.

Nina slid her arm around my shoulder, but that was the only thing I felt. The world was numb, empty. I'd never killed anyone. I'd come close to it. Wade was truly a lucky man to be alive. But I'd never crossed that line.

What would I feel after? Relief? Pain, for the relationships that would never be? Did it matter? I'd find out soon enough. There was no stopping Quintin and Raiena. No reasoning with them. The only thing that would stop them was death.

A mini-van screeched up outside the tent. A van I recognized. There wasn't anyone there to stop it, with all of the soldiers between the city and the fae.

Rosie was in the driver's seat, rolling the window down. How she was managing that with her leg, I had no idea. But she looked mad. Really mad.

"Trisha Penchant!" Oh yeah. Really mad. "I've been calling and texting you all day!"

"Who is that?" Kormann asked. "Do you want me to have her escorted away?"

Oh, so now that he knew my father was the king of the fae he was actually asking what I thought and wanted. "No. Give me a second." I walked over to the van. "Rosie. It's not safe to be here. You need to go home. Or better yet, somewhere with a basement. I don't know what's going to happen."

"Shut up, Trish." Her tone made me snap my mouth closed. "I have a friend. In Florida. She's got these bracelets that make the person wearing them unable to perform magic without permission from the person who put the bracelet on them. The person with the bracelet basically has to do anything their handler says. She's trying to get them here, but is still hours away. And I don't know how to get her through the dome."

"Where are these bracelets from?" I didn't want to totally dismiss Rosie trying to help, but I'd never heard of these kind of bracelets before. Surely Starren would have mentioned them if she knew anything about them.

"Some other world. She has a friend that comes through a portal. But I lost contact with her when the dome went up."

A friend who comes through a portal?

"This doesn't sound like a fae device." Wraith's voice in my ear made me jump.

"It wasn't from Faerie. Some place called Arnath, I don't know. But she swears it will work, and I trust her."

A small spark of hope lit inside my chest. If what she said was true... No murder. I could live with no murder a lot easier than with murder.

The rest of our group had gone quiet behind me, and moved our way.

"How do we test them?" Starren asked.

"That's the thing. Once they're on, there's no getting them off. I don't know for sure they'll work for the fae, but you can't try it on anyone or we'll lose them. But they work for humans." A confused look covered her face. "Well, I guess people from Arnath might not be human either, but it works on them."

"Wonderful," I muttered.

"It's a big risk," Wraith said. "If you chance putting the bracelet in place and it fails, you're unlikely to get another go at a sneak attack."

She was right. And now everyone was looking at me. Did I risk a literal war to try to save two evil people? And try was the word, because it might not even work.

"Any ideas how to get the bracelets here?" I asked. "All this is a moot point if we don't even have them." I checked my watch. "We only have thirty minutes until we're supposed to meet Quintin and Raiena."

We all stood there, looking at each other.

"The portal," Starren finally said.

"The one the fae showed up in?" Kormann asked.

"No. There's another one," I answered for Starren when she didn't even acknowledge him speaking. "A permanent one." But I didn't tell him where it was.

"Give me your phone." Starren stuck her hand out toward Rosie. "I'll go through the portal and call your friend. Find out where she is and get the bracelets."

"You don't even believe in this plan," I said.

"I believe in you." Starren kept her hand out until Rosie placed the phone in it.

"You can't go," Dan said. "Quintin and Raiena will know something is up if you don't go to the meeting with Trish on time. And there's no way you'd be back before it started."

He was right. But who else was there?

"We'll go," Carver said from behind Starren. Cray stepped up beside him.

Wait, Cray was volunteering for a dangerous mission?

"No," Starren said. "Absolutely not. Getting to the portal itself is dangerous enough, but neither of you know how to function in the human world outside of this city and your routines. You can't go."

Carver put his hands on Starren's arms, rubbing up and down. She'd probably kill anyone else that tried that, but for him she just looked mildly irritated. "If we can get ahold of her and she can give me a good enough visual, I can make a pocket portal and she can place the bracelets in there. Then, we'll get back and I can reopen it from here and pull them out. We won't need to interact with any humans."

"You don't know that," Starren said. "It's too big a risk."

"We'll go," Dan said from behind me. I spun around to glare at him.

"Uh, no," I said. "No way."

Nina moved forward and the three of us faced each other. "It needs to be done," she said. "And we're the best ones to do it. You know we're no help here. I feel useless. Give me something I can do."

"I can send some of my people instead," Kormann offered.

Starren glared at him. "I don't trust your people. If Dan doesn't go, Carver and Cray don't go."

Did she not trust them to get our people to the portal, or not trust them with the portal's location? Probably both, plus seven other reasons that I hadn't thought of.

"Dan and Nina are civilians," I said. "They can't go."

"Trisha," Dan said. The way he said it, I knew I wasn't going to like it. "We let you take point on these things because-" stopped himself and considered his answer. "You're more likely to know the best way forward. But we are your parents. You can't tell us not to do anything. Thank you for your advice, but we've decided this is the best way forward."

Ouch. He'd brought me to the top by saying they were my parents, and then knocked me all the way back down by stating the obvious, that they didn't have to listen to me.

Crap.

I couldn't live without them. Couldn't see Nina like I had before, pale and cold, everything that made her herself, gone. "I could stop you." It came out quiet, but everyone heard it.

"Don't you talk back like that, young lady," Nina said. It wouldn't have sounded threatening to anyone else, but it hurt me down to my soul. Even back in D.C. when I'd pulled all kinds of crap, she hadn't really raised her voice.

"I could though. If I stepped over the border, I could stop you. Easily."

"And then you'd be just like Quintin or Raiena," Starren said.

The words hit me worse than a blow would have. The last thing I ever wanted to be compared to were my biological parents.

"We're wasting time." Dan held his hand out to Kormann, who placed a handgun in it. "The sooner we leave, the more lives we save. You aren't going to be able to stall them without a fight again."

He was right. I was risking lives. But that didn't mean I didn't want to keep them here as long as possible. "Please." I waited until they were both looking at me. "Don't go."

"Do you think they're any safer here, where a great battle is about to commence?" Ferid spat on the ground. "I'm beginning to think that you aren't fit to be queen."

"I don't want to be queen!" I shouted. But he was right. This option would at least get them away from where the fighting would be heaviest. As much as I didn't like it, it was going to happen. "Fine. Go."

"Trish, I-" Nina started to say something.

"Just go, Nina. It's okay. Please. Be careful."

She pulled Dan and me into a group hug, somehow getting Starren to at least hover on the edge. "We'll be back as soon as we can." Her eyes filled with tears. "If there was some way I could help you here-"

"There isn't," Starren said in her usual blunt way. "Don't die." And then Starren walked over to tell Carver goodbye.

I gave Nina a strained smile. "I think she just told you she loves you."

"You know, I think so too." Her eyes were watering, but she held it together. One of the SUVs we'd rode over in pulled up, Dan in the driver's seat. "Goodbye, Trish. We'll see you soon." The side of her mouth tipped up. "Don't die."

I waited until she was in the SUV with the door closed. "You either, Nina. You either."

"Are you ready to strategize?" Kormann asked from inside the tent.

"Leave her alone," Starren hissed, and I almost went over and hugged her right there, just because she was actually thinking about my feelings. No reason to punish her for a good deed though.

"No, he's right," Wraith said. "Your parents will be back soon. We need to know how to keep them distracted long enough for your other parents to get back."

"Quintin and Raiena are no longer my parents." I walked into the tent and faced everyone else. "What resources do we have?"

"My people," Kormann said.

Ferid snorted. "Useless, except to draw some attention. It will be my ogres who bear the brunt of this battle. We can hold, but not for long. I don't know all of the fae your-" he stopped at the look on my face. "That the king and queen brought with them, and so I don't know what we're up against."

That was not great. A bang behind me made me jump. Rosie. Getting out of her van. I'd just left her there. "Excuse me for a moment," I told everyone else before marching over to confront her. "What are you doing?" I hardly recognized my own voice. I needed to get a lid on this anger, before it made me do something stupid.

"Staying here to help. I know the magic words we need for the bracelets."

This was beginning to sound crazy. I trusted Rosie's heart, but did that mean I could just believe she had something of this magnitude right? Yes. I trusted her heart, but also her judgment. She'd never led me wrong on anything before.

"Then tell me the words and get out of here. There's about to be a battle."

"I know. And I'm staying." She dropped her chair out of the side van door, unfolded it, and maneuvered herself in. She'd gotten really good at that in the short time she'd needed it.

She gave me a look, and then left me behind, heading over to the tent. Poor Kormann watched with his mouth half open. This had to be frustrating for him too. He was used to being in charge, and no one would listen.

What was he going to do? Lock us all up and risk the entire city?

"Rosie, I-"

"Don't have time to argue," Starren said. "Look."

I checked where she had nodded toward. Quintin and Raiena were walking toward us.

"But it's early," I got out.

"Yeah." Starren didn't seem surprised. But then, she rarely was.

"What do we do?" I asked.

"Two options," she answered. "We meet them now, and they show the fae who's in charge."

"Or," Wraith added. "You wait until the specified time, and make them so mad they kill everyone anyway." She laughed at what she apparently thought was a joke, no doubt making everyone who could hear her a little worried about her sanity.

Everyone but me. I already knew.

"Do we really want to let them have the upper hand?" Kormann asked.

"They already have the upper hand," Ferid answered. "The real question is, do we want to make them stop pretending to care what happens to us all?"

They were both right. And looking to me to make a decision.

"Send two of your soldiers, human," Starren said. "They must tell Quintin that we will be there shortly. While they will be unhappy at our play, they will have no excuse to feel slighted."

Wow. She was good at all this fae crap. The stuff I hated. The pretending, scheming, back-biting.

"We can't just put them in danger like that," I said.

"If it will help, I'll do it myself," Korman answered. "I would never send one of my people to do something I wasn't willing to do myself."

"We need you here," I said.

"No," Wraith interrupted. "He's right. They have even less to be offended about if it is one of the enemy leaders who comes to them. It's a good play."

"Then it's decided." Kormann snapped his fingers and Halder came over. "You're in command until I get back. Don't start anything, but if they do, finish it." He adjusted his Kevlar and checked his sidearm. "Anything you can tell me that could help me out?" he asked me.

"Don't trust your gun. Metal works oddly around the fae."

"Don't show weakness, and don't trust anything that comes out of their mouths," Starren added.

"Don't give them any details about why Trisha is meeting them,"

Wraith threw in her two cents. "They'll twist whatever you say around to mean what they want it to. In fact, say the least amount of words possible."

Kormann's face didn't betray him, but the fact that he was keeping such a tight lid on his expression gave him away. He was freaking out.

Good. Maybe it would help keep him alive.

He stopped in front of me and held out his hand. I took it, and we shook.

"You're a fine young woman," he said. "I hope to get to know you better. But in case I don't, I'd like to let you know that you've earned my respect. I hope things go your way." He cracked a grim smile. "Of course, it doesn't hurt that you seem to be the only leader here that cares about human life."

"I'm not a leader," I said automatically. "Just deliver your message. I'm busy, and I'll meet them at the pre-decided time. Then get out of there. Get back over the line as soon as you can."

He nodded, hesitated a second, and then started toward Quintin and Raiena at a brisk walk.

I almost followed, but Starren grabbed my arm and pulled me back into the tent. "It won't help him if they can plainly see that you could have come if you wanted to."

She was right Of course she was. But I hated it. I was sending him into danger instead of going myself. But it would buy Dan and Nina a little more time.

Nina. I needed to hear her voice. Everyone who was left had collected in a small circle in the middle of the tent, watching the screen where the camera feed of Kormann stepping very carefully around Storm who was laying with his head on his paws taking a nap and crossing the line.

I slipped to the back of the tent and pulled out my phone, hitting my number one favorite. It didn't even have a chance to ring.

"Is everything okay?" Nina didn't take the time to say hi.

"Hi," I answered. "Everything is fine." Uh, no, not exactly. "Everything is the same as when you left. I just wanted to see how far you'd gotten."

"We're on the lane up to the farm house right now. We have to be close." We sat there in silence for a moment, neither of us having anything to say, but not wanting to be the one to hang up. Gravel crunched on the other end, and doors slammed.

"I'll check the perimeter." Carver's voice came through, and I almost wished I'd let Starren be a part of this conversation. Almost.

Nina's breathing came in short bursts. She was close to flipping out, even if she wasn't saying so.

"It's a weird feeling, going through a portal, but it'll be fine," I said.

"I remember."

"It's all going to be fine," I said again. We both knew it wasn't her I was trying to convince.

"Carver knows exactly what he's doing. We'll pop through this portal, talk to Rosie's friend so Carver knows where to place a portal, grab the bracelets. Piece of cake."

"Piece of cake," I repeated.

"Good to go!" Carver called.

"Once you go through the portal, we won't be able to talk until you get back."

"I know, baby. I know."

"Tell her I love her," Dan's voice came through.

"Dan loves you," Nina said.

"Love him too."

"We're here."

I clenched my eyes closed. I would not cry in front of all of these rough and tough warriors. I would not snot up in front of an ogre army. I would not.

"I'm about to step through, Trish. Love you."

"Love you too." And then the phone lost connection. "Nina?" I asked anyway. "Nina?" I pulled the phone away from my ear and stared at it. One minute and thirty-seven seconds. Maybe the last minute and thirty-seven seconds I had with them.

How we were all going to make it out of this, I had no idea.

A shout rang out inside the tent, and I whirled around to the TV screen. Kormann was on the ground, Quintin standing over him with blood dripping down his blade.

CHAPTER FIFTEEN

I froze in shock. Humans weren't covered under Sanctuary, but surely they were covered under a council. And even if they weren't, he was working with me, which should have protected him.

I looked to Starren. She stared at the screen, a muscle in her jaw jumping. Around us people fluttered, not sure what to do.

Halder moved up beside me, her eyes also glued to the screen. "What now?"

"They can't attack without breaking council," Starren said. "Hold."

"But they just did," she argued.

"No. They executed a human. It isn't seen as the same thing," She sounded weird. Like she was bluffing. I didn't know enough about the fae to know if she was or not, but it didn't really matter. I couldn't possibly be more freaked out at the moment.

And then Quintin and Raiena started walking toward us, jockeying for position.

"You," I said to Halder. I would call her by name if we survived this. I hadn't been a fan of Kormann, but every time I thought about him being dead, I nearly hurled. "Keep her safe." I nodded at Rosie.

She nodded, but I wasn't too confident that Rosie would be a priority for her. There wasn't anything I could do about it.

"Oh, I almost forgot." Starren reached into her portal pocket and pulled out the clothes she'd had for me so long ago when we'd gone to that meeting and met Wade instead of our parents. She must have seen the look on my face. "Get in these. Quick. You heal crazy fast, but no injury is better than healing."

I grabbed the clothes and looked around before settling on Rosie's van. I popped in for a second and changed, the leather feeling both weird and natural at the same time.

By the time I'd gotten back out of the van, our parents were nearly to the line.

"What are they doing?" I asked Starren.

"It looks like they are forcing council. It's a stupid power move, and it could have serious consequences."

"What do we do?" I asked.

"We meet them. We can't risk what could happen if a council is broken."

"What does that mean?"

"I don't even know. Breaking council, breaking Sanctuary... The stories are far older than I am. Who knows if they're even true. I choose not to find out." She straightened and walked toward the line, almost leaving me behind.

I scrambled to catch up, and Wraith and Ferid fell in on either side of me. We reached the line together, and both of them instantly changed into their fae forms, taking up far more space than they had before. Somehow I'd forgotten how intimidating Wraith was when she was over eight feet tall and covered in scales.

Good. They looked a whole lot more intimidating. At least to me.

"Have you decided?" Quintin asked when we got closer, ignoring everyone but me.

His smug face made me want to put a fist through it.

"We will stand with the humans, against you," Starren said.

I almost smacked her. Yes, it was very satisfying to tell off Quintin, and part of me was jumping up and down that she got to do that, but we were supposed to be stalling.

"Then you will die with your humans," Raiena hissed.

Ferid caught her sword with his own right above my head.

She'd tried to kill me. Truly no-back-from-the-dead miracle healing kill me.

"Our one true failure," Quintin said. "No matter. We'll have another chance, if we decide we want to try and raise another brat."

I didn't have time to process the fact that neither of my parents cared if I died before Raiena took another swing. This time it was me who blocked it.

They were breaking council. And obviously without a qualm.

Wraith snarled and leapt at Raiena. The sound of swords clashing came from Quintin and Starren, but I didn't get a chance to look that way. "Help her!" I yelled to Ferid, hoping he knew who I meant.

He grunted, but obeyed. Which left Wraith and me fighting Raiena.

We exchanged blows, mine half-hearted, hers hard.

"Come on, Trisha, I taught you better than this. Surely some of the things we worked on stuck." She upped her attack.

But Wraith had apparently had enough. She roared, a full-throated hyran scream, and came at us, ramming Raiena, who stumbled back.

Her face melted into hate, and she paused. Golems took shape behind her. "Attack," she screamed, and it wasn't just the golems who obeyed her. The line of fae who had followed her through the portal all took up her scream and ran forward as one.

"Get back across the line," Starren yelled from somewhere.

I obeyed. Wraith was extremely formidable, but I doubted even she could take on three golems.

We ran. Full speed. But the fae behind us were gaining ground. What happened when we crossed the line? I couldn't heal there. Storm stood up in the tent. He bounded for the line, bursting into dragon form when magic could touch him again. He jumped into the air and let out a massive bellow, making the line of fae falter.

Storm flew past, blasting fire in front of him and giving us a small space of no man's land.

Until another golem formed, this one made from flames.

The ground shook, and I fought to get my balance. While I'd been staring at the sky, trolls had started through the portal. They carried pieces of some kind of weapon.

"Trish," Starren yelled. "Get Storm out of here!"

Oh crap. They were starting to throw together some type of giant crossbow.

"Storm!" I screeched at the sky, unsure if he could hear me.

He did, and banked toward the trolls. He sucked in a huge breath, but before he could breathe it out, a smaller version of the dome over the city popped into existence, covering the trolls.

I waved my arms to get his attention. "Get out of here!"

Ignoring me, he dive-bombed the dome, letting loose an inferno.

It did nothing against the dome.

"Go," I shouted again.

The dome flickered for a second, and a shot flew toward Storm. He dodged, but it clipped his wing, sending him into a tailspin, screaming. Far behind enemy lines. Fae swarmed him.

"No," I screamed, and ran forward. No one tried to stop me. Ferid and Wraith stuck close on either side. We were almost to hit the first of the fae running at us when I realized we'd left Starren to fight Quintin and Raiena alone. Stupid, stupid, I could never see big picture.

I spun around just in time to see Quintin knock her to the ground. "Wraith!" I pointed at Starren. She grimaced, but did as I asked and bounded over to crash into Quintin, knocking him back.

Storm roared and a burst of flames burned through the fae closest to him. Tears filled my eyes, but he was going to have to take care of himself.

A swarm of fae hit Ferid and me then. I swung my sword indiscriminately. One on one with an opponent, I'd gotten very proficient with a lot of weapons. But this was full on chaos.

The other ogres joined the fight with a loud battle cry.

I fought my way back toward Starren, sick that I'd left her. There. Still on the ground, with Wraith standing above her, dripping purple blood from several open wounds.

Raiena and Quintin ignored the rest of the battle, the two of them working in tandem to take down Wraith.

I ran at them and took a swing at Quintin. He dodged easily, and laughed.

Behind me, the ogre line was already buckling. There were just too many fae against us. Where were Dan and Nina? How many people would die because I didn't want to kill my parents?

Quintin swung at me and I scrambled backward. It was too late to take them out now. Maybe, if I'd had the element of surprise. But not now.

The sound of gunshots rolled out over the clash of weapons and screams of the wounded. The fae had reached the city line.

Quintin paused, and almost smiled. "If you beg, I may still allow you to surrender."

A wave of fighters, from both sides, got thrown as Storm forced his way over to us on the ground.

"Are you talking to yourself?" Ouch. A dumb comeback. "Because you're about to get pulverized."

As he spun to look at what I was talking about, I ran and slid past him to Starren. She was unconscious, a large gash oozing blood on her temple.

I almost screamed for Wraith, but she was still holding back Raiena.

"Just you and me, Star." I grabbed her under the armpits and tugged her toward the line.

Bodies littered the ground, making it nearly impossible for me to get her anywhere.

"Raiena!" Quintin yelled from where Storm was keeping him occupied.

Raiena left her assault on Wraith, and went to join him, golems forming around her as she ran.

Once her attention was elsewhere, Wraith rushed over, assessing the situation in a glance and picking up Starren. We stumbled toward the line.

Storm roared in pain, and I looked back. A giant arrow stuck out of his side, two golems beating on his back.

By the time I could tear my eyes away, fae blocked our path back to the command tent.

There were at least twenty of them, heavily armed.

Wraith carefully sat Starren down, and moved up beside me.

"Let's do this." I hefted my sword.

She didn't answer. Her eyes darted around, terror obvious in them, but she didn't move. One of the fae had her eyes closed, face strained in struggle. She must have some type of ability that was affecting Wraith.

Without pause, the rest of the fae charged. It was just me and my sword.

I blocked a thrust and dove under a swing. Several of them rushed past me and began to hack at Wraith.

"Stop it!" I lunged at one of them, only to get knocked sideways by another. The leather Starren had gotten for me kept me from getting wounded.

My parents had picked the perfect place. There were no trees here, no vines. Nothing to help me. My dragon and friend were getting overwhelmed, and my sister was down. I screamed in rage and hacked at anything that moved, the tears flowing freely now.

No friends here, to worry about injuring.

Somewhere behind the line a horn sounded. The skirmishes all around us paused, and as one we all looked that way.

Jaden. Standing in front of an army of fae. Guj stood on one side, and Martha on the other. He'd brought the refugees. "To Trisha." As one, they all ran forward, screaming different war cries.

The two lines clashed, the few ogre who were left falling back to the city line.

"Help Storm," I yelled to anyone who would listen.

The fae surrounding Wraith attacked again, with twice the vigor. I jumped one, screeching in his ear and beating him with the hilt of my sword until he threw me off.

And then there was a hand there to pull me back up.

I grabbed on, and when I was back on my feet crushed Jaden in a hug.

We didn't have time to talk. I nodded toward the fae whose ability was holding Wraith prisoner. "Get her."

Jaden nodded, and without question started her way. He was somewhere between Starren and me in his talent with a sword, and flowed through the fighting toward her.

I went back to the fae trying to kill Wraith, getting in jabs whenever there was an opening, keeping them distracted.

The second the fae went down that Jaden had gone after, Wraith snapped back to life. She gave a demon-banshee scream, and let loose her fury.

In that moment, I learned why the fae were truly scared of hyran. I leaned over Starren, covering her with my body, doing my best not to see the things Wraith did to those who had almost killed us.

A gentle hand on my shoulder almost made me gut Jaden. But I noticed the jeans in time.

"Let's get her out of here," he said, and leaned down to throw Starren's arm over his shoulder. He probably could have carried her on his own, but I took the other side, and we ran for the city limits.

Fae clashed around us in small groups. Sick, I tried not to look as we passed them. They were here because of me, and I was hauling for the safer area.

Once Starren was out of immediate danger, I'd be back.

We floundered across the line, and instantly I felt every move I'd made in the last few hours. Aches and pains weren't too bad as everything had mostly healed, but exhaustion like I'd never known before almost dropped me.

Human soldiers rushed to us, and I passed Starren over to a woman in a medic uniform. Starren groaned, the first sign of life. I squeezed her hand as they threw her on a cot.

Rosie was almost to us by then, and I waved her over.

"Oh Trish," she said, tears in her voice. I must have looked terrible, but it didn't matter.

"Watch Starren for me," I said. "I'm going back out there."

Determination went across her face and she wheeled around, moving after the medics.

Jaden and I exchanged looks. I almost expected him to tell me I couldn't go back out, but he didn't. He nodded, and we turned back together.

Our people had lost a lot of ground in the time I'd been distracted.

"We need to get them over the line," Jaden said.

"If we do that, we're way out-numbered and don't have a dragon and ogres. I don't know if they are as strong in human form as ogre."

"The dragon isn't helping us at this point. We don't know if it will affect the ogres or not, but it will take out your mom's golems."

He was right. We'd be bringing the fight into the city though, closer and closer to innocent people. But we had no choice.

"We have to get Storm out of there. He needs us."

"We can't give up that many lives, Trish. I'm sorry." Jaden looked sorry. But that didn't help anything.

He pulled a horn over his shoulder and blew out two loud blasts. The fae who'd come with him began to retreat, the few remaining ogres sprinkled in among them.

A golem began to form, blocking their retreat. Raiena would show no quarter. I knew that now. "We have to help."

Jaden nodded, and took off.

After crossing back over the border, I caught up with Jaden easily, passing him quickly. I slashed at the thing, my sword cutting right through it. But mud just oozed back into place, filling any wound I left.

"Get across the line!" I yelled to anyone listening.

A banshee shriek distracted me long enough to get hit from the side and flung away, crashing to the pavement. A rib groaned and I held in an angry scream.

I didn't wait for it to heal. The golem moved to block several fae's retreat. I bit my lip, focusing on the golem. This was something I could help with. I didn't even know where Wraith was at the moment, there was nothing I could do for her.

Fighting the golem was only a stall tactic. Without the trees to help, there was nothing I could do. "Hey, you!" I threw a dirt clod at the thing. "Pretty sure Raiena wants me first."

It turned, processed for a second, then lumbered forward.

The fae it had stopped got around it, making for the line.

I grinned for .2 seconds, then panicked. This thing would have no trouble tearing my head from my body.

With its full attention, running seemed like the best plan. I took off, and it followed, gaining ground quickly.

The sound of wings made me change direction. Storm was back on his feet, shaking fae off. All but one fae. Wraith sat on his neck, a feral smile on her face. She must have gone back for him. She saw me and nudged Storm in the direction of the golem.

He roared and the ground shook. He jumped into the air and was on the golem in a flash, crashing into it at full speed.

Dirt rained down from the sky. Jaden appeared beside me and grabbed my hand, pulling me toward the city line.

Storm and Wraith got there at the same time we did. They transformed when they hit the line and tumbled to the ground, Wraith rolling straight back up and cackling in glee.

Storm didn't move.

"Medic!" I shouted, running his way. A vet would be better, but anyone would be more help than me right now.

I slid to the ground at his side, checking for breathing. There. A slight rise and fall. I checked through the blood covering him, trying to find the worst wounds.

He whined, sending my heart soaring and crashing at once. "You're going to be fine. Really. It's all going to be fine."

The medic who'd taken Starren earlier moved in beside me with her cot. She stood with her hands on her hips for a second, taking stock.

"I'm going to be watching your every move," Wraith hissed to the medic. I hadn't seen her come up behind me, but now that I did, I couldn't miss how bad she looked. She'd taken quite a beating. I hadn't seen Ferid in far too long. He was probably dead. All of my champions, down for the count.

Chanting started over with Quintin's troops. It wouldn't be long before they reformed and tried another assault.

"We've got him," the medic said. "And your people just got back."

My head whipped toward the tent. There. Carver. Where was Nina? "Thank you," I got out, and took off toward the tent. Leaving Storm crushed my soul. But stopping this was the only way to save him. To save everyone.

I burst into the tent, Jaden right behind me. There were fae and humans covering every space inside. The injured moaning, some calling for help. I shoved down the guilt trying to overwhelm me. Either Quintin or Raiena would have done this eventually, even if I wasn't here.

The first person I saw who I knew was Cray. "What took you so long? Where are the bracelets? Where's Nina?"

"Here," Nina stepped around one of the soldiers and ran to me, pulling me into a hug. "I was so scared you were dead. When we pulled up..." she choked. "I'm not made for this."

"Did you get the bracelets?" I asked.

She held them up. Two savage looking metal rings, with spikes on the inside. My stomach roiled.

"Jaden," I waved him over. "I need you to call a council with Quintin and Raiena. Make them believe whatever you want, that we're surrendering, whatever. I just need a little time."

He nodded and took off.

"Where's Starren?" I asked.

"On the other side of the tent wall. We thought maybe she'd calm down if she couldn't see what was going on."

A small hit of relief went through me. She was well enough to be throwing a fit. I followed Nina around the tent. There, Dan was trying to convince Starren to stay in a cot, gently pushing her back. If it had been almost anyone else, Starren probably would have just killed them.

Rosie sat in her chair beside the cot, face white and drawn. Everything going on was a big distraction from the pain, but at some point, it was all going to come crashing back.

"You have the bracelets," Starren said. "It's time. Tell this buffoon to let me go."

The fact that Dan was able to keep her here at all was a bad sign. She was in much worse shape than she was letting on.

The sound of a horn rang out, and all the chanting stopped, leaving a strange, blissful silence, broken only by ambulances coming to take away the injured.

"I think that means Jaden was able to get Quintin and Raiena to agree to talk," I said.

"Agree to talk?" Dan asked. "That didn't help very much last time."

"Yeah," I held up the bracelets. "But this time we have these. Star. Are you well enough to get one of these on Raiena?"

"I'll take Quintin," she growled.

Okay. Fair enough. They had quite a history. But that meant I had to face my mom.

"Help her up," I told Dan.

She waved him off and struggled to her feet herself, swaying slightly. Her face had already bruised, the purple stark under the swelling. I handed her one of the bracelets.

"You'll have to say these words when you put it on," Rosie said, and then said something in a language I didn't recognize.

"Where's that from?" Nina asked.

"Who knows," Rosie answered. "But they won't work unless you get this right. Repeat after me." She said the words again, and both Starren and I said them back.

I'd better not forget them when I was out there trying to get this thing on Raiena.

Jaden came around the tent wall. "They agreed to talk. I think they're losing a lot more troops than they expected. Who knew Trish had a hyran and a dragon hanging out ready for a fight?" He tried to smile, and I loved him for it.

"Okay then. We should try to get them inside the line," I said. "Those golems are destroying us."

Jaden nodded. "I thought of that. I showed them exactly where to meet, and it's well inside the line."

"I'm surprised they agreed to that," Dan said.

"They would show weakness if they did not." Starren stretched a little, and then bent down to pick up her sword lying on the ground by her cot. "It would look like they fear us. Now let's get this over with."

She led the way back through the tent. Around us, fae watched as we walked past. A strange range of despair to hope covered their faces.

No doubt all of them would die for siding with us if this didn't work.

The last person we passed was Guj, from Jenny's. He was missing a hand, the stump wrapped tightly. He nodded at me when we walked past, and the faith in his eyes almost sent me running.

No. I would not run. I would see this through. It would all be over soon, one way or another.

When we stepped out of the tent, I checked the line first thing. Quintin and Raiena stood far closer to the tent than I'd like, far over the line. Fanned out behind them were what was left of their people.

Both sides had taken heavy losses.

"Nina," I said.

She flapped a hand. "I know, I know. We'll wait here. But I won't be happy about it."

I smiled at her. "I'd be upset if you were happy about it."

Dan and Nina both leaned in for a hug. I clung a little longer than I should have, but then took a deep breath and started toward the meeting spot.

Behind me, Starren and Jaden followed, with Cray and Carver behind them. I didn't try to convince them to stay behind. I knew better by now.

"We need them to let us close," I said. "We need to get them to drop their guard. Keep them talking, get them to relax."

The strange metal bracelet bit into my hand, my fingers threaded through the spikes. This was an insane plan. How were we supposed to get close enough to get these on the two most evil fae I knew?

Getting the bracelets on would be difficult enough. What if they didn't work?

There should be a plan B, but there wasn't. We didn't have anything left. This had to work.

I stopped three feet from Raiena. She would be suspicious if I tried to get in too close. Stick to the plan. Get them to relax a bit. My body ached. Bumps and bruises that hadn't had a chance to heal before I jumped back over the line protested every movement.

A gash I hadn't noticed on my face stung when I closed my eyes just to take a moment.

"What did you wish to discuss?" Raiena asked.

"Nothing less than total surrender, I assume," Quintin said.

"We want to keep the losses on both sides to a minimum," I answered. As soon as I said it, I realized it was true. Many of the fae here probably didn't want to be. They had about as much a choice in the matter as I did.

"Then admit defeat. Choose the next ruler of the fae." Quintin stretched high, giving his speech. "Join us, and rule both worlds. It's the only option you have left."

"Not exactly," Starren snarled. She leapt forward, latching onto Quintin's arm.

In a fraction of a second, Quintin grabbed Starren, jerking her out of the air and knocking her to the ground.

"Let her go," I shouted, but when I tried to get to them, Raiena blocked me.

What was left of my parent's armies surrounded us, attacking Jaden, Cray, and Carver, while Quintin leaned in harder on Starren, grabbing her around the throat.

I pulled my sword on Raiena. "Let me pass!"

She pulled her sword and smiled. "Name me ruler of the fae, and I will help you save your sister."

I couldn't. She could help me save Starren, but then kill Dan and Nina. She'd shown herself just as bad as Quintin. I looked around wildly, but there was no help in sight. Jaden, Carver, and Cray were struggling to hold their own against the press of the fae coming against them.

An empty field started on the other side of the line. Even if I got my parents pushed back there, nothing would be able to help me, and I'd have Raiena's golems to deal with. But there was no way I could take Raiena on my own. She'd already proved that.

Here, in Sanctuary, a small copse of trees lined the road.

My only hope.

Please, I begged the trees. *Please, I need you. Help me.*

The closest tree creaked a little. The branches of all of them moved like the wind had picked up, but there was no wind.

Quintin would kill Starren. Any moment, and I would lose my sister. He squeezed tighter, and she choked, slapping at his arms with no effect.

I know you're not supposed to help me here, but please.

A branch lashed out, grabbing Quintin around the wrist.

"Mareena," he said, his voice odd. "You don't want to do this. Not in Sanctuary. Starren has broken the law, but you haven't caused harm yet. Let me go. Choose me, and I will leave the ruling of Earth to you once we conquer it. I swear."

Leave me to rule Earth? I didn't want to rule anything. Sure, it would save people, but no one would want me to rule them either, and then I'd just be in a whole other mess.

I didn't even need to communicate with the trees. Branches wrapped around Quintin. He let go of Starren and hacked at the trees, but every time he got free from one, two more replaced it.

The fae surrounding us stopped their attack on Jaden, Carver, and Cray, pausing to see what happened next.

The branches didn't stop at Quintin. One grabbed Raiena's leg. She growled something in another language and the branch paused, for a fraction of a second, then continued its creep. She slashed at it, but as soon as she did, branches flew in from all directions, pinning her arms to her sides.

I walked in close, getting in Raiena's face. "You brought this on yourself." I shoved her sleeve up and clamped the bracelet into her flesh, latching it together and reciting the words Rosie had given me. The bracelet glowed briefly.

Beside us, Starren put her sword to Quintin's throat. She kept it there, staring at Quintin for far too long.

"Star?" I asked.

She swung her sword, cutting Quintin's sleeve off and slamming the bracelet into place. She said the words and we stood there, exhausted, afraid to let the trees free them.

"Well?" Jaden asked. "Did it work?"

Thank you. I told the trees. *You can let them go now.*

Reluctantly the trees let go.

"What is this pathetic thing supposed to do?" Raiena asked.

"Touch your nose," I said.

Raiena looked at me like I was crazy. At first nothing seemed to happen. But then her face changed. Fear, the first true fear I'd ever seen her show, covered her face. She gritted her teeth and fought back against whatever force was trying to make her obey, but couldn't stop it. Her hand raised toward her face, shaking.

"Bow to me," Starren growled at Quintin.

Okay, that was uncomfortable.

Quintin fought hard. His face turned purple, and his eyes bulged, but eventually he fell to his knees, bowing to Starren. I saw then why she'd forced him to do it. The rest of his people still alive dropped to one knee as well.

"You are to perform no magic unless clearly ordered by me in person." Starren stepped back. "Now go back to Faerie. And never hurt anyone again. Never scheme against another person. And you are not to step foot on Earth ever. You will obey all orders given to you by any of my friends unless it includes violence. Understood?"

Quintin didn't look up. His entire body shook with rage.

"Understood?" Starren shoved him with her boot, and he automatically drew back to strike, but couldn't.

"Understood," he finally said.

Yeah, Starren was much better at this stuff than I was. "The same goes for you," I told Raiena. "Get out of here."

They stood, stiff, faces twisted in terrible expressions. By now our people had made their way from the command tent, backing us up.

"Can you disobey my orders?" I asked.

"No," Raiena bit out. I tried to control the relief making my muscles weak. Unless for some insane reason the bracelet allowed her to lie, she would never be a threat again.

"Are you able to do any harm to any other being without my permission?" Starren asked Quintin.

"No."

Starren waved Carver forward. "Take Goiut and three others. Escort these two to the line. Make sure nothing changes outside of Sanctuary."

Carver nodded, and Cray moved forward to join him, carefully keeping Carver between him and Quintin and Raiena.

"As for the rest of you." Starren turned to the other fae. "Do you swear allegiance to Trish?"

"Who me?" I squeaked out. "Huh uh, nope. No way." I grabbed her arm and pulled her a few steps away. "I don't want anyone's allegiance!"

"If you don't accept it, someone else will. Possibly someone as dangerous as those we just fought."

She was right. The fae needed someone to keep them in check. I turned to the remaining fae. "You need a ruler. Someone who understands your ways and respects your culture. Swear your allegiance to your new queen, Starren Penchant."

"Trish," Starren hissed.

I ignored her. Fae didn't have last names like humans did. Giving her mine showed my support.

It started with a fae in front. "I swear." And from there, it spread through the rest of the ranks, until all of them had sworn to follow Starren.

"Escort my parents through the portal," Starren said. "Place them in the deepest, darkest hole you can find. It will be some time before I trust the bracelets completely."

I got hit from behind by a hug. It took me a second to wiggle free enough from Nina to get turned around and return it.

"How are Storm and Wraith? Uh, Hazel?" I asked.

"They're both going to be fine," she answered. "You did it. Somehow, you did it again."

Dan wrangled me away from Nina and crushed me even tighter than she had. I groaned a little, but it wasn't really in protest.

They each crowded in on both sides, an arm over each of my shoulders. We watched Carver and Cray escort Quintin and Raiena to the portal. Wherever these bracelets had come from, I was beyond grateful. Rosie's friend was about to get the biggest thank you possible. Especially now that I could leave Sanctuary. I glanced back at what was left of the human soldiers. Hopefully I could leave. If I wasn't locked away forever.

Quintin stepped through the portal without looking back. But Raiena paused. She met my eyes and her face screwed up in a snarl.

To think that at one point, she had been my whole world. Had I ever truly meant anything to her? It didn't matter now. I had a whole new family. She was pushed through the portal by one of Starren's new minions, and the hope that I would never see her again flooded my soul.

"Now what?" Dan asked. "Is it truly over?"

No one had an answer for him.

Starren strapped her sword over her shoulder and walked over. She stopped in front of me. "Good work." She paused, looking at a loss for words.

"You too," I answered. "Queen."

She rolled her eyes. "That's your fault. It could have been you."

"And then the entire universe would be in trouble, not just our two worlds."

We stood there and grinned at each other.

"I'll miss you," Starren said.

Uh, what? "Miss me?"

She gestured behind her. "Faerie is going to need healing. I'll be quite busy for some time."

"What?" I pulled free from Dan and Nina. "You can't just leave like that."

"You could come with me." Her voice was odd. Like she knew the answer. "Or at least visit."

"You'll get tired of me visiting," I got out even though my voice didn't want to cooperate. Of course she had to go. How else was she supposed to rule the fae? How had I not thought about this before I'd pushed her into being queen?

"Walk me to the portal?" she asked. Of course I couldn't say no.

We moved along slowly, her stopping to check on fae she knew who'd fallen on the battlefield, and waving medics over for the ones who were still alive. There weren't many.

Part way back, Carver and Cray joined us.

As we got closer, our pace slowed even more, until we totally stopped about ten feet away.

"Do you have to go right now?" I asked.

"Until I can be sure that those bracelets are going to do what was promised, I need to be near Quintin and Raiena. I'll visit as soon as it feels safe." She leaned in close. "I am worried." What? Starren, admitting that she was worried? "We broke Sanctuary, Trish. There are consequences. Watch yourself, and stay in close contact."

"Nara could help with that," I said.

"If I find her and she will be loyal, we'll see." She didn't sound hopeful.

"What kind of consequences are we talking about?" I asked.

"The stories are too old. It isn't clear. But it's said that those who break Sanctuary will suffer. And fae stories..."

"Are always based on truth." I shivered.

"But we'll worry about that when it comes to it." Her cheery tone sounded so odd coming out of her mouth. She gave me a hug, pulling me in tight. "I'm going to miss you."

And then she left me standing there, with my mouth hanging open. "What just happened?" I asked Carver and Cray.

Carver slapped me on the back. "See? I told you she can be affectionate. I'll miss you too, Trish. See you soon." He followed Starren through the portal.

It took me a second to get my tear ducts under control. I couldn't have all these fae who were now my sister's loyal people see me cry. "Ready to go?" I asked Cray, my voice soggy.

"About that." He rubbed his neck. "I'm sorry, Trish. I truly love Faerie. I couldn't be there, because. Well. You know. But Starren will need help now. That's something I'm good at."

I stared at him, speechless. I was losing everyone today. It wasn't like we could be texting with him in an entirely different realm.

"It could change, eventually," Cray said. "But you know how I've always been with humans. I'm still not quite comfortable. If I go home, I can just be me."

I couldn't argue with that. I pulled him in close, and couldn't stop the tears this time. I cried into his shirt for a full minute before he gently moved me out to arm's length.

"They're getting a pretty big head start."

"Go," I said, waving my hand.

He nodded. "Goodbye, Trish." And then he stepped through the portal.

Fae filed by me over the next couple minutes as I tried to regain control. They drug the wounded between them. Soon all of the fae here would be gone.

All of the fae, but me.

I walked back toward the command tent. Dan and Nina were right where I left them, waiting for me.

"Where's Cray?" Dan asked.

"He decided to go with Starren."

"What?" Nina yelled. "And he didn't even say goodbye?" She noticed the look on my face then, and pulled me in tight. "I'm so sorry, sweetheart. We're all going to miss him. A ton. And Starren too, though I never thought I'd say that."

Over her shoulder I caught a glimpse of Jaden back at the command tent, helping with the wounded who were too injured to be moved.

Okay. So I wasn't the only fae. He met my eyes and gave me a tired smile.

I still had the one that I would have missed the most.

"I need to talk to Jaden," I told Dan and Nina.

"Okay." Nina said. "I need to find Wren anyway. She hasn't answered my messages."

Jaden and I met halfway between them and the tent. We stopped close, but not quite touching.

"Are you hurt?" Jaden asked.

"No," I answered. Physically, I wasn't.

"Good. I came back up to make sure Rosie was okay when I saw that you and Starren had everything under control."

"Starren's gone."

He took my hand. "I know."

"Cray's gone too."

"I know." He pulled me in and rested his chin on the top of my head.

"Everything is going to be different now. Better though. We won't have to hide what we are. I won't have to worry about my parents all of the time." He didn't answer, so I tipped back to look up at his face. "What is it?"

"I hope you're right." He looked over my head avoiding my eyes.

"Jade?"

"I saw... That night, in the truck." Now he did look down, and smiled. "It's fine. Surely we changed that future today."

He wasn't sure. He couldn't hide anything from me.

But for now, I was going to ignore it. There was no use worrying about something I didn't know about. I needed peace. Time to decompress, to explore what Jaden and I could be.

Anything else we'd deal with when it got here. Together.

ABOUT THE AUTHOR

Growing up, it was impossible to catch Cassie Greutman without a book in her hand, even at the most inappropriate times. Since then with the rise of ebooks, it's only gotten worse. With her full-time job of caring for over thirty horses, some of that has changed to audiobooks, but you can bet there is always some type of story rattling around in her brain. She has always loved stories in any format, whether that is a movie, video game, or book form, and hopes to tell stories that catch a person's imagination and interest like so many have done for her.

A finalist in the Cinematic Book Competition with Screencraft out of over 1200 entries, and five star ratings with Reader's Favorite, and a win with The Indie Author Project, Cassie has been throwing all of the extra time she has into building worlds for everyone to enjoy. When she isn't stuck in a book, of course.

I so hope you enjoyed Trish's latest adventure! There are a couple ways we can keep in contact about new books below!Follow me on Facebook and TikTok for updates on new stories!

https://www.facebook.com/cassiegreutman/

https://www.tiktok.com/@cassiegreutman

Or join my newsletter for a free short story about Trish first coming to live with Dan and Nina:

https://dl.bookfunnel.com/pq98nn1jof

If you'd like early access to stories as I write them and behind the scenes posts, check out: https://reamstories.com/page/lh4u19l5l3